Sarah Harrison becam
with the publication o
of the Field, an intern
unanimous critical ac
with equal success, by *A Flower That's Free, Hot Breath, An Imperfect Lady, Cold Feet* and *The Forests of the Night. Foreign Parts* is her seventh novel.

Sarah Harrison lives with her husband and children in Cambridgeshire.

Foreign Parts

Sarah Harrison

WARNER BOOKS

A *Warner* Book

First published in Great Britain in 1992 by
Macdonald & Co (Publishers) Ltd
This edition published in 1993 by Warner Books

A CIP catalogue record for this book
is available from the British Library.

ISBN 0 7515 0175 1

Photoset in North Wales by
Derek Doyle & Associates, Mold, Clwyd
Printed in England by Clays Ltd, St Ives plc

Warner Books
A Division of
Little, Brown and Company (UK) Limited
165 Great Dover Street
London SE1 4YA

For

M & D W

CHAPTER ONE

'*Reste tranquille*,' said George, patting my knee. 'The Périphérique'll be a doddle at this time of night.'

'You think so.'

'I know so. Even the Parisians have to get their beauty sleep on a Sunday night, with the working week ahead.'

He began tum-te-tumming to himself, one hand tapping the steering wheel, the other resting on the gear lever. It was a signal that the exchange was at an end.

Mind you, it was about as far as our respective tethers would stretch at this stage in the holiday farrago. Shattered by several weeks of intensive debate about arrangements, followed by the carrying-out of the arrangements themselves, culminating in the savage trauma of departure with its accompanying dog fights, we would now remain in a state of armed truce until we arrived in Tarn et Garonne.

One of the chief benefits of my year's separation from my husband had been the absence of any need for a family holiday. I had travelled a good deal in the interests of research and book publicity, and the children were happy enough with their own arrangements, so the months of July and August had passed ruction-free in a pleasant haze of minor socialising and sunbathing in the garden.

But our reconciliation had occasioned, at least on George's part, an urge to reinstate this annual trial-by-travel.

'We should get away for a few weeks,' was what he'd said back in March.

'Yes – yes, we should.' I read the right magazines and knew that quality time together was essential to a relationship, especially one like ours built on somewhat shaky foundations. 'We need some time to ourselves.'

'That's not exactly what I meant,' said George.

'What, then?'

'I was thinking more in terms of getting away as a *family*,' he said, making it sound as though we were to slip out of the country in disguise.

'I see.'

'It's important to include the children, don't you think?' he went on. 'I mean, this is a new start for all of us.' I forbore to point out that the children's lives continued largely undisturbed by our comings and goings. The image of our family in the Louisa M Alcott mould – cosy, united, selfless, all for one and one for all, had a certain quaint, fantastic charm.

'I expect you're right,' I said.

He wasn't. Gareth, enjoying a year off between school and university, justifiably pointed out that he had outgrown family holidays, and anyway had already spent a month touring the sex capitals of Europe on a student railcard. He was sure no one would mind if he stayed at home and got a job.

Clara, too, was against the idea, and mutinous with it. 'For how long?'

'Four weeks, we thought . . . give us time to really unwind.'

'*Four weeks*?' You'd think I'd suggested trepanning. 'We can't go for four weeks!'

We adjusted it to three.

'But in France!'

'What's the matter with France?'

'Why do we have to go there the whole time?'

'We didn't go anywhere last year.'

'Yes, and it was a brilliant summer.'

'It'll be brilliant in France. We'll have a pool.'

She glowered. 'I suppose that means you and Dad will do lengths to make me feel guilty.'

'I gave up on that long ago.' Since selling her pony Clara's exercise had been confined to combing the music and clothes emporia of Barford and Basset Regis, and what she described as 'mellowing out' in such low dives as these towns afforded. You might have thought that this inertia, combined with a four-bar-a-day chocolate habit and a high-tar nicotine addiction, would have made her fat and spotty, but she remained as lissome as ever, her sultry fallen angel's face innocent of the smallest zit.

She tried another tack. 'You're not making Gareth come.'

'I'm not *making* anyone come,' I said. 'I foolishly supposed that you'd enjoy a few weeks in the sunshine in rural France with a fifty-foot swimming pool.'

'That's not answering the question.'

'Gareth is two years older than you. He's legally an adult, he can stay and look after the place, and the pets—'

'Huh!'

'What?'

'You know perfectly well he'll have filled the place with his disgusting friends before we've even got to Dover.'

'I don't know any such thing,' I snapped.

Later, when Clara was out, and Gareth just returned from work, I asked him: 'Gareth, if you

6

do stay here, you must behave responsibly.'

'Chill out, Ma,' he replied.

'Look after the house. No nonsense.'

'Keep your hair on. What do you think I am?'

I spared him that. 'No parties.'

He took my head in an arm lock and waggled me gently from side to side. 'Take it easy.'

I told George about Clara's reaction.

'She'll be fine,' he said. 'Let her bring a friend.'

This she agreed to. 'At least I'll have someone to talk to.'

Naomi Neville was a well-upholstered brunette with a personal stereo grafted to her skull and the heaviest suitcase George had ever come across.

'What in God's name has she got in here?' he snarled, as he lashed it to the roofrack and I tried to fit the rest of our luggage in the boot. 'Are you sure she's not a descendant of Burke and Hare?'

The conversational side of things had not yet, as far as I could see, come up to expectation. Clara and Naomi claimed to be bosom friends, but so far they had scarcely spoken. Clara was busy demonstrating her disapproval of the whole enterprise, and Naomi had retreated with INXS. Southern England and northern France had passed without comment.

Now, at about eleven thirty p.m., we were bowling through the outer suburbs of Paris. It never failed to surprise me that the outskirts of a glamorous city are every bit as seedy and uninviting as those of an industrial war zone. The view from the car window, bathed in smeary yellow light, comprised the usual run-down tower blocks and litter- and graffiti-strewn walkways. A faint but noticeable smell of drains invaded the car.

'Ugh,' said Clara. 'France, here we come.'

'Now then,' said George, 'so far so good. Harriet, can you remind me of the signs we should be looking out for?'

'Er – yes.' I picked up the road map of France and opened it at the page indicated by a slip of paper inscribed Marker One, thoughtfully placed there by George the day before. As I did so I experienced a small twang of anxiety. By the very act of handling the road map I was accepting shared responsibility for our circumnavigation of the French capital. From now on my husband would behave like someone partially sighted, only barely literate and incapable of empirical thought. I had become the Routekeeper and the Mapmaster.

'We're closing on the centre,' George said. 'Jog my memory.'

'Umm . . .' I peered. The car accelerated. 'I wonder if we could pull over for a moment, the light's bad.'

'Pop your glasses on,' George suggested.

'Slow down a bit then.'

He braked, and swooped into the slow lane as I was opening the holdall containing the entire group's life-support systems for a twenty-hour car journey. Of course, I dropped the road map, and not only Marker One, but Markers Two, Three, Four and Five cascaded to the floor.

'Dear God,' said George, 'I don't believe it.'

I ventured the view that it was not the end of the world.

'No,' he replied, 'just a nuisance. The markers do make things so much simpler.'

I pointed out that since I was the Mapmaster, it was I who would have to suffer any inconvenience as a result of my clumsiness.

George agreed. 'But do you think you could find my first page reference again? I really do need to know which turning to take before I'm committed to going round for a second time . . .'

Another ounce or two of responsibility shifted from his shoulders to mine. Outside, the tower blocks and flyovers were beginning to give way to busier, more humane, better-kept buildings interspersed with the odd row of trees, though the smell of drains remained.

There was a tinny yammering as Naomi removed her headphones.

'Where are we?'

'Paris,' said Clara, 'can't you smell it?'

'Oh,' said Naomi, brightening, 'are we anywhere near Bastille? My uncle and aunt live there.'

'A hundred and six, north tower, eh?' asked George.

'Pardon?'

'We shan't be going near Bastille,' I said. 'We're going round the city on the Périphérique.'

'The M25 with garlic,' offered Clara. 'And sewage.'

'More like the North Circular actually,' I said.

I could imagine the down-turned mouths and up-rolled eyes in the back seat as I continued my search for the correct page in the road map. But the hint of asperity in my tone had the effect of drawing the girls together.

'Hey, Nev,' said Clara, 'fancy a Cola chew?'

'It's perfectly simple,' said George through barely open lips. 'Is it Tours we want or Nantes?'

'Well,' I replied, holding the road map up to the window and squinting for the umpteenth time at the spider's nest that was Greater Paris, 'it looks here as though either would do.'

'That's sorted that out then,' said Clara from the back. Both girls were greatly refreshed by a shot of refined sugar and the atmosphere of impending disaster with which the car was now charged.

'Spare us the sarcasm,' I said. 'Look,' I added, 'do let's try and stop somewhere.'

'Where would you suggest?' asked George, indicating with a sweeping gesture the lanes of fast-moving traffic on either side of us, and the dizzying web of criss-crossing carriageways beyond and above. He glanced sharply at me. 'By far your best bet is to find my first marker. I had the target towns listed on it.'

'Don't say that.'

'What?'

'Target towns.'

'Why not?'

'It's like rumpus room.'

'Just a spot of self-parody.'

He beamed with the not quite innocent vanity which had always been one of his more engaging qualities. But I was not to be engaged.

'The trouble with self-parody,' I said, 'is that it pretty soon becomes the real thing.'

'Oh dear,' he said, 'I'm sorry.'

I felt bad then, of course. We were, after all, in the business of trying to make things work.

'That's all right. I'm sorry, too.'

With my peripheral vision I saw Clara making violin-playing motions, but decided to deny her the oxygen of comment.

'Sign coming up,' said George. He did not, however, pull into the inside lane, nor slow down. I rummaged furiously amongst the fallen markers.

'Tours!' he shouted suddenly. 'Any good?'

'I don't know.'

'Probably Nantes,' he said cheerfully.

I found Marker One. 'Tours it is,' I said. 'Was.'

'I say, Nev,' said Clara. 'There's Bastille.'

'Oh yes . . .' The two of them peered out of the window at the sign with what I considered to be an exaggerated degree of interest. I tried to gauge George's mood by the position of his hands on the wheel.

'You said we wouldn't be going anywhere near Bastille,' said Clara.

'We're not,' I said. 'That's only the sign.'

'Why don't we call in on Nev's relations? They could probably tell us how to get off this blasted road.'

'Language.'

'Yes, they would be able to,' confirmed Naomi. 'They've lived here for ages. Marie-Laure is French. When they first got married they lived in Wembley, but then they decided to come back. They have this really wicked art shop, with posters and cards and all these lovely boxes and notebooks and what have you, and their flat is absolutely amazing, it's completely white with hardly anything in it, and those tubular steel chairs. They have this big glass table, and they always have the same white flowers in this square vase . . .'

She burbled on, but I'd heard quite enough to convince me that I wouldn't call in on Alex and Marie-Laure if they were the last people on earth.

'It's out of the question,' I said. 'It's one o'clock in the morning, for heaven's sake.'

'One forty-five,' said George. 'Shit. S-H-I-T.'

'This time round we'll do it,' I opined, unwisely.

'You mean *I* will do it. And incidentally,' he added, 'if you don't want our bleached bones to be found on the middle lane of this palsied road a week from now, be kind enough to sing out if you spot a filling station.'

At the garage the girls descended like dope fiends on the all-night confectionery and cigarette dispenser and I sat in the car and watched George as he contrived to ask directions of the youth behind the counter without seeming to do so. When the youth pointed and gestured vigorously with both hands, George chuckled and chatted as though the whereabouts of the main autoroute to Bordeaux was a mere *divertissement* to an Englishman with a car full of luggage and mutinous females on the outskirts of Paris at two in the morning.

His expression altered as he herded Naomi and Clara, jeans pockets bulging with *Disque Bleu* and chocolate bars, out of the shop and back to the car.

'Right,' he said, settling himself once more behind the wheel. 'No problem. It's exactly as I thought.'

It was just possible that George had already worked out the correct route for himself. But his prognostications concerning the Parisians' beauty sleep proved unreliable. Not only were there several thousand motor vehicles creeping nose-to-tail back into the capital from assorted *maisons secondaires* and camp sites, but the southbound commercial traffic was well under way, no doubt anticipating the flood of half-baked foreign holidaymakers who would be clogging the main roads from dawn till dusk.

'At least it's moving,' said George, as we sat staring at the monumental backside of a tanker full of yoghurt. 'And we're on the right track. All right in the back there?'

The girls had finally fallen asleep. George sighed happily and glanced at his watch. 'Good thing,' he said, 'if they sleep for a bit. Since we haven't progressed that far south I should be able to pick up the *Today* programme in a couple of hours. When they come round we can stop at some nice little *brasserie* or *crêperie* and have a spot of breakfast.'

Sadly the volume of traffic interfered with reception of Radio Four, and when the girls woke up we were still hemmed in by juggernauts and travelling (intermittently) at about fifteen miles an hour.

'Nadgers,' said Clara. 'What a nightmare.'

'Don't dramatise,' said George. 'It's only traffic. We're on holiday, remember? There's nothing to hurry for.'

'But I'm absolutely starving,' protested Clara. 'And we're both bursting for a pee.'

'Not long now,' said George comfortably, a prediction that flew in the face of all the evidence.

'Poop-poop!' he cried. 'Hooray for the open road.'

The rest of us stared jadedly out of the window. There is something peculiarly unwelcome about the dawn when one has scarcely slept, and when one is suffering from an empty stomach and a full bladder.

'*Courage mes braves*,' continued the irrepressible George. 'We are about to reap the benefits of opting for a pleasant, sensible A road instead of that noxious motorway.'

'What are they?' I asked.

'Well for one thing there won't be anything like

the number of lorries. And for another we won't be stuck with those ghastly service stations. As I said, we'll be able to stop at whatever pleasant provincial caff takes our fancy.'

'So long as it has a bog,' said Clara.

I turned, smiling brightly. 'How are you doing, Naomi?'

Naomi removed her headphones for a second. 'Sorry?'

'How are you doing?'

'Surviving.'

She replaced her earphones and closed her eyes. I recollected dimly how I had behaved at sixteen when being taken on holiday by the family of a friend. Slavishly, humiliatingly polite, painfully enthusiastic about everything, never allowing a word of complaint or dissent to pass my lips even when my friend's younger brother was sick over me on the ferry. How times had changed. The thought of three weeks exposed to Naomi's air of taciturn censure froze my blood.

'Here we are,' said George. 'Just the job.'

We climbed stiffly from the car. The place was a large wooden roadside chalet with a verandah and a metal sign advertising *Pschitt!* and cold beer, neither of which was a very appetising prospect at seven in the morning. It would not have surprised me to find a couple of cross-eyed, gap-toothed hillbillies sitting on tipped-back chairs chewing quids of tobacco.

'Where are the loos?' asked Clara.

'We'll ask. *Sois calme*,' replied George.

Naomi suddenly became animated. 'I'm going to have brioches and hot chocolate,' she announced. 'And a nice French ciggy.'

'Damn,' said George, 'I've left my *Economist* in the boot.'

We got as far as the steps when a girl about the same age as Clara and Naomi, and of about their combined weights, emerged from the door and indicated that the café was closed.

'*Nous voudrions le petit déjeuner*,' explained George, as if that were likely to make any difference. He tapped his watch. '*Il est sept heures*.'

'*Non*.' The girl shook her head. The rest of her quivered like a great, greasy duvet. '*Sommes fermé*.'

'Come on,' I muttered, thoroughly intimidated. 'Let's find somewhere else.'

'But it's ludicrous,' protested George. 'Apart from anything else, where's their business sense? Think of the passing trade they must be missing by not opening at a respectable time in the morning.'

Naomi came forward. '*Avez vous des toilettes s'il vous plaît?*'

'*Non!*' The huge girl looked murderously at the perpetrator of this solecism. '*Sommes fermé!*'

'Pardon us for living,' said Naomi, and led the way back to the car.

'You'll have to go behind a bush,' said George, the edge of his pleasant mood now well and truly blunted.

'Thanks a bundle!'

'Everyone does in France,' I said. 'They're far more relaxed about that sort of thing.'

A mile or so further on George pulled into a lay-by bordered by trees. The girls surveyed the terrain suspiciously, but I was out of the car like a shot.

When I returned, sunny with relief, the girls were still surveying the lie of the land while George fiddled with the knobs of the car radio.

'Get a move on,' I said. 'Breakfast calls.'

'Okay, okay!'

They began to move in the direction of the woods, but at that moment half a dozen French youths on motorbikes roared up the road and snarled to a halt in our lay-by. The atmosphere changed in an instant from one of womanly intimacy to one of twanging sexual tension. The youths dismounted and formed a loosely-knit group, leather collars up, hips cocked, hands in the back pockets of their 501s. Cigarettes were passed and lit. Comments were made. The girls' eyes glittered and their bodies underwent those subtle alterations that denote acceptance of a challenge.

George switched off the radio and leaned out. 'Girls, are you going to stand there all day or what? I want my coffee.'

Clara and Naomi lit up rival cigarettes, dragging and puffing like a couple of old tarts in a drinking club.

'Come on,' I said. 'To the woods.'

They didn't even deign to reply. It was a lost cause. The early morning air quivered with the throwing-down of gauntlets and the emission of rogue pheromones.

'Okay.' I admitted defeat. 'Back in the car.'

I returned to my seat. The girls remained where they were, but then the leader of the pack separated himself from the group and advanced on them, sending them scuttling for cover like a couple of terrified rabbits.

'That was a prize waste of time,' commented George.

Clara sighed heavily, but happily. 'What a bunch of chronic posers!'

We stopped half an hour later at another wayside establishment, which was open and which had all the usual offices. George dug out his copy of the *Economist* from the large case in the boot and we sat at a window table. We were the only customers. The girls returned from the loos with whitened faces.

'What's the *matter* with them?' complained

Clara.

'Nothing,' said George. 'They're the most civilised nation on earth.'

'They don't care about their toilets,' said Naomi self-righteously. George gave her a withering look, and then beamed brightly at the patron, whose villainous moustaches now hung over us.

'*Petit déjeuner pour quatre,*' he said.

'*M'sieur.*'

George turned back to Naomi and Clara. 'The French have perfected the art of living. It's simply that the British have an obsession with bodily functions. We like to pretend they don't happen.'

'My own I can put up with,' said Clara. 'It's everyone else's I have a problem with.'

'Look,' I said, 'do you think we could drop it? I want to enjoy my breakfast.'

This turned out to be a forlorn hope. It seemed we had hit on a stray pocket of French who had not matriculated in the art of living. Chipped mugs containing grey and gritty coffee, or in the girls' case tepid chocolate, were accompanied by hunks of desiccated bread, tiny cartons of the sort of highly coloured jam usually immured in a doughnut, and no butter. George pretended it was all good peasant fare, but it wasn't. It was outstandingly nasty. And on top of everything else a huge, scrofulous mongrel appeared from behind the bar and sat watching us at close range, emitting warm waves of halitosis.

'Poor thing,' said Naomi. 'It doesn't look well.'

'It's all right,' I said briskly. 'I bet it eats a lot better than the customers. Half a horse a day by the look of it.'

At this the dog stood up and shook violently, its great tatty pelt shuddering and flapping and sending out clouds of grizzled hair and grit. As it settled down once more, Clara peered closely at it.

'It's got the most awful eye bogies.'

We left soon after.

CHAPTER TWO

By eleven a.m. we were approaching Cahors and were within an hour or two of our objective. George announced that he was handing over the wheel to me.

'You should be fine,' he said grandly. 'We're on the home straight now.'

'Except for actually finding the place,' I pointed out.

'You'll be okay.' I noticed there was no question of a 'we' this time. 'You've got that letter with the details, haven't you?'

'Yes.'

'Well then.' He settled himself comfortably in the passenger seat and closed his eyes. 'We're home and dry. Wake me up if you have a problem.'

I glanced over my shoulder at the girls, but there was no comfort there. They were both plugged into their stereos. I negotiated Cahors in a sweat of anxiety in case the furious shouts of the indigenous drivers should wake George. When I finally emerged, I pulled over at the first lay-by and consulted the agent's instructions.

'The Villa Almont,' I read, 'is a miraculously restored farmhouse with many features typical of the Quercy area . . .' I skimmed to the second page. '. . . As you approach from the main southbound autoroute from Bordeaux—' Well, here was a problem for a start. Because of the traffic and George's desire to take breakfast at a pleasant provincial café we had opted for the A road and were consequently approaching from the opposite direction. I checked the name of the nearest small town: Lalutte. If I could get that far I could turn left instead of right, and then I'd be on course.

I wasn't over-confident. Still, this was a country road, we were closing on our destination and for the first time I began to feel I might enjoy the holiday. I am not one of nature's holiday-makers, being one of those who take a week to unwind and another week worrying about the return journey. But on this occasion I had taken the precaution of bringing along the work in progress to ease the strain.

After my flirtation with the serious novel, *Down Our Street* marked my return to popular fiction and the warm approval of my publishers, Era Books. But it was no bodice-ripper. My agent, Lew Mervin, had pointed out the unwisdom of going back to where the tights bulged and the rapiers flashed.

'That's had its day,' he told me. 'You've only got to see how many there are on the shelves. Every housewife in the land is dusting off her hot historical and the result is the shops are stuffed with quasi Blairs, and they're truly dire. It may be the sincerest form of flattery, Harriet, but it sure as hell means it's time to move on.'

'Well what,' I asked, 'would you recommend?'

'Clogs and shawls,' he replied. 'Mills and gloom.'

I demurred. 'I'm not sure it's me.'

'No one thought a literary novel was you,' said Lew. 'But look what you achieved!'

I looked, and in truth it wasn't much, but it was always nice being hosed down with Lew's admiration.

'I suppose so. I just feel – well, those sort of novels are so clannish. So parochial.'

'Can't you locate even the tiniest dash of northern blood?'

I thought about it. 'Sorry.'

'Personally,' said Lew, 'I think that's all to the good. Your speciality has always been bringing a freshness to established genres.'

So I had resurrected my impetuous, head-strong, not conventionally beautiful heroine, divested her of chemise, laced bodice, pannier and hoops, draped her in a plain wool skirt and black shawl and renamed her Mattie Piper. Thus equipped she had begun a new existence in the mean, cobbled streets and rain-lashed moorlands of Marsdyke, an apocryphal northern town where men were men, women were women, and old passions ran deep as the coal face. But the black shawl covered shoulders white as milk and hair the colour of burnished copper; and woe betide the man who by his importunings caused Mattie's eyes to flash green fire. I had lobbed in a spot of doubt as to Mattie's parentage, and a couple of suitors, one blond, rugged and of humble stock, the other suave, dark and moneyed, son of the local mill owner.

The presence on board of *Down Our Street*, snug in its box-file in the boot, was a great comfort. The smouldering resentments and quickening affections of Marsdyke would bear me company through the uncharted wastes of the holiday like old and trusted friends.

Lalutte was now only a few kilometres away. To left and right little lanes scuttled off between the dense crowds of watching sunflowers, and roughly painted signs beckoned to local *auberges*, and *dégustation de vins régionaux*, and *vente de melons*. Rustic *pigeonniers*, with charming timber frames and pointed roofs, stood in fields where fat white cows grazed like becalmed yachts. I was glad the others were asleep. I pictured rousing them cheerily as we pulled in at our destination, able to fill them in on the pleasant detail of the area which I had noted as I cruised independently along. When Lalutte appeared on the horizon – a clock tower, a wall and a jumble of red rooftops on top of a sugarloaf hill – I was almost lightheaded with exhilaration. I pulled over again and consulted the instructions.

'Turn right opposite the Lalutte junction,' advised Crispin Rutherford-Pounce, the English *chargé d'affaires* of France Vacances, from whom we had rented the Villa Almont. That meant I must turn left. I hummed along until I reached the foot of the sugarloaf hill and, yes, there was a narrow white road leading up to the town. And here a left turning with a small bridge over a stream, also mentioned by RP.

'Follow this road up the hill, passing the double-fronted farmhouse and the track sign-posted Forge. Over brow of hill take hairpin left and watch out for driveway entrance marked with John Bull teatowel.'

Piece of cake. I zoomed up the hill, marvelling at the view, the sunshine and the lack of traffic. Here was the farmhouse. It was a little further than I thought to the track. There was a sign, though I couldn't read it. But several kilometres went by and there was no hairpin left. I had already, as I thought, driven over the brow of the hill – there was yet another patchwork panorama shimmering before me to prove it. A small worm of doubt nibbled at my confidence. I pulled over and switched the engine off.

Rutherford-Pounce's map was rendered in a series of geometrically straight lines and crisp angles. This made it look wonderfully simple, but bore absolutely no relation to the curving, untidy, rural reality in which I now found myself. I stared fixedly at it, trying to relate my current position to some point on the neatly annotated graph.

'Don't tell me,' said Clara, now awake, 'we're lost.'

I smiled brightly without lifting my eyes from the map. 'No, we're not lost. I'm just getting my bearings.'

'So where are we?'

'Virtually there. In fact I think we're probably within a couple of hundred yards of the villa.'

Clara wound her window down and peered about. Naomi woke up and Clara filled her in on the bad news that we were more or less there. I felt it incumbent on me to make a move. As I started the car George regained consciousness with a sound like a cat coming in from the rain.

'I say, this is jolly nice. Where are we?'

'Almost there.'

'But not quite,' put in Clara. 'We're lost.'

'Don't be so silly,' I said testily. 'I know exactly where we are. It's merely just a case of pinpointing the villa.'

'Hm.' George pulled himself up in the seat with an 'if you want a thing done you'd better do it yourself' expression which I found totally enraging. He held out his hand. 'Let's have a dekko at RP's instructions.'

I turned the engine off again and silently handed him the sheet. He studied it, looked out, gazed round, looked at it again. Then said dully: 'It's at times like these I wish I hadn't paid the full rental in advance.'

'What on earth are you implying?'

'Nothing, nothing at all.'

'You're thinking it doesn't exist, aren't you?' said Clara with a quaver in her voice.

'I never heard such nonsense,' I said, with greater firmness than I felt. 'No one could look less like a crook than Rutherford-Pounce.'

George frowned at the map. 'But what does a crook look like? The days are long gone when the criminal fraternity obliged by wearing black masks and striped pullovers.'

'I think we should drive on down here a bit,' I said. 'It does say "over the brow of the hill" and we haven't gone that far.'

'I agree,' said George, surprisingly, adding, 'Any movement is better than none.'

I glanced in the rearview mirror and saw that for the first time Naomi appeared a shade tense.

Perhaps this was what made me over-eager to identify something – anything – as a hopeful sign.

'Look,' I said, 'down there.'

They all looked dutifully. 'What?'

'That could be it.'

A grey roof and a glint of window was just distinguishable among the trees on the hillside. Almost at once we came to a gateway – or at least gateposts, there was no gate – from which an unmade drive led to a large house. A square of material hung from the branch of a tree.

'Here we are!' I cried.

'What about the hairpin left?' said George, but I'd already turned in.

We were on what must once have been an open forecourt, now a sweep of grass, gravel and stone spiked here and there with leggy weeds. Straight ahead was the house, an enormous off-white building with rows of shuttered windows and a whimsical hexagonal tower at one end. To the right was a ramshackle wall with an archway leading into a large courtyard, also grassy and weed-strewn. There was no sign of life, no vehicle, no animal, no sound. An air of romantic dereliction hung over the whole place.

'Amazing,' said Naomi.

'Yes, it certainly is,' said George. 'And not a bit like its photograph.'

'You can't go by that,' I pointed out. 'They take photographs from funny angles.'

I switched off the engine. Clara got out and wandered away from the car, lighting a cigarette as she did so. In spite of the many windows I did not feel that we were being watched. The three of us sat there in silence, stupefied by the heat, and the sudden silence, and the long, long drive. Was this it?

'Hey Nev! Cop the pool!'

Clara was now at the far end of the house, looking at something beyond and slightly below it. Naomi baled out and walked over to join her.

'See that?' murmured George. 'Her backside winks at you.'

It was true. The crease beneath either pneumatic, denim-clad buttock opened and closed rhythmically as Naomi swayed away from us.

'Did Clara say she'd found the pool?' George asked.

'I think so.'

We got out of the car and strolled through the stunning heat to where the girls stood.

'Some pool, huh?'

It was if anything even bigger than the fifty feet

mentioned in Rutherford-Pounce's brochure. And it was surrounded by a paved area between the stones of which wild flowers, moss and weeds grew in abundance. At the far corner was a small, single-storey rectangular building with transom windows set high in its brick walls, and wooden swing doors like those of a western saloon.

'I suppose it really is a swimming pool . . .?' said George.

'Of course it is,' said Clara, 'it's got those little ladders.'

'And measurements on the side,' pointed out Naomi.

They were both enjoying the joke. And indeed George could be forgiven for his doubts, because it must have been years since this pool had been used for swimming. The light blue tiles with which it was lined, and the measurements to which Naomi referred, were coated in spinach-coloured slime. And in the water which half-filled it, villainous-looking giant carp slunk and loitered beneath huge lily-pads and a green canopy of algae.

'Okay, Dad,' said Clara, 'let's see you do a few lengths.'

George, arms folded, began a slow circuit of the poolside, clearly trying to think whose fault this was. The girls sat down on the stones and smoked happily. Perhaps they imagined this latest setback would lead to the holiday being cancelled. I glanced up at the house and noticed, from our new vantage point, that a French window stood open at the top of a flight of stone steps.

'I don't think—' I began.

Just then a naked man and two dogs came out of the house. At least, this is what I later realised had happened. At the time all I was conscious of was a jet-propelled nailbrush charging at me and making a bloodcurdling noise as it leapt to within striking distance of my throat.

'Help!' I shrieked.

George, safe on the other side of the pool, recommended me to calm down. The girls withdrew to the top of the bank.

'*Asti! Asti!*' called a voice. This was when I noticed that there were two figures following in the wake of the nailbrush, one squat and black, the other large and pinkish.

'*Asti! Méchant! Viens ici! Tais toi, Asti!*'

Asti, a miniature Yorkshire terrier with its topknot tied with tartan ribbon, took not a blind bit of notice of these orders. But the arrival of its friend, a great black beast like the scourge of the Baskervilles, seemed to calm it a little, and when the man called a fourth time it took a flying leap into his arms.

The big black dog stood stolidly staring at me,

at George and at the girls who had now recovered their composure and come to my side.

'*Comme tu es méchant, Asti!*' cooed the man, without a trace of real censure. He was completely naked except for a pair of flip-flops and a threadbare pink towel around his neck.

'Hallo,' he said, one finger scratching Asti's ruff. 'Is there something I can do for you?' He spoke English with an exceptionally fruity French accent.

He didn't seem in the least surprised to find us there. I could sense the twin laser beams of the girls' stares coming from behind my right shoulder and fixing on his private parts which were hairless and chubby, like a cherub's.

'I do apologise if we're intruding,' said George. 'We're not quite sure if we have the right place . . .'

As he launched into a graceful explanation of our presence I kept wondering why our host didn't lower the dog to cover his modesty. But when I caught the animal's eye and its lips ruched into a snarl of naked ferocity I had the answer to my question. The large dog flopped to the ground and lay there panting.

'. . . and we ended up here,' George finished.

'You are most welcome!' said the man, beaming. 'But this is not the Villa Almont.'

I was overwhelmed with relief. 'But what about the teatowel?'

'Teatowel?'

'We were told to look out for a John Bull teatowel, and we thought we saw one hanging over your gate.'

'Ah, that is my *drapeau* – my flag!'

I could feel the movement of air which meant the girls were starting to giggle. It was time to make our excuses and leave. George obviously had the same idea. He stepped forward with his right hand extended. The dog growled. He withdrew it.

'I'm so sorry we disturbed you. I'm George Blair, this is my wife Harriet.' The man gave a little bow over the dog's quivering topknot. 'And that,' continued George, with the slightly glassy smile which indicated he would kill anyone who sniggered, 'is our daughter Clara and her friend Naomi.'

'Hallo,' said the girls.

'*Enchanté, mesdemoiselles*, said the man. 'And to introduce myself, I am Guy de Pellegale.'

Our turn now to smile and bow. 'The rest of my family are still in Paris now, which is why it is so quiet,' he explained. 'It is so exciting for me to have visitors!'

There was a loud snort from behind.

'We'd be enormously grateful if you could point us in the direction of the villa,' said George. 'And then we'll get out of your hair.'

This provoked another snort, since Guy de

Pellegale was as triumphantly hairless as a newborn babe. There was something almost sinister in such gleaming all-over baldness.

We returned to the car, the girls jack-knifing into the back seat like rats into a hole. De Pellegale explained with the utmost charm and courtesy that George had taken the wrong turning off the Cahors road.

'My wife was driving, actually,' said George, ever the gentleman.

'I followed the agent's instructions,' I said. 'I turned off opposite the Lalutte junction.'

'But you took the first, Madame. And it is the second you want.'

De Pellegale explained that we were no distance from the villa as the crow flew, *en effet* he could actually look down on our garden from the edge of his garden, but in order to drive there we must return to the main road and take the next turning on the left.

As we bumped away across the grassy gravel he stood there, his *embonpoint* gleaming in the sun, the nailbrush twitching with frustrated fury in his arms.

The girls exploded. 'What a basketcase! What a headbanger!'

George – back at the wheel for safety's sake – said: 'I thought he was a charming chap.'

I said, 'But a little eccentric, you must admit. I

mean the place was weird, for a start.'

'Oh I don't know. I'm quite disappointed it's not where we're going to be.'

As we paused between the gateposts Naomi peered out of the window. 'I wonder what's on his flag.'

'Family crest I shouldn't wonder,' said George.

Speaking for myself, I was thrilled to bits that we weren't going to be spending the next two weeks *chez* de Pellegale with his homicidal nailbrush, his well-aired privates and his pool full of killer carp.

And when we caught our first sight of the Villa Almont I was delirious. In seventh heaven. This was the Business. Even Clara and Naomi conceded that it looked pretty good and George (overlooking the fact that I had organised the entire holiday) asked if anybody had any complaints now?

It was a building of mellow stone, sprawling up the grassy lower slope of the wooded hill upon which, I now realised, the de Pellegale house was situated further up. A verandah ran along the whole of the front of the house garlanded with honeysuckle and hung with trailing geraniums. Easy chairs and a wooden refectory table stood in the shade. On three sides of the house was a rambling garden – fruit trees (amongst which we caught a tantalising glimpse of two hammocks), flowering shrubs, acres of daisy-spattered lawn, all brought to that state of artful artlessness which is so monstrously difficult to achieve. There was also a rough stone barn converted into a spacious garage, and a pool to die for – a glittering oblong of flat, blue water surrounded by white paving that hurt the eyes, and flowers of flame red and yellow. All this and utter, perfect seclusion . . .

'Hallo, good afternoon and welcome!'

We were standing by the car breathing it in. I could not at first believe I'd heard the voice. 'You made it all right then?'

We blinked, and refocused unwillingly on the intruder. He was in his early thirties, shock-headed and dressed in an emerald and turquoise shell suit and sparkling Reeboks, like a fugitive from *Brookside*. We stared.

'I do beg yours.' He shook our hands in turn, a liberty to which we nervelessly acquiesced, hoping it was a bad dream. 'I assume Crispin warned you about me.'

We shook our heads.

'Annexe Man.' He laid a hand on the front of his shiny jacket. 'The sitting tenant. Mine's the purple Mini, but you have sole use of the garage.'

Something did cry faintly from the deeps of my memory. Yes, somewhere there had been mention of an 'unobtrusive regular tenant' in the villa's adjoining annexe. But surely, surely, this couldn't be—?

'You must be the Blair clan,' said Annexe Man. 'And I'm Royston Sinclair. You're most welcome. And if there's anything, I mean anything, I can do . . .'

As we went into the cool, herb-scented interior of the house, Clara spoke for everyone.

'Come back, baldy-bot, all is forgiven.'

CHAPTER THREE

George and I lay side by side, soaking up the sun. Tucked beneath the barn at the top of the sloping lawn was a *sous-sol* containing the owners' wine cellar, and here the girls had set up camp, their stereo playing at the permitted level.

'If he invades our privacy just once,' I said, 'just once, I shall be on the phone to Rutherford-Pounce.'

George chuckled. 'We mustn't prejudge the fellow. He may not be our type—'

'I don't care whose type he is, I don't want him on our holiday.'

'—he may not be our type but he was nothing if not civil. If we strike any hitches it may even be useful to have an English speaker about who knows the ropes.'

'I have no intention of asking him anything. I have no intention of speaking to him at all.

Knowing he's there is bad enough.'

'You're making too much of it,' said George. 'You mustn't let it spoil things for you. Besides,' he added lightly, 'the telephone's in the annexe and I may need to make the odd call.'

As if we had summoned him up the bell on the corner of the verandah jangled. 'A rustic intercom' Royston had called it when showing us around. 'You ring it if you want to speak to me, and vice versa.' I had vowed at that moment never to touch the darn thing, and I had innocently supposed that if Royston rang it he would then wait discreetly round the corner until we arrived.

This was not to be. Even as George rose from his towel to answer the summons the beastly man appeared at our end of the verandah, raised his hands as if blessing us, and called: 'Sorry to disturb! I remembered something I meant to tell you. If you're wireless addicts like me you may be interested to know that it's possible to pick up Radio Four from the top of the hill.'

He really was unbelievable. George, standing halfway between him and me, made a strange little movement which I interpreted as trying to put his hands into nonexistent pockets.

'Thanks!'

'My pleasure. Up by old de Pellegale's château, the place where you went by mistake.'

'Right – much appreciated.' George took a few rocking steps backwards. The whole exchange would have been great material for Jacques Tati.

Royston did not, as he should have done, withdraw at once, but stood there grinning, and then nodded in the direction of the *sous-sol*. 'Girls enjoying themselves, I see.'

I gritted my teeth. He annoyed me so much that I felt I might simply levitate, rigidly at the horizontal like a conjurer's assistant, lifted by the heat of my irritation. But George was determined to be polite.

'Oh yes, happy as sandboys!'

I'd have given a lot to see Clara's face on hearing this comment.

'Right, I'll leave you to it then. *A bientôt!*'

'Yes! Bye!'

I felt George thump down next to me again.

'I swear I'll kill him,' I said.

'A very trying man.' He laid his hand on my thigh. A long, hot pause ensued. 'Still, handy to know about the BBC reception. I'll be able to keep up with the Archers.'

I had the same feeling that I used to get as a child when I snuggled down in my bed only to spot a spider scuttling down the opposite wall into obscurity. It didn't have to be a very big spider. Knowing it was there, going about its spidery business among my possessions, was

41

enough to keep me awake for hours.

I could not ignore Royston Sinclair.

It's different, of course, when you're travelling alone, when the hourly expectation of disaster keeps you pinging with tension all day and sleeping like the dead at night. The previous spring, following the publication of *A Time to Reap*, Era Books had seen fit to despatch me on a month's PR tour of Australia and New Zealand. George had moved back to Basset Regis for the duration. In retrospect I realised this had probably been instrumental in our reconciliation, since four weeks' intensive exposure to the fruit of his loins in their natural habitat had convinced him that I was a wonderful woman. Overlooking the fact that it was I who had given him the elbow he decided in my absence that we should try again. As it turned out he was lucky: I was sufficiently grateful to him on my return to consider the idea, and agree to give it a go.

The antipodean branch of Era Books had gone out of their way to guide, cherish and fête me as befitted an author upon whom several thousand pounds' worth of first-class travel had been lavished. They were tireless, nay zealous, in their attentions. When I arrived late at night in Perth, bug-eyed, dehydrated and brain-dead after twenty-one hours in the air, I was met by a wiry redhead in batik culottes who began talking as I came through the barrier and did not draw breath until she left the honeymoon suite at the Perth Transglobal three hours later. During this time she made a speech of welcome; ran through her CV and qualifications for the role of Minder; told me she'd had hell with Jeffrey but that Jilly was bliss; gave me an exhaustive run-down on the many special features of my room (including circular four-poster, courtesy vitamin tablets, quadrophonic sound and a view over the Swann River estuary); established that I had taken the wrong suitcase from the carousel and effected the changeover with the furious Scotsman who had mine; told me I would need only flat, comfortable shoes; and presented me with a red leather folder containing my schedule and itinerary. Her name was Monica Ball.

'I'd better leave you to your beauty sleep, Harriet!' she said, bouncing to her feet. 'And have a lie-in, do. The jogging photo isn't till nine thirty.'

Jogging photo?

' 'Night Harriet!' Monica spoke in exclamation marks. 'It's really great that you're here!'

I crawled to the four-poster and slumped across it. Jogging photo?

Of course I should never have mentioned the marathon. This weird excess, jotted down in a desperate attempt to make my author notes more interesting, had been seized upon by the Oz Erans as a major selling point. I wasn't just any old housewife wordsmith with a string of popular successes to my credit, I was a *jogging* housewife wordsmith etc. And I was never to be allowed to forget it.

Fortunately Monica had booked me an alarm call so that I might luxuriate in my lie-in until all of seven a.m. This gave me the opportunity to cast an eye over my schedule as I awaited a room-service breakfast. Yes, dammit, it was true. A local paper wished to photograph me in shorts and singlet jogging along the prom. And what was this? Dave Cuthbertson, veteran reporter and fellow marathon-runner, was looking forward to interviewing me on the run.

Cuthbertson turned out to be a desiccated little man the colour of tea who had run across Australia for charity. He surveyed my specially bought new kit with the utmost scorn from the unassailable jog-cred of his own threadbare, sweatstained garments. It was no contest. He was several inches shorter than me, but still contrived to conduct the entire interview over his right shoulder without breaking sweat. That morning set a precedent from which there was to be no turning back. In every major city on the continent features editors dug out the fun-runners, the marathon veterans and the cross-country stars from among their staff, ordered a period of intensive training, and prepared to see whether this particular whingeing Pom could cut the mustard. It was a tribute to Monica's PR skills that they all seemed to think they were the first people to have the idea.

'I read somewhere that you're a bit of a runner . . .' the voice over the phone would say, and before I could demur: 'We thought it might be fun to do a piece with that sort of angle – you know, you in your running gear, out in the park in the morning . . .' Yes, yes, I knew. And next morning, bright and early in the hotel foyer, there would be the super-fit representative of the local press while out on the pavement Monica briefed a baffled photographer.

I suppose I should have been glad of something – anything – which boosted my column inches, especially after the dash cut by Jeffrey and Jilly. But I could not escape the worrying impression that it was my fitness, not my book, that the interviewers were interested in. It was hard enough to produce telling quotes about one's work at the best of times, let alone on one's third pre-breakfast circuit of an inner-city park, with the heat and the lead levels rising rapidly.

Monica was nothing if not appreciative.

'You're such a sport, Harriet! I don't think I've

ever had an author who was so positively bounding with energy!' She spoke as if I had personally requested this madness. 'I talked to your lovely Vanessa on the phone last night,' she went on. 'And she said she wasn't a bit surprised you were taking us by storm!'

Suddenly I saw that Monica was Vanessa's precise Australian equivalent – effusive, energetic and rabidly ambitious. It was crucial that I make a good showing on this tour: I represented one of the rungs on Monica's ladder to the top.

Her friends and acquaintances were legion.

'I want you to have wonderful weekends!' she announced early on, not recognising that my idea of a wonderful weekend was one of zombie-like isolation by the hotel pool. 'I'm going to introduce you to some really beaut people. And food! You haven't eaten till you've eaten well in Australia – and drunk Australian wine, of course.'

Eating out, and food and drink generally, turned out to be a key factor in Monica's pitch on behalf of her fellow countrymen.

'We're not all Surf 'n' Turf you know, Harriet,' she confided, filling my head with images of burly lifeguards and peplum-jacketed ladies at the Melbourne Cup, before adding: 'Not all prawn cocktails and steaks. We have the most wonderful natural ingredients in the world, and some of the greatest cooks. I want you to go back home and tell them you had the best meals of your life when you were in Oz . . .'

She was as good as her word. In and out of innumerable bistros, brasseries and sushi bars we trooped with members of Monica's immense social circle. We consumed prawns so huge they must have been stopped with a Kalashnikov, calamari so fresh its tentacles threatened to grab you by the throat, salads so various and crunchy that to eat them was to sound like an army on the march . . . Oh yes, the food was superb. And the company amiable, vibrant and possessed of the kind of healthy good looks that would have made even the fittest Brit feel like a species of slug. After every social engagement Monica would gaze into my eyes and ask: 'What did you think of them, Harriet? Aren't they great? And wasn't that dinner just the best . . .?' And every time I'd assure her that the whole thing had indeed been wonderful, too chicken to confess that my dearest wish was for a night in front of the in-house video in my dressing gown eating a soft boiled egg with Marmite soldiers.

It wasn't only the social demands of all this carousing. There was also the issue of Monica's private life, the complexity of which was awe-inspiring. She had a man in every state as well as a live-in boyfriend at home in Sydney, and a married man to whom she referred as her bit of 'arvo delight' as though he were a trifle topping.

At every gathering of Monica's friends the conversation – after the obligatory topic of me, my books, and my reaction to Australia – was taken up with in-depth discussion of matters so personal they quite put me off my buttered brains with capers. I'd never thought of myself as easily embarrassed, but Monica and her cronies had me disappearing under restaurant tables from coast to coast.

At one place in Adelaide, where about eight of us were eating pasta al fresco, Monica suddenly clasped my wrist with a shriek, and said: 'Hey guys, you know we should really tone this down! Harriet here is a happily married lady!' This was the one aspect of my life which the Erans had implored me to regard as holy writ engraved on tablets of stone.

'Really?' Cliff from local radio looked at me in wonderment. 'How long you been married then, Harriet?'

'Twenty years,' I said apologetically. You'd think I'd just told them I'd been born a man.

'No! Twenty years? Unreal! That is totally unreal! Twenty years with the same bloke?'

'Yes,' I muttered shamefacedly.

Monica put her arm across my shoulders. 'I think it's marvellous, I do really. You're the last of a dying breed, Harriet. Even my mum and dad are divorced.'

Eventually they composed themselves sufficiently to get on with their dinner, but even then I caught the occasional bright, incredulous glance. I could almost feel the collagen draining from my skin, and the liver spots appearing on my hands.

It was unbelievably frustrating to have to submit to this youthful incredulity, and not be able to capitalise on my adventures with Kostaki, and more recently with Edward, disastrous though their outcome had been. I promised myself that if I ever needed to I would produce my falls from grace like rabbits (oh unfortunate simile) from a hat, and even Monica would be gobsmacked.

The opportunity never arose. Like the jogging, the twenty years of marriage became instant myth. There was no escaping it. Monica contrived to build it in to every exchange. George, who had always been a shadowy figure as far as my publishers were concerned, had now sprung into focus. A helpmeet of more than two decades' standing had won his spurs.

So now there was another inevitable question to be addressed.

'And your husband, Harriet – George, isn't it? – how does he react to your success?'

'He thinks it's marvellous,' I would reply.

'You've been married for more than twenty years, so he must have seen you through the tough times—'

'Well yes, of course . . .'

'All those rejection slips. How much difference does a stable relationship make, Harriet?'

I was only glad none of my family could hear me as I said: 'Oh, an absolutely crucial difference. I couldn't have done any of it without George.'

This was at least partly true. To be fair to George he had always been a perfectly supportive husband. The hiccups in our marriage had not been of his making, or only indirectly. I suppose any wife is fully justified in saying she couldn't have made it without her husband. This begs the question of how much more she might have achieved without his clothes to wash, his house to maintain and his appetites to accommodate.

Still, it ill behove me to complain, especially in public. So the Great Twenty-Year Marriage was at my shoulder as I jogged round Australia.

'What the—?'

This is one of those exclamations which, like 'Oh, and by the way' and 'Here, drink this' and 'I might say the same of you', are usually only employed in TV plays. But there was no doubting George's genuine alarm.

'What's the matter?'

Leaning against George's shoulder was the biggest domestic cat I'd ever seen – coal-black, long-haired, with eyes the colour of barley sugar, a tail like a lavatory brush and voluminous feathered trousers. The girls came rushing down from the *sous-sol* and picked it up.

'Oh, he's really swee-eet . . .!'

'Christ, it scared the living daylights out of me,' said George grumpily and flopped down again. The cat reposed in Clara's arms, emitting a thunderous purr, its enormous gut dropping like a furry hammock. Despite its size it was a cuddly animal unlike our own cat, Fluffy, who was shifty and combative.

'I expect it's a neighbour's,' I said.

'I see you've found Teazel!'

It was Royston, passing by on the far side of the pool in the direction of the compost heap, a dripping bin liner in one hand. At that moment he was the man for whom the expression 'blot on the landscape' had been created.

'Sorry to intrude,' he said, 'just recycling. Jules and Antoinette are very hot on their compost.'

For some reason I had a fleeting vision of our landlords coupling wildly on a mound of steaming rubbish.

'Is that his name?' said Clara. 'Teazel?'

'It is. He's my best boy, aren't you, Teazy?' Royston made a smacking sound with his lips that sent a cold shiver down my spine.

'Where does he live?' George did not like cats and only tolerated Fluffy at home because of his hostile and reclusive nature.

'Where does he live?' Royston echoed, with a stupid expression of incredulity. 'How can you ask? He lives here, of course.'

'Brilliant!' chorused the girls. 'He's so gorgeous!'

'Yes,' said Royston, 'he's a real *mensch*, isn't he, girls? And this is his manor, his domain. Teazy rules the roost.'

'You look after him, do you?' said George.

'Well, it's a joint effort really.' Royston stepped on to the poolside, his bin bag dripping dark spots on the white stones.

'Joint effort?'

'We'll look after him the whole time, won't we, Nev?' said Clara.

Teazel's purr had now risen to a sound like an approach- ing helicopter.

'By all means,' said Royston.

George stood up. 'No, I don't think so.' He grinned tetchily. 'Minding the owners' cat wasn't part of our remit. We come on holiday to get away from pets.'

'Speak for yourself!' Clara and Naomi bore Teazel away to their camp by the *sous-sol*.

Royston smiled. 'It looks as though you might

have a spot of bother reaching a consensus on that one.'

George sat down. 'It looks as though we'll have to put up with him being about – we haven't much option – but there's no way I'm feeding him. The thing's the size of a small panther, for God's sake.'

'Amazing, yes,' sighed Royston admiringly. From his expression I had a nasty feeling he would have liked to be up by the *sous-sol* luxuriating in the girls' attentions along with the laid-back Teazel. 'Well, I'll leave you to it.'

We lay down. The sun beat. The ghetto-blaster played Madonna's 'Cherish'. The girls cooed over the cat. But I could just hear the squelch of Royston's bin bag evacuating on to the compost.

I got up and leapt into the pool, sending a shower of cold drops on to George and disturbing him again.

As our first day was a Monday and the shops were closed we were using up such supplies as we'd brought with us, and those things which RP had requested Royston to get in on our behalf. Knowing that the *baguettes*, cheese, pâté and salad had been purchased and handled by Annexe Man rather took the edge off my appetite. I gave a saucer of the pâté to Teazel, guiltily aware that I was thereby binding him to us with hoops of steel. Tomorrow there would have to be a foray to the *supermarché* in Lalutte.

In the evening after supper the girls went for a swim. Their splashes and shrieks floated to us as we sat on the verandah in the golden glow of the dying sun. From beyond the corner of the verandah I could see a bright shaft of light emanating from the annexe, and wondered what Royston was doing. Teazel appeared from the undergrowth and sat on the grass, feet together, gazing at us from his ruff like some pampered Elizabethan favourite.

'Maneater,' said George. He sounded quite mellow. 'Think I'll go for a bit of a walk,' he added. 'Fancy coming?'

We strolled up the side of the house, where the bedroom doors opened on to the garden, and down the driveway in the direction of the lane. As we passed the annexe we saw Royston sitting at his desk, tapping busily on a keyboard. The VDU in front of him was packed with text. On a table next to him a fax machine spluttered forth documents, the first few sheets of which had already slipped to the floor.

At the top of the drive, on the other side of the road, a broad track led on up the hill. We could make out the top row of the château's many windows glinting in the afterglow.

'Shall we?' said George.

We walked through the woods, bypassing the château's garden, and emerged near the top of the hill in the road I had first taken. The view was charming – lush, domestic, profoundly and mysteriously rural as only the landscape of a peasant economy can be.

We walked along the lane as far as the entrance to the château. As before there was no sign of life, and no sound from inside. We stood staring, enjoying the peace. The tattered 'flag' hung limply from its branch. It wasn't a flag at all but a square of material on which someone had written some words in smudged gothic script:

'Backpackers and Wayfarers Always Welcome.'

'Crumbs,' said George. 'Castle Dracula.'

CHAPTER FOUR

All her life (I wrote) *Mattie Piper had known that Seth Barlow would wait for her. No matter what she did, no matter how many other hearts she broke, no matter how long she went away for, Seth would be waiting at the corner of her street when she returned.*

Writing *Down Our Street* was comfortable. For one who felt like a foreigner after Scratchwood Services I was remarkably at home with it. In fact I felt set to out-clog allcomers.

Not (I added) *that she had any intention of encouraging Seth. Quite the reverse. As she tripped down the cobbles in her bright new shoes, the skirt of her dress lifted daintily in one hand, she was conscious of being watched from the narrow, darkened windows of this street where she had been born and raised. Watched, and envied . . .'*

My heroine was not to know that come-uppance time was nigh. Like Scarlett, Amber, and scores of other fiery and impulsive heroines before her, Mattie Piper needed bringing to her senses. Mattie was a good girl at bottom (I was beginning to think in the vernacular), but had got a bit above herself since turning her back on her humble origins and the devoted friends of her youth and swanning off to the bright lights of the apocryphal city of Haddeshall. There she had knocked about a bit on the halls before catching the eye of a bewhiskered, cigar-chewing impresario and carving out a reputation as a singer: The Northern Nightingale. But Mattie was soon to discover the hard way how ephemeral was the nature of fame. The Nightingale would be sick as a parrot by the time I, and the residents of Marsdyke, had done with her.

Halfway down the street she passed Seth's doorway. It was evening and he would likely be in. – I allowed a hint of colloquial speech to colour my style here and there – *She kept her chin lifted and her eyes straight ahead, conscious of the pert beauty of her profile beneath its becoming city hat. Caleb* – I referred to the leering impresario – *had often told her she had the profile of a princess, and now she wanted Seth to see it too. During her time away Mattie Piper had learned to collect men's admiration like the flowers they threw on to the stage: she scooped them up with a smile, and threw them away a moment later.*

'Mattie! Mattie Piper – is it you?'

It was Seth himself, opening wide his door and stepping out to greet her.

'Mattie – I can scarce believe it!'

She stopped and turned to face him. 'You had best do so, Seth Barlow, for I shan't be here long.'

His blue eyes drank in her smart clothes, the fetching hat, the dainty red shoes. He ran a work-roughened hand through his fair thatch.

'Not staying?' There was naked disappointment in his voice.

Was nakedness audible? I often wondered. Anyway.

Mattie tossed her head. 'I should say not!'

'But you've been away so long, Mattie girl. And by – you look fine.'

I wasn't dead sure whether I was the right side of the Pennines with that 'by', or even in the right latitude . . . But this was only the first draft, so I circled it and moved on.

'And that's the way I intend to stay,' said Mattie. 'I just came back to see Uncle and Auntie, and then I'll be away back to Haddeshall. I've a tour coming up.'

Seth beamed. 'I heard you were doing well. Top of the bill, I heard.'

Mattie didn't bother denying it. It was almost true, wasn't it?

'I must be on my way, Seth.'

He stepped aside humbly and she walked off down the street with her head held high, feeling his eyes upon her every step of the way.

I closed the A4 pad, laid down my Biro ('Another bonkbuster from the ballpoint of Ms Blair', one past reviewer had written) and stretched luxuriously. I was aglow with virtue. Only eight o'clock in the morning, the sun barely warm on the surface of the pool, and I'd already done an hour's work! I owed myself a tranquil swim and a coffee before the girls rendered the day unholy with pop music and wrangling over sunbeds.

I got up from the table in the large gallery *atelier* which I'd appropriated as a study. Near the balustrade that overhung the kitchen area on the level below was a jigsaw belonging to the owners, a five-thousand-piece behemoth depicting 'The Building of Stonehenge'. Thousands of tiny, simian figures, heavily bearded and scowling, stretched away into the distance. Acres of storm-tossed clouds melted into vast areas of shadowy downland from which the giant rocks jutted in their grim uniformity. Come to think of it, the landscape had a lot in common with that featured in *Down Our Street*. A few satanic mills would have been perfectly in keeping. The jigsaw had only two helpful landmarks. One was an overseer, or foreman, just left of centre (as was only proper). In spite of the inclement weather he looked a bit more cheerful than the others –

access to Management amenities, no doubt. The other was the Chief Druid, all in Persil white.

I crouched down and peered at the sea of grey-green pieces. There were a couple of paler ones where a shaft of dismal sunlight slanted through the storm clouds, and I homed in on these and stuck them in. Then I went downstairs.

George was still asleep, covered by a sheet which protected his modesty in the studiedly casual way of sheets in PG certificate films. There was no evidence that his dreams rated an '18'. I didn't disturb him. Instead I removed my 'I've Got the Fiction Addiction' T-shirt (a gift from Barford Central Library on the occasion of their Historical Romance Festival in 1987), and got into my new bikini from Medusa Modes. The bikini represented the ultimate triumph of market forces over common sense. How else could I have been persuaded to buy two strips of nylon bunting for a price in excess of twenty pounds?

And there were the hidden costs involved in the wearing of such a garment. My entire body from the hips down had been subjected to a waxing so intensive that my follicles had gone into permanent retreat. The handmaidens at the Oasis Health Club had then declared open season on cellulite with a motorised rubber hedgehog which had my fatty cells running for cover.

Still – I did a quick twirl in front of the

full-length mirror – it had been worth it.

I stepped out of the bedroom door into the early morning sunshine. I was not quite alone. In the melon field on the hill opposite a man in blue overalls was doing something complicated with rolls of wire. He was far enough away for me not to be able to see his face, so perhaps that meant he was also far enough away not to be able to see my hips, which now felt unpleasantly exposed.

My other companion was Teazel, who sat like a teapot by one of the pool's overflow ducts, staring down through the grille. I knew what this meant, and steeled myself. First I picked up the cat and carried him, stiff with outrage, to the bedroom, where I shut him in. I then lifted the grille, revealing the wretched shrew that was paddling round and round with nightmare slowness inside the duct. I picked out the shrew, placed it in the shelter of the plants, and replaced the grille. My next move was to take the six-foot pool net and trawl the surface for the flies, moths, harvesters, spiders and other winged beasts who had dived in overnight. These I carefully emptied out on to the grass where, we quickly learned, they dried out in record time and plunged straight back in, repaying one's kindness by closing their mandibles on the first bit of human flesh they encountered.

Having thus cocked a snook at Nature red in

tooth and claw I dived in and began a leisurely fifty lengths.

This was the holiday fantasy I entertained on those dark days in the new year when the temperature plummets, the mucus rises, and the only thing keeping the wolf from the door is the log-jam of manila envelopes. This morning sun, and blue water, and perfect silence broken only by the soft gloop of breaststroke . . . this, indeed, was the Business . . .

'Aaaargh!'

It was George, adding to his lexicon of exclamations previously encountered only in fiction.

I continued swimming.

'Get off, damn you! Ouch! Piss off!'

I turned, and swam on.

The bedroom door burst open and Teazel shot out like one of those gremlins in the Spielberg film, all staring eyes, ears and fur *en brosse*. He did not even pause to check out the shrew, but raced to the top of the garden and disappeared amongst the fruit trees beyond the barbecue.

George appeared, stark naked.

'What the bloody hell was that cat doing shut in the bedroom?'

I stopped. 'Sorry. I had to rescue a shrew.'

'Oh, well, of course that makes it all right. You know perfectly well I hate a cat on the bed, and yet you lock me in so the creature can dig his claws into my leg while you rescue a rodent which will probably die anyway.'

'We're all going to die,' I said philosophically.

'Okay.' George held up his hands. 'Okay.' He examined his thigh. 'See that? Severe lacerations.'

'Come on in, it's gorgeous.'

He looked huffy. 'Someone had better go and buy the bread.'

'Okay, but cover yourself. Farmer Giles is in the field opposite.'

'Farmer—?' George's hands flew with maidenly swiftness to where they were most needed. 'So he is.'

He jumped in and did a storming crawl up to the far end. When he got there he shook the water out of his eyes and said, 'What's he doing?'

'I don't know. Something with wire. Mending fences?'

George peered over the side. 'Looks more as if he's planning to blow us up.'

When I got back from Lalutte with the shopping Prince was warbling improper suggestions in the girls' room, but George was nowhere to be found. I made coffee, dolloped apricot jam into a croissant, and carried both on to the verandah. In the field the farmer had finished unrolling his wires and was busy erecting something in the far corner. It was ten o'clock and getting hot. I heard voices from round the corner, and braced myself for an encounter with Royston, but it was George who finally appeared.

'Hello,' I said. 'Where've you been? Coffee's made.'

'Thanks.' George disappeared and came back with breakfast.

'Actually Gareth rang up, and Royston came to get me to take the call.'

'Gareth?' I put my cup down. 'Oh, no. What's wrong?'

'Why should anything be wrong? Honestly, darling, you're paranoid. No, he just wanted to ask about our journey, see how we were. Rather a pleasing impulse, I thought.'

'He didn't say what was wrong?'

'Will you stop that? Nothing is wrong. He's probably missing us.'

I treated this unlikely suggestion with the contempt it deserved. 'I hope Royston didn't mind being disturbed. We only gave Gareth that number for emergencies.'

George dusted croissant crumbs off his palms, but overlooked the ones enmeshed in his chest hair. 'He didn't mind. Couldn't have been pleasanter about it, as a matter of fact.'

'Ingratiating, you mean.'

'No, no,' said George in the tone of one who

has the patience of a saint but finds it running out. 'I think you've got the wrong idea about him. He's okay.'

'What does he do?'

'Researcher. In exile pro tem from the Commission writing a few reports.'

'Reports on what?'

'Umm ... what did he say? ... Training initiatives in rural areas.'

'I see.' In the field the farmer had now moved down to the corner nearest us.

'He's got a pretty smooth set-up round there,' went on George. 'He's got some absolutely state-of-the-art desktop technology.'

Here were a couple of phrases which, like target towns, rumpus room and ETA, made my teeth itch.

'Good,' I said. 'Lucky him.'

'Another thing,' said George. 'He has a glass eye.'

There seemed no possible response to this. But I was spared having to find one for at that moment the farmer completed his work, and the boom of a cannon made George spill boiling coffee over his lap.

'I wonder,' I said, as we sat down at a table in the town square at Lalutte, 'whether that cat is Royston Sinclair's other eye.'

'Mmm?'

George was extracting the last ounce of nourishment from his copy of the *Economist*. I was reminded of a starving man eking out a single square of chocolate.

'I think it spies on us and reports back to the annexe.'

'Probably.'

It was very hot. We had parked the car in the lower reaches of the town and trudged up through the narrow mediaeval streets to the square, which crowned the hill. The girls had stopped off at a less picturesque café on the way to take iced Coke and a reviving fag.

'You want to stick with us,' George had told them. 'It'll be marvellous up in the old part.'

'That's all right,' said Clara. 'We like it here.'

'So what will you do?'

'Wait for you to come back down.'

The café where we left them had speckled metal tables, a mass of rusty advertising signs and a condom machine near the door. Inside in the gloom two or three locals in flat caps and braces kept their smeary glasses company at the long bar. The *patron* was pale, dour and exhausted-looking, with hair brilliantined straight back à la Valentino, and plimsolls. It was difficult, from looking at his premises, to deduce what he did that wore him out so.

'Please be sensible,' I said as we left them.

'Certainly not,' said Clara with leaden sarcasm. 'We're going to drag those hunky Frenchmen off their stools and indulge in perverted practices with them the moment your backs are turned, isn't that right, Nev?'

The town square was worth the climb. A cobbled expanse surrounded by buildings of such enchanting, crooked antiquity they might have come from a Disney film. Shutters, windowboxes, a cool, paved cloister with one or two interesting shops. A stone church with a great black bell hanging beneath a red-tiled campanile. And two cafés.

We had chosen to sit in the one with the most shade. A blackboard suggested various *spécialitiés de la région*, and a set lunch for a price which, George pointed out, was almost laughable.

'We'll have to come here to eat,' he said. 'Real French bourgeois provincial cooking.'

'It's awfully quiet,' I said.

At this point a door at the rear of the café banged open and a pack of dogs raced out, hurtling between the tables and knocking over chairs in the process. Once in the square, a dachshund settled down to defecate in the middle of the cobbles and a great Dane with cropped ears like Scooby-Doo allowed itself to be mounted by a long-haired Alsatian.

'Oh dear,' I said. 'Everywhere we go.'

George put down the *Economist*. 'But it's typically French. People talk about the English obsession with pets, but the difference is we keep them properly under control. *Au continent* they're either chained up and kept at boiling point, or rushing about everywhere creating a health hazard.'

He seemed quite satisfied with this analysis of a state of affairs which in Basset Magna would have had him firing off choice letters to the Parish Council, the local paper and the police. 'Ah,' he added. 'Here comes someone.'

A tall, bony young woman, a-flap with Indian drapes, approached the table. Like the *patron* of the girls' café, she had the deep pallor of someone long disenchanted with heat. Her hair was a khaki-ish blond, and her big dirty feet had trodden down the backs of her whiskery espadrilles.

'Good morning, what can I get you?'

George grinned. '*Non, non! Parlons français.*'

'If you insist.'

'But you're English, aren't you?' I asked.

'It takes one to know one.' She held out a huge hand covered in elephant's hair rings. 'Priscilla Shaw.'

George stifled his disappointment and ordered *citron pressés*.

'Would you credit it,' he said as she went to fetch

our drinks, 'all this and we're being served by an English girl.'

The Alsatian had transferred its dishonourable intentions to the dachshund, and was thrusting absentmindedly at the air several inches above the little chap's back as it nosed round a plant tub.

'Never mind,' I said. 'She's bringing up her dogs in the great Gallic tradition.'

Priscilla returned, put the glasses, sugar and lemon juice on the table, and then banged the tin tray vigorously with the heel of her hand, shouting: 'Heinz! Pedro! Zac! Here!'

The dogs cantered back and leaped on to a painted metal park bench that stood against the café wall.

'Sorry,' she added. 'They think they own the place.' She had a plummy voice with a clipped, rather offhand delivery. I had heard such voices ringing out from the collecting rings, tea tents and Volvos of a score of village gymkhanas.

'Working here for the summer?' asked George.

'No, actually. I own this place.' She was unsmiling, obviously used to this question and a touch tired of it.

'Gosh,' I said. 'How long have you been here?'

'Ten years.'

'Did you have any connections before that? I mean, friends in the area or anything?'

'No, but my then-lover did,' boomed Priscilla.

'We were on our way back from Nepal and we stopped off here. When he moved on, I stayed.'

'I suppose,' said George, 'that property was cheaper then.'

She shrugged. 'Possibly. Cash wasn't a problem, actually.'

She loped off into the interior and the dogs jumped down and followed her, their paws rattling on the lino. I was left with the impression we had been put in our place.

'What a caution,' I said. 'Straight off the hippie trail.'

'Anyone who uses that word in all seriousness,' said George, stirring his lemon, 'is suspect, in my view.'

'Hippie?'

'No, lover.'

We picked up the girls on the way back. They had moved inside, and were perched at the bar at a safe distance from the men in caps.

'What's in those glasses?' asked George suspiciously.

'Chill out, Dad, we moved on to the Orangina.'

The *patron*, studying a folded newspaper at the far end of the bar, gave us a nod as though we were collecting empties.

'So what was it like at the top?' asked Naomi

generously as we walked to the car.

'Lovely,' I replied. 'Very pretty. Very old.'

'Very French,' said George, conveniently overlooking Priscilla Shaw.

As we turned into the drive of the Villa Almont we encountered Royston, who was walking down from the post box with a handful of letters and a screwdriver. He waved them at us and George drew to a halt.

'Good morning! Want a lift?'

'Good grief, thank you but no, this is practically the only exercise I get,' said Royston. He wagged the screwdriver. 'Darn thing's broken. Morning, girls!'

'What a lot of mail. That's working from home.'

'That's the reason I flagged you down. You've got one.'

'A letter? For us?' said George in his TV-play mode.

Royston passed it through the window. 'Nothing very exciting, I'm afraid. It's from the agency.'

George dropped the letter on my lap as though I were an in-tray. Royston peered into the back. 'By the way, girls, I hope the bird-scarers aren't disturbing your sunbathing too much.'

They looked blank. 'I don't know anything

about them,' said Clara. 'Do you, Nev?'

Naomi shook her head. Royston made a silly face with his eyebrows raised. 'What? You haven't heard the cannons going off every ten minutes?'

'They have music on,' I explained.

'Perhaps that's as well,' said Royston. 'Guy de Pellegale is always on at Rindin about his cannon, but it does no good. Your French farmer is nothing if not a free spirit. The next thing will be the all-night pump from the pond so he can water his wretched melons.'

The letter turned out to be a pro-forma communication, obviously sent out by Rutherford-Pounce to all his tenants on a certain date, which explained its early arrival.

'Dear—' (and here our names were filled in in ink). 'This is to inform you that it is the policy of France Vacances to inspect its properties on a regional basis each year. This summer we are trying to cover the area south of the Dordogne, which includes Tarn et Garonne, and the property where you are staying.' Here 'Vila Allmont' was filled in. 'These inspections are for the benefit of all our clients, both present and future, and we do hope that the visit of our representative will not inconvenience you in any way.

'May we take this opportunity to wish you a

very happy holiday with France Vacances, Yours sincerely, Crispin Rutherford-Pounce, Managing Director.'

'What is it about us,' asked George rhetorically, 'that we come to a paradise in the sun only to be plagued by the proverbial mad dogs and Englishmen?'

There was a sharp report from the hill opposite and Teazel exploded from the hedge behind the compost heap, a rodent draped between his jaws.

'Never mind,' I said. 'You'll be able to lodge a complaint about the cat.'

CHAPTER FIVE

That night I lay awake long after George, and even the girls, had gone to sleep. I was suffering from that curious sense of overview that happens when you're away from home and can observe your circumstances without the usual smokescreen of day-to-day responsibilities.

On the whole I was optimistic. George and I seemed to have settled into a relationship very like that we had enjoyed pre-Kostaki, but with a not unpleasant edge. This turning back of the clock was enhanced by my own return to the fictional form in which I had first succeeded. The children were growing up. Clara had mercifully lost interest in horse-dealing, and Gareth had got a place at Bristol for the autumn. There were occasional flashes of maturity and amiability, like the lights of a car on a distant motorway. It was becoming possible to envisage a time when

George and I could flee Basset Magna and its works and live in a place of our own very like the Villa Almont, but perhaps nearer the sea . . . We would look back, as they say, and laugh . . .

Suddenly, I heard something – I wasn't quite sure what – that snapped me out of my reverie like a bucket of cold water. Come to think of it – it *was* water. The clop, clop, clop of water bring drunk noisily by someone, or something, with a large tongue and a stupendous thirst.

I froze. I was suddenly aware of the fragile glass-panelled door that stood between our bed and the outside world. We were in deep countryside. We didn't even have a telephone in the house. Had I locked the verandah door? And would holiday insurance cover attack by a cross-eyed, thirst-maddened Anglophobe armed with a pitchfork?

I was so rigid with anxiety that my teeth ground together with a noise like chalk on a blackboard. George moaned and rolled over with a great lurch that rocked the bed. He was an untidy sleeper, but a notoriously deep one. Many was the night he had snored tranquilly through bouts of infant sickness, cat fights, the death of pets, and teenage soul-searching: nights when the entire household, both human and animal, converged on our bed to air its problems and afflictions, and he had never stirred. A little thing like the Missing Link stalking the garden of the Villa Almont with murderous intent would scarcely make his eyelids flutter. I was fearful of shaking him too hard in case he woke with a trumpeting snort and advertised our whereabouts to the putative assailant.

Very, very gingerly, I folded back my half of the sheet as though it were made of some unstable substance, and swung my bare feet – poor bare, unprotected feet – off the bed. As they touched the floor there was a tremendous, crashing splash – no ordinary splash but an explosive displacement of water such as could only be made by the Creature from the Rue Morgue doing a honeypot into our pool.

The splash was followed by a brief silence and then the muted gloops and hisses of limbs moving in the water. Trembling with dread I crept to the door and moved the edge of the provençal print curtain aside with my finger. In the moonlight I could make out the gleam of the cannons in the melon field . . . the glimmer of the dewpond in the spinney below the compost . . . the rippling silver of the swimming pool broken by great dark shoulders, and a shaggy head making a bow wave as they forged towards the far end—

I leapt back into the bed and pressed myself cravenly against the back of the sleeping George.

The steady swimming continued for another minute or so, and then there was the slosh, slosh of the creature emerging via the shallow pool steps. It must have cut across the grass, for the next thing I knew there was the pad of footfalls on the verandah, not three feet from the window by the bed, and the sound of heavy breathing. This was followed by a brisk slapping sound, and then the footfalls moved away.

I must have remained completely motionless for about five minutes, for when I did decide to rouse George I found my arm had gone to sleep.

'George! George! Wake up! There's been an intruder!'

'Sorraworrawossamarrerwothewhotimeisit?' said George.

I explained. He was not impressed. 'Steady on, love, it's only some animal or other.'

'But it was huge! And so close!'

'Like me, eh,' said George.

Following an interlude which, in fairness to George, put all thoughts of the marauder quite out of my mind, he fell back into the deep, untroubled slumber from which he'd emerged to such good effect. But as the sky began to lighten, I was still awake. And to make sure I didn't drop off, there was the dull drone of machinery starting up in the hollow: the farmer's drainage pump.

I knew it would be hours before the others were on the go, so I got up, let in Teazel who was glaring sphinx-like through the (yes, unlocked) verandah door, and went up to my table in the *atelier*.

As I passed 'The Building of Stonehenge' I noticed that someone, possibly the girls during one of their late-night rap sessions, had begun on one of the stone crossbars. There was something encouraging about this, like finding a homemade pie on the doorstep when one is recovering from the 'flu.

I sat down at the table. The drone of the drainage pump had already become almost unnoticeable. Through the small window at the side of the atelier I could just make out the figure of the farmer walking backwards across the field unrolling a giant hosepipe. Still agitated by the events of the night I wondered whether the phantom swimmer might have been the farmer himself. He must resent the presence of a bunch of foreigners splashing about in a heated pool when he was having to pump water from a stagnant pond. What better way to take revenge than by stealth, polluting the pool with sweat (and doubtless worse) at dead of night . . .? His small, overalled figure took on a distinct air of menace.

I shivered and addressed myself to *Down Our*

Street. Mattie was still flouncing along the road having left poor, loyal, worthy Seth gasping in her slipstream. It was the time to set the cogwheels of her nemesis in motion . . .

I wrote: *Now that Mattie was in sight of Uncle Gransden's front door, the corner house where so many of the Piper women had slaved and suffered and worried for their menfolk, she slowed down. A little of the spring went from her step.*

A little of the spring had also gone from my writing as I considered the women of Marsdyke. A southerner, separated from O-level geography by nearly three decades, I wasn't sure whether mines and mills went together. Could the more enterprising wives be at t'mill while the men were down t'mine? Or would they all be at home blancoing their front steps and blacking their grates, not going out to work? I quite liked the idea of a reformed and politicised Mattie rallying the mill girls one moment and standing at the pithead in the driving rain the next, her shawl drawn about her shoulders, waiting for her man to come back . . . but was it authentic? Not for the first time, I was confused. My policy of 'story first, facts afterwards' did have this drawback. I scribbled 'mills/mines?' in the margin, and continued. I was about to enter territory which I knew well, and had made my own in the deer parks, manor houses, hayricks and castle keeps of innumerable bodice-rippers.

Mattie wanted more than anything to impress her uncle and aunt: to show them that she had done well for herself and was not the mere fly-by-night gadabout that some of the hard-faced street gossips took her to be. She tilted her chin upward defiantly and drew back her shoulders. She regretted nothing. Pace Piaf. *Just then the clatter of hooves cut across her thoughts, and she had to leap aside to avoid being trampled by a great black horse. She glimpsed reddened nostrils, a wild, white-edged eye, and a foaming mouth fighting at the bit.*

Mattie shrieked. She was unhurt, but her heel had caught in the hem of her skirt and ripped it, and she was spattered with mud. Instinctively she lifted her fist and shook it at the rider, shouting as she did so: 'Mind where you're going, can't you?' To her surprise, the horse was reined in and walked back, flanks heaving, to where she stood.

It was a massive creature, but Mattie did not give ground. It stood between her and the pale winter sun, so that at first it was hard to see the face of the man who sat astride it, his hands holding a whip which rested on the pommel.

'So, Matilda Piper' – the voice was low and silkily threatening – 'you haven't changed.'

'You have the advantage of me,' lied Mattie.

'Oh, no.' In a single, lithe movement the man had dismounted and was standing next to her. 'You know me.'

'And what if I do?' said Mattie. 'You may have a fine horse and expensive boots, Oliver Challoner, and you may be the mill-owner's son, but you are no more a gentleman now than when you tripped up the girls on the way home from school!' (I thought this may possibly have been rather too much re-capping in one speech, and scribbled 'disperse' in the margin.

'And you, Matilda,' replied Oliver, with that smile that was like the flash of steel, 'are no lady, no matter what you have been doing in Haddeshall this past twelve months.'

'How dare you!' Mattie's cheeks burned with rage. 'I have been earning my living by my own talents. The only talent you have is one for spending your father's money!'

For a moment she thought he would hit her. His face whitened, and a muscle throbbed in his cheek. Their eyes locked together and neither would give way.

Then his manner changed with disconcerting abruptness.

'Go your way, Matilda. Your uncle is waiting for you.'

As Oliver swung back into the saddle, Mattie glanced over her shoulder and saw that the door of the corner house was open and her Uncle Gransden stood there, looking up and down the street.

'He's getting old,' said Oliver from his great height. 'But then you may yet be able to keep him in his twilight *years, Matilda, with your'* – he allowed a slight, insulting pause to elapse – *'talents.'*

Before she had time to retaliate he had struck the horse's flanks with his spurs and was gone, leaving Mattie smarting with indignation.

I was quite pleased with this. It would do. It was perfectly standard love/hate stuff. There would be at least three more similar encounters before Mattie made her final choice. And of course it would be the unreconstructed male chauvinist who would win hands down (or up). He of the cold smile, threatening voice and curling lip. This was written in tablets of stone in the Chapel of Romance. But there always remained the problem of what to do with the disappointed suitor. Sometimes it was possible to lay on – unfortunate phrase – a sub-plot containing some nice, homely girl who could team up with the disappointee in the final chapter. But on this occasion, I thought I might be able to do better. Especially if there were mines . . .

I got up, stretched, and yawned. As I went over to the jigsaw I glanced out of the window and saw that there was someone in the field with Rindin. Whoever it was wore a shiny red, all-in-one suit. I concluded that it must be some fellow farm-worker kitted out for crop-spraying. He seemed to be gesticulating a good deal. Perhaps they were discussing where work was to take place.

We took the girls to lunch at Priscilla's café (known as Pru's Bar) in the square. We had located a parking area overhanging a sheer drop on the far side of the church, so the steep trudge through the narrow streets could be avoided. Heinz, Pedro and Zac were careering round the perimeter of the square barking wildly with their tails in the air, ignored by everyone. We walked along in the shade of the cloisters past the shops. The girls scrutinised them as if hoping to come across a branch of Jean Machine or The Gap lurking under the crumbling overhang of the ancient houses. In reality there was an ironworks, a nightmare hotchpotch of giant flies, fighting cocks, lizards and creepy candelabra spilling out over the pavement. In the dark interior lurked a dwarfish man with wild dark hair and eyebrows which ran continuously from one side of his face to the other like a headband. There was a shop with local handicrafts – belts, candles, ceramic reconstructions of the church and town hall, and quaintly-shaped gourds tricked out to look like geese and owls. A third shop was a food shop of sorts, but there was nothing fresh: the bottles of wine, oil and vinegar, and the inevitable jars of honey, had the deeply undisturbed look of artefacts in a pharaoh's tomb.

The square's second café had a thin, dark *patron* with an expression of the deepest melancholy. He had one or two customers of the cap-and-braces variety, but no food was advertised. Inside was a pool table. A baby cried from an upstairs room.

'Are we going in here?' asked Clara loudly.

'No,' said George, 'we thought we'd try the other one. They advertise rather a nice lunch over there.'

'What a shame, he's so *sweet*,' said the girls.

In contrast to its rival, Pru's Bar was doing good business. Several immense motorcycles were parked nearby and the local bratpack, tattooed, bandannaed and with their old ladies in tow, were lolling about at the outside tables. A barbecue made out of two oil drums split lengthwise and filled with charcoal stood on the edge of the square emitting a column of dark smoke.

I sensed the girls stiffen. 'Are we still sure?' I asked diplomatically, not wanting to take anyone's attitude for granted.

'Certainly,' said George. 'Why ever not?'

He led us to a free table and we sat down. The dogs, scenting fear through the smoke, thundered back to base and flopped down on their bench like a heap of discarded coats at a bottle party. The bratpack greeted their arrival with empathetic whines, yelps and howls.

'Interesting clientele,' I said.

'More French posers,' observed Naomi, adjusting the shoulders of her boat-necked T-shirt as she did so. She and Clara lit up the cigarettes without which no display of withering scorn is complete.

'Honestly, you're hopeless,' said George, 'all of you. What chance does the single market have while attitudes like yours exist?'

His own attitude was the polar opposite of the girls', and no more rational. This unedifying rabble of sleazy riders, with whom in England he would no sooner have dined than flown, didn't give him a moment's perturbation in the square of Lalutte, because they were French.

Priscilla emerged from the bar and bore down on us with her long, loping stride. She wore a beaded tunic with what used to be called 'trumpet sleeves' (I had them on my wedding dress) and jeans with more than a suggestion of flares. Her feet were bare. Naomi and Clara went quite rigid with shock.

'Hi there,' said Priscilla. 'What can I get you?'

'*Des boissons, s'il vous plaît,*' cried George genially.

'Fire away,' said Priscilla. It was quite surreal.

George ordered drinks, adding: '*Et nous voulons aussi manger.*'

'Fine, we're just waiting for the charcoal to settle down,' said Priscilla. 'I had an absolute mother of a head this morning and I was a bit late lighting it. If you don't mind waiting a minute or two we'll bung the meat on shortly.' The girls drank in this exchange with fascinated attention.

'Are you the chef?' I asked.

'No,' said Priscilla, 'cooking's not my bag. I leave that to Max.'

She flopped away. George closed his eyes as though luxuriating in the sun but actually, I knew, to avoid looking at Clara.

'Dad.'

'Hmmm?'

'Dad!'

'Yes?'

'She's English.'

'That's right.' George tilted his straw hat over his nose. 'Gone native in the best tradition of adventurous Englishwomen abroad.'

'But English.'

'Sure.'

It was a very palpable hit. Clara did not need to say more. Naomi glanced at where Priscilla stood in the doorway with our drinks, shouting something over her shoulder.

'And she's a right old hippie, too,' she said. 'Check out those flares.'

The lunch, as it transpired, was a success. Max the chef, while looking as though he got his kicks from despatching the fatted calf as painfully as possible, had a way with a marinade. And there was more than we could fit on our table, so we split and multiplied like a self-propagating organism. The dogs lined up on their bench and watched us with eyes filmy with greed, long stalactites of saliva drooping from their jaws. George smacked his lips and told us repeatedly that This Was the Life and Where Else Could We Have Enjoyed a Feast Like This For a Few Bob?

The Sleazy Riders and their molls ate an awful lot of meat – it was like watching lions at a kill – and great platters of *frites* washed down with beer. They got very noisy but what with the sun and the food and the *pichets de vin du pays* which Priscilla replenished unasked, we didn't care. George even raised his glass and cried '*Salut!*', and they roared back. Mad Max presided over the barbecue, his sweat running down to join the spitting fat below. The dogs cracked bones amongst the chair legs. Priscilla sat in the doorway with a glass of whisky and a panatella, and read a battered Erin Pizzey.

The horrors of the night seemed a long time ago.

That afternoon, however, there was a reminder. At about five, as we lay about the pool, there was the stutter of an engine coming down the drive, and shortly afterwards we heard Royston talking to someone round behind the annexe. This was sufficiently unusual for George and me to prick our ears up.

'A visitor?'

'Not for us, thank God.'

We were wrong. The bell jingled and Royston appeared on the verandah in his customary pseudo-apologetic attitude.

'George! Harriet! I've got someone here who'd like to see you.'

'Oh, right . . .' We clambered unwillingly to our feet. Clara looked up from the lilo in the middle of the pool and hissed: 'Don't ask them round here!'

We pulled on T-shirts and followed Royston. The visitor sat astride a Honda motorscooter near the front door of the annexe. It was Guy de Pellegale, resplendent in cerise motorcycle leathers which clashed with his tomato-red face.

'You've met the Count, I believe?' said Royston.

'Yes, we have. *Bonjour, m'sieur le comte,*' said George.

'Only we didn't know you were a count,' I added.

De Pellegale laughed heartily at this. 'I was not in uniform at the time.'

I realised, as we all joined in the merriment, that this gleaming cherry-red figure was the one I'd seen that morning in the melon field. I also noticed that the nailbrush dog, Asti, was packed into the scooter's saddlebag. Its fringed ears, quivering with malice, and its bright, lozengy eyes, were clearly visible beneath the half-zipped flap.

'I came for two reasons,' announced the Count. 'I want to apologise for the noise of the cannons and the water pump. I have had strong words with Luc Rindin on the subject.'

'That's all right,' said George. 'We've got quite used to it, haven't we, darling?'

The Count shook his head so violently that his leathers creaked. 'No! That is not the point! It is *affreux! Hideux!* He is my tenant. I feel responsible.'

'There's no love lost between the Count and M'sieur Rindin,' explained Royston unnecessarily.

'It's very good of you to intercede,' I said. 'But please don't worry about us.'

'Excellent,' said the Count. 'Please call me Guy. My son is coming from Paris for the weekend. Would you care to come to the Château Forêt Noir for dinner?'

'Well, it sounds—'

'I don't see why—'

'On Friday? At seven o'clock? It will be perfectly informal,' he said. I wondered if by informal he meant bollock-naked. 'Royston, you will come too?'

'What a treat, that does sound nice,' said Royston.

'Good. You can come together then!' The Count's manner was an interesting blend of old-world charm and high-handedness. I could find it in my heart to feel quite sorry for M. Rindin.

'I see your dog enjoys a ride,' said George indulgently.

'Asti? Yes, he loves the wind in his hair.' Realising we were talking about him the nailbrush bared his horrid little fangs.

'Is that Asti as in Spumante?' I asked.

'No!' The Count sounded triumphant as though I had fallen into a cunningly laid trap. 'Asti as in Asterix!'

'Ah,' said George, 'so the big dog is Obelix.'

'Obi, *c'est ça.*'

'Obi likes a dip,' put in Royston. 'Don't be frightened if you hear splashing at the dead of night. She wanders down through the woods to cool off.'

'I know,' I said. 'She was here last night.' I suppose I was waiting for the Count to apologise, but I should have remembered that his sense of social responsibility did not extend to keeping his wretched pets in order.

'She likes to wander, my Obi,' he said proudly.

'But she is gentle as *un agneau*. And the English are such dog-lovers.'

And with that he kick-started the scooter and puttered away up the drive with the nailbrush yapping and snarling in the saddlebag.

'What a kind invitation. But I didn't ask whether he meant all of us,' said George.

'Oh goodness yes,' cried Royston. 'Guy is a great family man. You must bring the girls.'

'They may not be keen,' I muttered as we walked back along the verandah.

'*Tant pis*,' said George. 'It will broaden their horizons. And they'll enjoy it when they get there.'

CHAPTER SIX

George was right about the broadening of horizons but not, I suspect, about the enjoyment. The girls didn't even have the quiet satisfaction of being bored out of their skulls. It was that most uncomfortable of experiences for the young – a concentrated display of adult eccentricity. At the Château Forêt Noir no one commented on their hairstyles, or the brevity of their skirts, or their taste in earrings. They were given wine to drink, and Gauloises to smoke. They were included in the proceedings without hesitation or concession. They were quite simply left with nowhere to go.

Over the intervening day and a half we had agonised long and hard about the clothes angle. Royston would only say that informality was the keynote up at the château, which was no help whatsoever. We had already seen the Count's informality at first hand, and it had not been comforting. In the end George had decided on cotton trousers, the Lacoste golf shirt I'd given him three Christmases ago, and a blazer. I wore a sun dress and a batik throw – it was the one which matched my bikini, and which was supposed to perform half a dozen different functions, for most of which it was not the right size.

The girls poured scorn on our craven casualness.

'For goodness' sake! We're going to *dinner* at a *château*.'

'Yes,' I replied, stung, 'but nobody told us that when we packed.'

'And besides,' added George, 'you heard Royston say it wasn't formal.'

'Still,' said Naomi, eyeing the batik throw as if it were an untreated pelt, 'the French are tremendously chic.'

We sat down on the verandah with a glass of wine to wait for them.

'I tell you one thing,' said George placidly, 'if this evening serves no other purpose it seems to have brought out a latent admiration for the French in those two.'

When the girls reappeared they were dressed to kill. I should have known they would not have been caught out filling their cases with only those clothes suitable for three weeks in the French countryside. They had had the good sense and foresight to throw in the outfits they normally reserved for the style temples of Basset Regis.

Clara wore a crimson, sprayed-on, satin-look bustier, with a seven-inch-wide black and gold belt, gold chandelier earrings and black laced ankle boots with needle heels. Naomi had chosen a cream crêpe wraparound shirt caught with a diamanté tarantula, smaller versions of which crouched on her earlobes, and black baseball boots. Each get-up was teamed with the black stretch microskirt and black tights which were the tribal markings of the honky-tonk angels of Barfordshire.

As we hoisted our jaws back into position, Royston arrived on the verandah and obviated the need for comment.

'Girls, girls! *Très* glam! It's going to be a pleasure to be seen out with you.'

Any idea George and I might have had about walking up to the château through the woods, and returning the same way in the moonlight, had been quickly dispelled by the girls' toilette, which had the kind of hard-edged urban glitz that crazes and disintegrates on contact with the open air.

We took the car, and I made Royston sit in the front with George. Naomi and Clara sat on either side of me, their faces turned outwards like bookends, somehow managing to keep their black lycra-clad thighs from touching mine.

Disappointingly, the château presented its usual desolate appearance. There were no lights on that we could see, and it was just as well there was a moon as we bumped through the archway into the side courtyard. Here, more encouragingly, were parked the Count's scooter, a battered 2CV with the soft top down, and a white Rolls the size of a mobile home.

'Marie-Laure and Alex have got a Rolls,' said Naomi.

We piled out and stood uncertainly on the tussocky grass, Clara gradually losing height as her heels sunk into the ground.

'Come on,' said Royston, 'everyone uses the back.'

We followed him through the further arch and round the side of the house. Here, sure enough, there were signs of life. Some battered armchairs and a sofa stood on the grass, rusty croquet hoops peeped above the plantains, and a flight of cracked stone steps led to open French windows, through which we could hear voices, and some sprightly music in a Latin American idiom.

'Hallo-ee!' called Royston. 'It's us!'

This was the cue for a frenzied fusillade of yapping, punctuated by deep, sonorous woofs. Voices called 'Asti!' and 'Obi!', a door slammed, and then the Count appeared at the top of the steps. He wore a full-length cheesecloth robe in orange and white stripes in which he resembled nothing so much as an ambulant marquee.

'Royston, my dear fellow! George, Harriet, and your charming family. Do please step this way.'

Again, that curious headwaiter's mixture of arrogance and obsequiousness. I didn't like to look at the girls as we followed him up the steps.

We entered an enormous uncarpeted room about the size of Basset Magna village hall. In contrast to that which we had seen outside, the furniture in here was all of the garden variety – tubular steel folding chairs covered in nylon, and a couple of loungers with cushions. There were three people in the room, but perhaps wisely, no one was sitting down. One, a young man with a big nose and a receding hairline, stood consulting what looked like a timetable. He wore a gingery suit with windowpane checks. Two smartly turned out elderly women were dancing a corseted version of the lambada in the centre of the room. It was the women who were talking: they spoke in French but their matter-of-fact tone was at variance with the sullen sensuality of their dancing. A vast chandelier hung from a carved boss in the centre of the ceiling at a very slight angle. The fireplace was full of chocolate wrappers and cigarette- and crisp packets. At the far end of the room there was a sort of audio-visual plant, a table with a CD and tape player (the source of the music), a television and video machine. Beneath the table were cardboard boxes stuffed with tapes, videos and discs. The light was dim. It was a relief to see a scattering of what looked like rather good paintings hanging on the walls. From far away we heard the barking of Asti and Obi.

The Count clapped his hands. 'Here are our guests, everyone!' he cried. The young man lowered his timetable, and the two women stopped dancing and wandered towards us, still talking.

'May I present,' said the Count, 'my son, Claude ... my wife, Isabelle ... and my sister, Véronique ...'

We all shook hands. Claude said, 'How do you do?' with an accent that would not have been out of place in the china department of Peter Jones. 'I hope you're having a good holiday down there,' he added, like a tactful doctor making some gynaecological allusion.

'Couldn't be better,' barked George. I detected an edge of anxiety in his voice and hoped it wouldn't infect the girls. The two elderly women beamed and brushed their cheeks against ours, with little moues and murmurs.

'A drink,' said the Count. 'Some wine, I think.'

A bottle, one or two glasses and a bowl of cheese footballs stood on a low table near the fireplace. Claude picked the bottle up and upended it over a glass.

'A dead man, I'm afraid,' he remarked. It was strange how this English idiom sounded slightly sinister in his mouth. The Count took another bottle from a wooden wine rack of the self-assemble variety to be had from DIY centres, and handed it to Claude to open. The two ladies beamed approvingly. They presented an interesting contrast in styles. Madame de Pellegale had her grey hair in a Cleopatra bob with a heavy fringe, and wore a brown embroidered dress and a lot of heavy red and brown jewellery. Her sister-in-law, Véronique, was the epitome of bourgeois chic, her hair lightened with blond streaks and teased into a feathery toque of rigid artlessness. She wore an emerald green silk shirt, black trousers and high heels. Waves of some flowery scent emanated from her. When the lambada tape stopped both sisters took it as their cue to retreat once more to the far end of the room.

As Claude poured the wine, George remarked: 'What an astonishing house this is. Has it been in your family for years?'

'No, absolutely not,' replied the Count. 'It is only a simple country retreat.'

'When was it built?' I asked.

'In the twenties. It is the folly of a zip-fastener king.'

'Splendid,' said George.

Claude gave us each a glass of wine, and handed round the cheese footballs which tasted rather musty.

Royston said: 'Well, what do you think, Claude? It's not often we have such a bevy of beauty here, is it?'

'No, indeed,' said Claude. He and Royston moved in on the girls. It struck me that Claude was nervous, and entirely devoid of humour.

Isabelle and Véronique embarked on one of those dances where the participants stand next to one another and repeat certain actions, facing a different wall each time. They performed it with such insouciant elegance that it took me a few seconds to realise that it was 'Aga-doo, doo, doo'. This was a firm favourite at the Basset Magna Cricket Club Dinner and Disco, but one would never have known the two versions had a common root.

The Count, noticing where my attention lay, remarked: 'Isabelle and Véronique like to dance. There is plenty of space here.'

'Yes, it's perfect,' I agreed. I was beginning to feel that we were the cast of some strange Fellini or David Lynch film, and that at any moment a voice might shout 'Cut! Print!' and we'd all be restored to normality.

George and I took simultaneous gulps of wine, and simultaneously almost choked. To describe

the stuff as rough would have been like calling
Old Spice piquant. This was to fine wine what the
Sun was to diplomacy. We glanced at each other
with streaming eyes as the stuff scored a gully
down our throats. It was like having your
stomach lining cleaned out with wire wool. Not
only that, but having hit the bottom it seemed to
leap straight up again, like one of those
test-your-weight machines in fairgrounds, and
jangle a bell at the front of your skull. It was both
uniquely disgusting, and totally intoxicating.
Château-bottled Skid Row.

'*Salut*,' said the Count. Unsteadily, we raised
our glasses. But such was the effect of the wine
that we then took another mouthful and found it
not quite as bad as we had thought. Wiping his
eyes with his handkerchief, George moved
towards the French window. As we followed I
saw that Royston was already replenishing the
girls' glasses. Claude was saying: 'I have a
business which makes bathroom fittings, chiefly –
er – *des robinets* . . .?'

'Taps,' supplied Royston.

'I see,' George croaked, and then cleared his
throat and began again. 'I see you play croquet.'
From this remark it was possible to deduce how
many thousand brain cells he'd lost in the last
minute. You'd have needed a flame-thrower
before attempting to propel a croquet ball

through the low-level scrub outside.

'Not really,' said the Count kindly. 'Because I am not cutting *la pelouse*.'

'The lawn, yes,' said George in case I hadn't caught his drift.

'Don't you have any help with all this ground?' I asked.

The Count made a movement between a head shake and a shrug. His paunch rose with this movement, as though on a pulley, and then fell back again.

'Rindin, the *fermier*' – he waved in the direction of the melon field – 'he was coming, but I have no more use for him.'

This we took to be a comment on Rindin rather than the grass, which was plainly crying out for the farmer's attentions.

'Why is that?' asked George, downing another large mouthful of wine. His face was taking on an unfocussed appearance. It was so long since I'd seen George drunk I couldn't remember what to expect – was he maudlin? Droll? Sick? A berserker, even?

'He is a peasant!' announced the Count in answer to George's question. 'Without sensitivities. You yourselves have been troubled with his fearful pump!'

There seemed no point in explaining, yet again, that we didn't mind the pump. The Count had cast us in the role of innocent victims.

'*Ecoutez!*' he cried. And sure enough, if you listened hard enough, you could hear the dim drone of Rindin's irrigation equipment like a swarm of distant bees on the evening air. The Count's face darkened. '*Connard*! Some more wine.'

He went to fetch the bottle. I said to George: 'I hope dinner's fairly soon or they'll have to carry me in.'

'Really? I'm rather enjoying myself.'

That was that then, there was no further point in trying to halt my husband's gentle slide into hog-whimpering rattedness. The music now was a treacly tango, 'Jealousy'. Isabelle and Véronique were giving it their best shot.

'Do you girls dance?' I heard Royston enquire.

'I must ask,' said George, as the Count returned with the Red Infuriator. 'Why is your house furniture outside and your garden furniture in here?' This from the man who was constantly upbraiding me for my lack of tact.

But the Count was unperturbed. 'When it is hot we spend all day in the garden, so naturally it is nice to be comfortable for that longer time.'

'Doesn't it get wet overnight?' George persisted.

'It does,' agreed the Count. 'But we rise quite late, and by midday it is dry again.'

This seemed like a perfectly lucid answer. I was

trying to work out why that bothered me when the door opened and a man I recognised as Mad Max from Priscilla's café announced that dinner was served. He wore the same greasy jeans but had pulled on a sweater.

As we headed for the door, Clara said: 'Isn't that the man from the café in the square?'

'That's right,' said Royston. 'You've been there, have you? She's a great girl, Priscilla. You don't get many of those to the pound.'

'She is English,' Claude pointed out. 'But Max is from Portugal.'

We trooped along a dark and winding corridor to the dining room, which was not quite as large as the room we had left, but rather more gloomy because it was at the side of the house with a window overlooking the courtyard. There was no chandelier in here, just a couple of standard lamps on either side of the table. The effect of this was that we were all seated with our backs to the light, which gave us a slightly sinister appearance, like participants in a seance. This impression was reinforced by a huge white cloth which enveloped the table, and a black iron candelabra in the centre which I recognised as one of those made at the forge in the Lalutte town square. As I sat down I noticed on the wall opposite a painting which seemed familiar. It was undoubtedly an old master, but the combined effects of poor light and killer booze prevented me from identifying it.

In keeping with Max's parentage, it was sardines to start with. He might with advantage have prised them apart a little more. The way each portion clung together in its surrounding puddle of oil betrayed the tin from which it had recently been extracted. Clearly we were in yet another household where the art of living had not merited close study.

The sardines were followed by couscous, the only course upon which the moonlighting Max had employed his proven culinary skills. It was homemade but had grown rather chilly on the long, weary way from the kitchen. Finally (a total cop-out of which the girls greatly approved) we were presented with a large art-nouveau china washbowl filled with assorted icecreams and ice lollies. Claude, the spoilsport, asked for a dish and spoon, but we took our cue from the Count and ate our choc ices direct from the wrapper. All three courses were accompanied by copious infusions of the savage red wine. On several occasions I indicated to the girls that they should slow down, or better still stop drinking altogether, and I think that in fact they were disposed to do so. But every time they took a sip, however small, Royston, who was sitting between them, topped up their glasses.

During the meal Isabelle and Véronique scarcely spoke, although it appeared they had some English, for they laughed and nodded a good deal in the right places. Claude explained to us how bathroom fittings would be adjusting to the single market (the Greeks were not great ones for mixer taps, apparently), and Royston said that the young had got to be trained in such a way that they stayed in the country and kept rural communities alive.

'Don't say that in front of them,' said George, nodding at Clara and Naomi. 'They think rural communities stink. Don't you, girls?'

'I never said that,' said Clara, in what would have been a scathing manner had she not been struggling with the last lump of a scarlet frozen sky rocket.

'You don't have to,' said George.

'The trouble with villages,' put in Naomi, 'is that there's nothing to do, and you can't get out of them.'

'Like straitjackets,' suggested Royston.

'Exactly.'

'But if there was interesting work in the area, and other young people about, that might change things.'

The girls didn't look at one another, but I could sense the tremor of feeling that passed between them. Work, however interesting, was not something they rated, except insofar as it was a source of ready cash.

The Count, perhaps sensing a natural break,

pushed back his chair and rose to his feet. 'Shall we go back to the salon for coffee?'

Isabelle and Véronique bustled ahead, and by the time we got there they had put on a tape. It was the 'Teddy Bears' Picnic', and from their encouraging gestures it was clear they thought it had some special significance for us.

Outside, dusk was falling and the air was criss-crossed with swooping bats. In the half light the easy chairs looked rather like picnicking teddy bears. Véronique and Isabelle (there having been no takers) bobbed about together happily. I realised I was quite pissed, and would have a horrendous headache tomorrow.

'Oh!' cried Royston, who had been to the lavatory, 'the "Teddy Bears' Picnic" is super! Come on, George.' George was so surprised, and so drunk, that his mumble of uncertainty never saw the light of day. Véronique and Isabelle bore down on him and pulled him on to the dance floor, and Royston grabbed the girls, one on each side, and followed. I suppose they too were suffering from the effects of the Infuriator because they did not, as one might have expected, fell Royston with a kick to the shins and then finish him off with a hail of blows to the body, but allowed themselves bemusedly to be put through the motions of the dance. This involved the two sets of three advancing and retreating rather in the manner of the

'Dashing White Sergeant'; then the ladies each twirled in turn; then there was a complex figure in which each set of three, holding hands, twined in on itself and emerged intact; finally (and this was obviously the purpose and highlight of the whole exercise) the man kissed each of the ladies in turn. Then the whole thing began again.

'It's meant to be progressive,' called Royston, 'but there aren't enough of us.'

It looked quite progressive enough to me. The Count watched benignly for a few seconds, and then announced that he was going to hurry along the coffee. Left alone with Claude, I was aware that my conversational reserves on the subject of bathroom fittings were running dangerously low. To my surprise he grabbed my arm and dragged me over to the window.

When he spoke, his voice was thick with emotion. 'Mrs Blair – Harriet – I am so sorry!'

'Sorry? Whatever for?'

'It is not what you are used to – not what you expected—'

Not being entirely sure to what he was referring I was guarded. 'We're on holiday. We wouldn't want everything to be the same as at home.'

'But they are mad!'

I laughed breezily. The Infuriator had ensured that it was poor Claude who seemed like the mad one. 'Not at all. Your family are charming. Really.'

'How can you say that?' His stage whisper lurched into a squeak of incredulity, and his eyeballs almost touched his lenses. 'How can you know?'

'Know what?'

'What 'APPENS . . .!' said Claude. There was no doubting his sincerity. He was telling me – all of us – to flee while there was still time. I could feel giggles, like a sulphur spring, bubbling up inside me. He could not be serious, man.

'He is disgusting!' whispered Claude, and pulled me through the French windows and down a couple of the steps.

'You'd better hurry up and tell me about it,' I said. 'He'll be back in a minute.'

Claude needed no second bidding. He unleashed a torrent of broken English and rapid French, shaking my wrist, on which he still had a tight grip, to emphasise his points.

I got the gist of it. Guy de Pellegale was not a member of the aristocracy. The handle 'Count' was simply a nickname. He was a successful entrepreneur in the field of what is euphemistically called adult entertainment. He was the Paul Raymond of Paris. Group sex was a speciality of his, both professionally and personally. He had a voracious carnal appetite and no scruples. The house in Paris was a den of vice, and the Château Forêt Noir would soon go the same way. Claude was so very, very sorry!

The Count came back into the room, accompanied by Mad Max with the coffee. Viewed through the lens of Claude's revelations, everyone looked slightly different. Why, no wonder Max looked cheerful. There had probably been time for some lightning hand relief while the coffee perked. The 'Teddy Bears' Picnic' finished, to loud applause, and was put on again.

Oh well, I thought as I went to collect my coffee, this is the sort of thing that absolutely makes a holiday. An old dark house, a roomful of perverts, tinned sardines . . .

I took my cup back to the window steps and sat down. It was still very warm, and there was a big mottled moon peeping over the trees on the hill opposite. The drone of the drainage pump filled the night air. I was having real trouble getting my cup to connect with my lips.

When I became conscious of someone watching me from the garden I wasn't in the least bothered. I had long since passed the point where anything could surprise me. The figure was small, dark, and carried a pitchfork. Old Nick himself, perhaps, come to goad us on our way to perdition. I smiled benignly. I had done nothing wrong. Yet.

The figure took a step forward. It was the farmer, Rindin. The Count burst past me, roaring with rage and nearly knocking me off the step, and for a split second I was blinded as the folds of his robe swished around my face.

The sounds of the ensuing confrontation brought the others hurrying to the French window to watch the fun. Rindin brandished his pitchfork, the Count shook his fist, they both shouted loudly and at the same time. The dogs bayed frantically from afar.

'Golly,' murmured Royston, 'fancy the old bugger turning up here like that.'

'Maybe he's involved as well,' I said flippantly. It was as well no one could hear me.

'What's he doing here?' asked Naomi.

'Who knows?' said Royston. 'But it certainly won't be a social call. The Count's telling him to turn the pump off or he'll report him to the police for noise pollution.'

We huddled together on the top step, spellbound. The Count darted and flapped about in the grass like a Goony bird trying to take off. Bit by bit, Rindin, still cursing and spitting, gave ground. By the time Max arrived from the direction of the courtyard with Asti and Obi in hot pursuit, the farmer had finally withdrawn into the trees. Obi jumped on the sofa and curled up. Asti set off after Rindin. The Count returned to the house, eyes gleaming with excitement.

'*Connard!*'

We all agreed.

*

'I thought that was rather a pleasant evening,' observed George, as we made our way back down the hill at a circumspect ten miles per hour. 'Rather eccentric, but the Count's not a bad fellow and his wife and sister were charming.'

I decided against telling him just now that our host was a ravening sexual predator and that we had probably unwittingly auditioned for a hard-core skinflick.

'What did you make of it, girls?' asked George. But they were deeply asleep, mouths open and emitting little crackling snores.

'Bit of a funny place,' he added, rolling gently over the verge and back on to the road. 'Not exactly luxurious.'

'No,' I agreed. 'But he spends his money on paintings, doesn't he?'

'Ah!' George lifted a finger. 'I meant to tell you about that. Those paintings are all jigsaws.'

As we reached the bottom of the hill I saw, in the wing mirror, Claude's Rolls Royce turn out of the château's drive and make off hell for leather north-ward, in the direction of the autoroute, Paris, and safety.

We were no more than halfway down the drive when the first defiant cannon popped.

CHAPTER SEVEN

*G*ransden Pythorpe, I wrote, *and his wife, Clarice,*
had brought up Gransden's brother's girl since that
terrible day twenty years back when her parents had
passed over of the fever. Gransden and Clarice had no
children of their own, and were so much older than
Mattie's parents that even then Gransden had seemed
more like a grandfather than an uncle. This, I realised,
was unwieldy, but not quite unwieldy enough to
elbow aside my headache and make me do
something about it. This morning merely making
marks on the paper was a triumph.

This was the first time they had set eyes on their
young charge since she had tossed her head and waltzed
off to Haddeshall, and not a minute had gone by but that
they'd worried about her and feared for her safety. One
Sunday Gransden had even spent money he could ill
afford on the train ride into the city on the off chance of
finding her, but it had been a long, cold, empty day and
he had returned to Clarice exhausted and saddened.

*'City folk don't give you the time of day,' had been his
only comment. But they both knew, as they sat by their
small fire that night, what he'd meant by it: city folk
wouldn't care about a young lass from Marsdyke, and a
pretty one at that.*

I paused. Gransden and Clarice were my
favourite characters. I pictured him, anachronistic-
ally, in a black jacket, cap and muffler à la Andy
Capp; and her in a wraparound print pinny with
a scarf over her curlers. They were not so much
late Victorian as early Coronation Street. Whenever I wrote about the Pythorpes my tale took on
a dangerous reality. The familiar speech patterns
of Granada's long-running soap weaselled their
way in amongst the eebygummery of my
mythical north. In my mind's eye streets of gritty,
rainwashed back-to-backs sprouted TV aerials,
back extensions, loft conversions and patios. The
corner shop was run by entrepreneurial Asians
and stocked hummus. Mattie's peers were PAs
and management trainees. Where Oliver Challoner's coal-black hunter had stood, its great
hooves striking sparks from the cobbles, there
were gleaming Polos and Metros . . .

No, no, it wouldn't do. That way disaster lay. I
decided to exorcise these demons by changing
point of view.

*

Mattie saw that what Oliver Challoner had said was true. Her uncle's big frame was stooped, and his hair was now quite white. It was clear, from the way he peered down the street, that his sight was failing. She raised her gloved hand, and called gaily:

'Uncle Gransden! It's me, Mattie!'

His big head lifted, like a dog hearing its master's whistle. And now, as she drew closer, he pulled himself upright and stood there waiting for her, not quite as tall as she remembered, but every bit as forbidding. She ran to him and stood on tiptoe to kiss his rough cheek.

'Hallo, Uncle. Don't look so grim, I've come to visit.'

'Happen you have,' replied Gransden, his voice gruff.

'And what do you think of me?' Mattie twirled right there, in the street, her arms held out.

'Very grand. Those clothes must have cost you a fair bit.'

'They did! And every penny of it earned by me!' She beamed at her uncle, though her heart was beating with anxiety. He was so stern, so straight, always so right. Still, she told herself, she no longer cared what he thought. Now his big hand came out and held her shoulder firmly, steering her towards the door.

'I dare say. Now get inside and stop parading th'sen in our street.'

Our street . . . Mattie sighed as she entered the narrow, dark hall with its familiar smell of washing and smoke and plain cooking. Its walls were like the affectionate, unwanted hug of some humble relation;

114

like the hug her Aunt Clarice would probably force on her any moment now.

The downstairs room was empty. Everything was just as she remembered it. Here I paused and mentally trawled half a dozen north country sagas for props. Specificity was the thing. What did it matter if the Pythorpes' room were not identical to all the others? I was in the driving seat, dammit. As long as there were no glaring anachronisms, all would be well. Just the same, when I got going the subliminally retained clutter came galumphing back.

The clothes horse, (always a safe bet) *hung with Uncle Gransden's thick striped shirts, and Auntie Clarice's'* – Auntie Clarice's what? My mind filled with huge corsets and bloomers big enough to stable a stagecoach as I slipped into panto mode. My clothes horse rapidly became laden with the sort of gear favoured by the Rev. Eric Chittenden as Widow Twankie. That wouldn't do, especially as Clarice was a tiny, birdlike woman, not in the best of health. I put a comma after *shirts,* crossed out *and Auntie Clarice's* and continued: *the table covered with the old red plush cloth edged with little bobbles; the kettle with its high, arched handle hissing on the black iron stove; the two upright chairs with their worn tapestry seats; Uncle Gransden's armchair with its spotless white antimacassar. . . .*

I realised I was sinking ever deeper into a

quicksand of adjectives, from which it was going to be difficult to escape. A change of tack was required, and smartish.

Only one thing was missing, I wrote.

'Where's Auntie Clarice?' asked Mattie. Her uncle did not answer immediately, and this caused Mattie to turn and repeat her question. (Though God knows why, since Gransden was a taciturn old sod whose words came out with the wild spontaneity of a dripping tap.)

'Auntie Clarice – where is she?' said Mattie – employing, as George was wont to do, one of those verbal patterns which have their spiritual home in the pages of schlock fiction. I didn't worry about it. Recognition was the thing here. A setting as warm and worn and familiar as a pair of woolly socks.

Gransden's craggy features softened, I wrote, and wondered if that sounded as though his face were melting, like something out of *Hallowe'en 2*. It was his expression that should have softened. I'd fix it later. The muse was putting on her coat and hat.

'Nay, lass,' he said. 'Your aunt's upstairs.'

'Upstairs?'

'In bed.'

'In bed?'

Mattie was displaying a tendency to converse by repetition, like the Queen. If I was ever to launch an offensive on my headache, Gransden must put a full stop to the exchange.

'Aye,' he said. 'It's time you knew, and then happen you'll stop gallivanting, our Mattie. Your aunt's proper poorly.'

Before going down to the kitchen I attached the heads of a couple of glowering ancient Britons. The jigsaw reminded me of George's observation, and brought the rest of the previous evening's events into focus. They loomed through my headache like bizarre rock stars through a cloud of dry ice. Of course I should have known it was unlikely that a minor French aristo (as I had then taken him to be) would have had The Wedding of Arnolfini hanging on his dining room wall.

Everything was quiet as I skimmed the wildlife from the surface of the pool. No drainage pump, no cannons – though the latter had punctuated our sodden half-sleep all night long. I scanned the melon field, but there was no one there. So where the dickens was he? I felt sure that after last night's episode Rindin would have lumped us, blameless holidaymakers though we were, together with the bogus Count and his retinue of perverts. The shallow valley that separated the villa's ground from the dewpond to the south and the melon field to the west was covered with prickly scrub and would provide excellent cover for any crazed homicidal Frenchman who might choose to lie low there.

I did a few lengths until my head felt better, or at least until the effort of swimming became equally uncomfortable. As I got out I heard Royston calling me, and saw that he was standing on the drive beyond the girls' room.

'All right this morning?'

'Never better,' I replied.

'Entertaining fellow, isn't he? The Count.'

He was coming across the lawn towards me, and I was glad I had on my relatively demure, striped Debenham's one-piece.

'I suppose so,' I said. 'But you should have warned us he was a fraud.'

'Fraud?' said Royston. He must have caught it off Mattie.

'Not a count,' I said. 'A porn king.'

'Aha, that,' said Royston. 'Sorry if you felt you'd been misled. I've got to know the de Pellegales so well I don't give it a thought any more.'

'The son told me about it.'

'Claude, poor old Claude . . .' Royston shook his head indulgently. 'Not exactly a child of nature.'

'He doesn't like his father. He apologised for him, in fact.'

'The trouble is Claude's frightened of his own shadow.'

'Who wouldn't be, brought up in that ménage?'

'Oh, I don't know . . .' Royston said reflectively. 'The girls had a good time.'

'They were drunk.'

'They weren't the only ones.'

He was now at the edge of the pool. I wrapped myself in my towel. I promised myself that when RP's representative showed up it would not be Teazel about whom I should lodge a complaint, but Royston.

'Look,' I said, 'I'm going to buy the bread. Is there anything I can do for you?'

'How jolly kind,' he said, taking my brush-off as an offer. 'You could pick up a *baguette* for me at the top *boulangerie* if you're going that way.'

'I use the one near the post office.'

'Do you?' His tone implied that there was no accounting for taste. 'Fine, that'll do.'

'Right then, if you'll excuse me—'

'I almost forgot, Harriet. Can you tell George he's very welcome to use my little work centre any time?'

'I'm sure he won't be wanting to,' I said coolly. 'He's on holiday.'

'Yes, but from what he was saying to me the other morning—'

'I'll bear it in mind.'

'Do. He can come round any time. I've got fax, word processor, copying facility – he knows that anyway. No need for him to use the front, he can come in the little back door and go straight to the work centre.'

'Right.'

'*Au revoir*, then.'

Not if I see you first, *mon brave*, I thought grimly as I showered. There was something so aggravating about people who insisted on the littleness of everything. 'Work centre' itself was bad enough, but a *little* work centre was the absolute end, especially when the room in question was as stuffed with gadgets as the cockpit of a jumbo jet.

George was sitting up in bed reading a novel by someone known in the trade as the Queen of Crime. It seemed that fake aristocracy was to be the hallmark of this holiday.

'How are you feeling?' I asked as I got dressed.

'Feeling?' Now everyone was doing it.

'Yes. After last night.'

'Fresh as a daisy. Never better.'

'I had a head like a bucket,' I confessed, hoping to tempt him into a damaging admission. But my husband's confidence was, as ever, dentproof.

'Really? No, I'm fine. I enjoyed it. We'll have to have them down here.'

'Must we?'

'Why not? We're on holiday. We're not likely ever to see them again. Might as well live dangerously.'

I sat on the edge of the bed. 'He's a fraud, you

know, the Count.'

'I don't doubt it for a moment.'

'I mean he's not a count, or anything like it.'

'You astound me.'

I felt a bit crestfallen. 'He's in the sex entertainment business in Paris. Count's his trade name.'

'Fair dos,' said George. 'Like Giant Haystacks. That would explain the jigsaws.'

I got up. 'I'm going to buy the bread. Any requests?'

He gave me his roll-in-the-hay smile, perfected (so he thought) over two decades of marriage. 'Yes. Don't go.'

'I've got to. I'm buying Royston's bread as well.'

'Jezebel,' he said comfortably, and returned to his book. As I left the room he added: 'She's good, this woman.'

I quite enjoyed these solitary early morning outings to the baker. It was hot but not overpowering, and the natives of Lalutte were out and about doing their shopping. I had no intention of going to the *boulangerie* near the town square favoured by Royston. Mine would have to do. It was presided over by a Gallic Dora Bryan, bright-eyed, hennaed and garrulous. She had no English, and attempted to keep me satisfied with her barracuda grin while she kept up a flow of piercing nasal French with the other customers or, failing that, with some unidentified colleague in the back room. The Lalutte dialect consisted of an impenetrable stream of honks and whines, rather like a bagpipe. But I could have sworn, as I left with my sheaf of long loaves, that I caught the unlikely phrase, 'Rutherford-Pounce' . . .

Sitting over a coffee at the café first patronised by Clara and Naomi, I realised that it was quite likely the woman in the *boulangerie* knew RP. He would presumably have visited the area several times when vetting properties for France Vacances. But if she had been talking about him, did that mean he was around now? His letter hadn't mentioned a personal appearance, just that of an unnamed representative.

Opposite the café was my next port of call, the *Tabac/Maison de la Presse*. It stocked copies of the *Daily Telegraph*, only slightly out of date. The trick was to get there as soon as they arrived – usually about ten – and before the other ex-pats, drawn like sharks by the scent of newsprint, descended and stripped the shelves.

But even the predators were preyed upon. George and I had noticed an estate agent's next door but one to the *Maison de la Presse*. It went under the name of Sprigg Associates. A gentleman whom we took to be Mr Sprigg, dapper in a dove-grey lightweight suit, was generally to be seen loitering near the news stand, or taking an espresso in the café, from the time the *Telegraph*s arrived to when the last of the eager purchasers had departed. He seemed to know everyone, and those he didn't know he quickly became acquainted with.

'Touting for custom,' George had remarked disapprovingly. 'Is there nothing these fellows won't stoop to?'

'Well,' I said, 'you said we should be ready for nineteen ninety-two. Mr Sprigg should be a man after your own heart.'

George had then spent the next half an hour explaining to me why Sprigg was not only *not* a man after his own heart, but an outrage, a bounder and a cad.

This aversion of George's to business acumen meant that we had so far avoided exchanging more than a raised eyebrow with Mr Sprigg. But from his glossy and benign appearance it was obvious that business was good, and that the fantasy of owning a rambling French farmhouse still flourished profitably in many an English breast. This morning Sprigg was hovering near the counter, a copy of the *Financial Times* in his jacket pocket. I suspected that it was always the same edition, kept for the purpose of identifying Sprigg as English, in the way that a gentleman on a blind date might agree to wear an orange rosebud in his lapel.

The papers were in situ, but there were as yet no other buyers about. I didn't particularly want to present the only target for the Sprigg sales patter, so I waited.

Unfortunately, just as I'd ordered a second coffee, he spotted me. I began writing a postcard as though my life depended on it, but not quickly enough to miss the beginnings of a cheerful smile. Sprigg was certainly about to make his way over to the café and subject me to a prolonged fusillade of house particulars.

'Dear Gareth,' I wrote, 'this is a lovely place, and the weather is superb. We miss you, of course, but I'm sure you're making piles of filthy lucre. I'm sitting in a café in the local town hoping not to get picked on by a marauding estate agent who preys on unwary Brits—'

It dawned on me that it would only have taken Sprigg a few seconds to cross the street, and he had not yet turned up. Furtively I glanced in the direction of the newsagent's without lifting my head. A white MG convertible – the old-fashioned sort, with spokey wheels – was parked opposite, and its arrival had stopped Sprigg in his tracks. A tall, bare-chested man in a straw hat and sunglasses climbed out of the driver's seat and entered the shop, tweaking a wad of notes out of the hip pocket of his shorts as he did so. I noticed idly that he had the sort of bronzed athletic legs not usually seen outside the international tennis circuit.

Sprigg's smile was now all for the newcomer, though not, I suspected, for the scandalous legs so much as the MG, the GB plates and the wad of notes. The legs and their owner disappeared to the back of the shop, ignoring the English newspapers, and Sprigg moved away from the door.

I finished off the postcard to Gareth, put it in my bag and signalled to the proprietor for *l'addition*. This was my moment to nip across for a paper and be on my way while Sprigg was still fully engaged with the new arrival.

I had paid and was about to leave the table when both men reappeared at the till near the door, chatting animatedly. The Legs had a *Figaro* and a magazine under his arm. He removed the dark glasses in order to peel off a note and receive his change. He smiled and laughed. A deep, crescent-shaped dimple appeared in his cheek. The girl behind the till – stout, spotty and a stranger to customer relations – blushed and bridled. And who could blame her? She was being treated to the sort of high-voltage allure that should never have been allowed out unchaperoned.

I should know. I'd been there. And there . . .
and there . . . and down there . . .

I slithered out of my chair and limped and
shuffled crabwise down the hill to the car like
some creature but lately risen from the primeval
soup.

It wasn't until I was turning into the drive of
the Villa Almont that I realised my shoulders
were winched up round my ears with nervous
tension, and even then it was an effort to lower
them.

'Where's the bread?' asked George.

When he'd gone to collect it from the café I took
the lilo into the pool and lay on it, face down,
feeling the gentle undulation of the water beneath
me.

In spite of the heat, I shivered. Someone had
just walked over my erogenous zones.

Kostaki.

CHAPTER EIGHT

I coasted through the next couple of days in a dream state, part fantasy, part heightened reality. As with most dreams, I recognised it for what it was, but was powerless to escape. Nor did I want to. That one glimpse of Constantine Ghikas had indicated how fragile was my carefully reconstructed normality. While the frontage was still in place – George, our family holiday, the folksy familiarity of *Down Our Street* – the hinterland had been reduced, at a stroke, to a smoking ruin.

In my lucid moments I told myself sternly that I would not be seeing him again. It had just been one of those chance sightings. He was probably not even based in this area. Ah yes, but there had been no sign of any luggage in the MG. This was a man on holiday, making a casual visit to the local town for a newspaper, exactly as I had been . . .

The possibility that Kostaki might be sunning himself by some neighbouring pool threw me into an agony of frustration. I found myself peering this way and that when we were out in the car in the hope of spotting him, scantily clad and plainly in need of female company. In spite of the fact that he had always drawn women to his side like tacks to a magnet it never crossed my mind that he would be anything but available. One of Kostaki's many charms was his continual, adorable, fatal availability. But to be available he had, alas, to be accessible.

I knew I only had to see him once more, and approach him with ordinary civility, to become the focus of his attentions.

Unless – ghastly thought! – he was married. But I dismissed this as ludicrously unlikely.

So there I was, dreaming yet alert, in a state of suspended animation. On hold.

The result was that I allowed various things over which I should normally have taken issue to go by on the nod. I scarcely noticed when George disappeared after lunch and spent the best part of two hours playing with Royston's work centre; and when the girls, after a morning on their own in the town, announced they had bought tickets for a dance, I heard myself saying that it was a nice idea; and when George said he'd invited the de Pellegales, Royston, and 'one or two others' to an informal supper at the end of the week, I acquiesced like a lamb. But my meekness on this score ran so contrary to my earlier attitude that it aroused his suspicions.

'You're sure?'

'Yes. Absolutely . . . why not?'

'No reason whatsoever!' said George emphatically. 'I'm delighted you feel it's a good idea.' He glanced at me. 'I'll do the shopping,' he added, obviously still feeling he needed to build up some credit. 'We can have something quite simple. I mean who wants to go to a lot of trouble in this heat? And we are on holiday . . .' He rattled on for a bit about *charcuterie* and ratatouille and local goat's cheese and fresh fruit salad. He had always been good at outlining astonishingly simple and attractive ways of entertaining. 'After all, what needs doing?' was one of his catchphrases. 'Couple of bottles of wine and a vat of your nice goulash . . .'

'Bob's your uncle,' he said now.

'Absolutely,' I said again. I noticed he was beginning to look dangerously baffled, so I lassoed my errant brain, hauled it back into commission and forced it to formulate an intelligent question.

'Who are the other people?' I asked.

'Other people?' There it was again. Perhaps it

was me. Perhaps my speech was going the same way as my brain and no one could understand me. I licked my lips and took a run at it.

'You said you were inviting some other people, as well as the de Pellegales and Royston.'

'Oh – yes!' George seemed to feel on safer territory now he was being interrogated. 'I thought it mightn't be a bad idea if we diluted the Count and co. a bit, as you're right, they are a little strange – and Royston suggested a very nice English couple who own a place down the road. Denise and Keith something or other. They sound perfectly sane and civilised.' On recent evidence I couldn't imagine why George should suppose these people would turn out as expected, but he prattled on happily. 'I gather the de Pellegales have a house guest, too. Royston says he met her and she's quite okay, and anyway it would be rude not to include her.'

'Of course.'

'It should be fun,' concluded George, a trifle lamely. He'd been anticipating a passage of arms and none had been forthcoming. 'Are you all right?' he asked.

'I'm fine.'

'Only you seem a bit subdued.'

'It's hot, that's all.'

'Certainly is.' Satisfied, George flopped back on his towel. 'And going to get hotter according to local radio.' Since Radio Four could only be received when entirely stationary at the top of the hill, and was sacred to the Test Scores and Ambridge, George had become a regular listener to QV Quercy, a mind-numbing stream of Franglorock, the sort of thing he would have rubbished out of hand at home. The jabbering of QVQ as we drove about in the car made him feel he was saturating the girls with idiomatic French. It also enabled him to pepper us with a small shot of local facts such as this one about the weather.

'Yes,' he repeated, 'we'll be able to fry eggs on these tiles in a day or two.'

You could have fried eggs on my brain. It was ironic that the more heated and turbulent I became inside, the more vacant and laid back I must have seemed to everyone else.

I overheard George and the girls discussing me one evening. They were in the pool and had not noticed me come out on to the verandah. Neither did they realise how clearly their lowered voices carried over the water.

'She's in a really good mood,' Clara remarked. And added: 'I wonder why?'

George, to his credit, took up the cudgels on my behalf. 'I don't know why you should say that,' he said. 'After all, we're on holiday.'

'But she hates holidays.' So it had been that obvious.

'No, she doesn't,' persisted George. 'She just takes a long time to unwind. Creative people do.'

Naomi, who had so far not joined in this discussion, now put in her four penn'orth.

'She's still writing here, isn't she? I think that's amazing.'

She was rather a nice girl, really.

Clara said: 'It's like dope. She can't live without it.'

'As I said,' said George, 'the creative urge isn't something you can switch on and off. I think your mother is feeling more relaxed because she's getting some writing done.'

That much at least was true. Clara's view that I was some kind of word-junkie was flattering in its way, but incorrect. I could very easily live without writing. It was pressure I couldn't live without. And now that the pressure to finish *Down Our Street* had been upstaged by the pressure to find Kostaki, I doubted my ability to write another word.

'Anyway,' said Naomi comfortably, like some indulgent elderly relative, 'she's certainly unwound now.'

QVQ were right. It did get hotter. It got so hot that the top three inches of the pool were like soup, and your wet footprints dried as soon as you left them as if you were a ghost. A piece of paper was delivered one morning announcing a hosepipe ban. Teazel lay against the wall at the back of the verandah, or in the woodshed, all day long, his eyes liquid yellow slits in his scorching fur. The shallow hills trembled under the heat. The sunflowers crisped and curled and hung their heads. Early ripened plums lay thick on the grass, decorated by drunken butterflies. A snake, sleek and black as liquorice, appeared on the bank by the compost heap and lay motionless in the shape of a shepherd's crook while we admired it from a safe distance. We gazed in astonishment at our cupboards full of clothes as we slipped lethargically from one state of semi-nudity to another.

In the early morning and the evening the sky was like mother of pearl: the rest of the time it was almost white. From eleven a.m. until six p.m. Lalutte was silent, empty and shuttered. Like the numerous lizards which kept us company we lay in the sun until the sweat had collected in warm puddles beneath us and we had built up enough energy to blunder into the cool house and fetch a drink from the fridge. Passion fruit juice, orange juice, apple juice, peach juice, Coke, Orangina, lemonade – however much we bought it was never enough.

Yes, it was very hot. And, like a mirage, Kostaki had disappeared.

*

'George! George! Fax!'

It was Royston, on the verandah. He had altogether given up ringing the bell. I was lying face up on the lilo in the pool, and the girls were hiding from the noonday sun in their room. The faint sound of Soul II Soul sifted through their drawn curtains.

'George!'

The more I thought about Kostaki's absence, the more I was annoyed by the ever-present Royston. The lilo was nudging the end of the pool nearest the verandah, so he probably couldn't see me. I wasn't going to help him. I knew George was sharing a hammock with the Queen of Crime in the trees behind the barbecue. Indeed, he was probably sleeping with the Queen of Crime. Nothing short of rope fatigue or snake bite was going to rouse him.

But neither was Royston easily deterred. I heard the faint slap of his footsteps coming down the steps of the verandah.

'Aha, Harriet. Lying low I see – no pun intended.'

I opened one eye and saw him crouching at the side of the pool, staring down at me.

'Where's George?' he said.

'In the hammock.'

'Only I've got a fax for him.' He waved a sheet of paper over my face. I pushed myself away from the side. I was not going to give him the satisfaction of asking him about the wretched thing, but a frisson of irritation with George actually penetrated my habitual daze and I promised myself that I would take up the issue later.

'In the hammock, you say,' said Royston.

'That's right.'

'Mind if I pop up and give this to him?'

'Go ahead.' I was now floating away from him towards the far end of the pool.

I heard Royston crunch away over the dry grass. I rather hoped to hear George start violently at this intrusion, and hit the ground with a crash, but there was only a brief exchange and then Royston came crunching back.

'Message delivered.' he said. I lifted a hand. 'I'm looking forward to our little party.'

So it was 'our' little party, was it? I rolled off the lilo and did a few strokes under water. When I came up for air, Royston had gone.

'I must say,' I said, 'I think you might have stayed away from the fax machine. We are supposed to be on holiday.'

'I know.' I could tell from his tone he was going to be all sweet reason and common sense. 'I know, and it won't affect that. I just like to keep in touch.'

'The idea of coming here is to be out of touch, surely.'

'Up to a point. But if I keep myself informed about what's going on I don't have the worry of getting back to problems.'

'You might as well cut out the middle man and stay at work.'

He leaned forward and put his hand on my shoulder. 'Come on, darling, don't be like that. You write, don't you?'

I remembered the conversation in the pool. It made me even more determined to nail him.

'Yes, but I don't go handing out contact numbers to everyone so they can badger the living daylights out of me.'

'I'd hardly call one fax badgering,' said George. But he withdrew his hand and sat back in his chair, employing a body language which unmistakably denoted guilt.

My marital antennae were not at their most sensitive, or I might have picked up on the reasons for the guilt. As it was I misinterpreted them.

'So what was the message, anyway?'

'Oh . . . nothing. They've struck a bit of a hitch on the London Recruitment and Training Seminar.'

'And they can't possibly manage without dragging you into it?'

I knew how strangely I was behaving, especially as it really didn't matter to me at this moment whether George spent the entire holiday organising residential conferences in London. What he did had become of minimal interest and importance to me. I was simply jealous because he was doing what he wanted, and I wasn't.

George's manner became one of studied patience. He gave a sigh. 'Eloise was bright enough to pick up on a small lacuna in the plans. Since the plans were originally drawn up by me, and she had the number—'

'You gave her the number.'

'—correct, she had the common sense to contact me. It's nothing that can't be sorted out down the line.'

Eloise was George's PA, a smart, single, independent woman in her early thirties who thought the earth circled George's backside. She managed to make the most flagrant brown-nosing appear like sound judgement tempered in the white heat of the workface.

'He's quite simply a first-class man, Harriet,' was one of her most frequent remarks to me. 'He's been positively inspirational to middle management. Since he's been in that job an unprecedented number of really bright people have come good in the jobs that count. His influence has been catalytic.'

I had often thought that if this kind of testimony were even a pale copy of what George received most working days in the office it was no wonder he was given to occasional flights of pomposity and self-satisfaction. Eloise on song would have swelled the massed heads of the Little Sisters of Humility.

'Fine,' I said, 'Let's hope it's a lacuna you can cope with.'

Next morning, bold as brass, George slipped round to the annexe for a bout of crisis management, and I took the girls to the street market.

They weren't exactly begging to be taken. In fact I had to prise them out of the murk of their bedroom and pledge an increment to the holiday wad to get them to come at all. But I sensed they were reaching that pitch of reclusiveness which might presage a rift in the friendship, and this I was anxious to avoid. Besides, my obsession with the near-but-far Kostaki was taking its toll. I wasn't writing. I wasn't eating. But I was drinking. And I had also been foolish enough to doze off on the lilo after Royston had gone, and had acquired a telltale bloated glow which was doing nothing for my *amour-propre*. I could hardly continue to sunbathe. A shopping trip incognito beneath dark glasses and a straw hat seemed the most diverting option.

The market was not in Lalutte. Presumably the one-in-five incline had discouraged the less hardy twentieth-century peasantry from carting their produce up to the town square. Our destination was Torcheron, a larger town to the south. It was about a half-hour's drive along serpentine roads which wound down the wooded flanks of hills to where the town quivered in a cauldron of trapped heat. The girls, greenish from the drive, gazed dispassionately out of the windows. Wanting to sit together, they'd left me on my own in the front of the car, like a chauffeur.

Torcheron was not as pretty as Lalutte. It was not pretty at all. It was a busy, functional provincial town complete with an industrial estate, roadworks, a cinecentre, various unlovely 1960s developments and a McDonald's.

As we drove in we passed a Mammouth hypermarket – several square acres of shopping made easy. Vast hoardings indicated that this was the place to purchase everything from DIY requirements to high fashion in perfect air-conditioned comfort, and with the opportunity to stop for cold drinks at the soda fountain and snack bar.

The girls brightened. 'Why don't we go there?' asked Clara. 'I bet they've got everything we need and it looks really cool.'

I knew she meant this in both the literal and figurative senses. I was annoyed that I was not immune to Mammouth's allure, and this made me even more determined to stick to the objective.

'We didn't drive all this way to go to a supermarket,' I said. 'The market will be much more fun. And more French.'

'But shopping's shopping,' explained Clara with irrefutable logic, 'and that looked like a really good place.'

'I'm sure it's excellent of its kind,' I said, 'but we're not going there. Now I wonder where the parking is . . .'

This, of course, was the sixty-four-thousand-dollar question. Torcheron was one of those places built on a system of ever-decreasing one-way circles converging on the hellish snarl-up of the market square. Unnervingly short stretches of dual carriageway would suddenly shrink into cobbled bottlenecks where optimistic restaurateurs had placed tables and chairs on the eighteen inches or so of available pavement. Parking was heavily circumscribed by lines, meters, notices, bollards and orange boxes, of which the native motorists were taking not the slightest notice. Vast ramshackle farm lorries were pulled up in the middle of the road, being unloaded by men whose sagging trousers revealed rear cleavages like the Grand Canyon.

'Check out those brickies' bums,' murmured Naomi, impressed. I knew that the more impenetrable the parking arrangements, the more vile my temper and the less appealing the locals, the more the girls' spirits would improve. It was a law of nature. So I tried to tell myself, as a twenty-stone farmer suggested I return to England at my earliest convenience, that unseen benefits would accrue from this nightmare.

After half an hour we had glimpsed the market about half a dozen times without actually being able to get out of the car.

Clara said: 'Why don't you do what everyone else does and stick the car on the pavement?'

'Because,' I snapped, 'with my luck I should get collared.'

'You can say you're foreign and didn't understand,' suggested Naomi. And added: 'You're a woman, too, so that would help.'

I should have heaped contempt on the sexism underlying this suggestion, but I didn't and shortly afterwards I slipped the right-hand wheels on to the pavement outside an optician's, and stopped.

'This'll do.'

With markets, it's a question of attitude. The English so often want to shop as they eat – in a spirit of let's-grab-the-fuel-and-get-it-the-hell-over-with. The buying of food is simply a case of making a list, working through it as speedily and cost-effectively as possible, and getting the stuff home prior to dispatching it with the minimum of fuss. Normally I adhered to this philosophy. Twenty years of accommodating the inner man, child, and domestic pet had rendered the culinary arts about as fascinating and sensuous as blowing my nose. But today, in the cacophony of the Torcheron market, I underwent my very own Road to Damascus. I couldn't help remembering the dinner I'd had with Kostaki in the baroque dining room of the Hotel Dynamik in Fartenwald, when every prawn, asparagus spear and sorbet had gleamed with erotic promise, and exuded lubricious juices on to the milk-white plates . . . I wandered in a trance, pressing the swollen flanks of giant melons, caressing glossy tomatoes, fingering the bloom on yellow plums and the stippled waxiness of ripe avocados . . . The girls didn't notice anything odd. They were too busy being shocked by old men with no teeth, and old women with beards, and live cuddly creatures being noisily assessed for the pot.

'Unbelievable,' I heard Naomi say. 'They are so gross.'

I almost wished George were with us to take issue about fresh produce and the art of living. But if he had been, I could not have sustained my mood, gravid with suppressed lust.

I bought a few things – some salad, some fruit, some cheese, a chicken (not one of the live ones) and some pollen in a jar which a young man assured me had miraculous properties of rejuvenation.

'*Vous êtes mariée?*' he enquired. I said I was. '*Votre mari sera très-très content,*' he assured me, with a black, burning look. How was he to know that it was not my husband's happiness that was at the forefront of my mind?

I've always believed in my personal fates. I can see them quite clearly, a bunch of old boilers in wraparound pinnies and Ena Sharples hairnets, their busts supported on folded arms, their mouths pursed like cats' bottoms. Most of the time they kept themselves to themselves and only peered disapprovingly round their damp washing as I passed by. But occasionally they would step out into the street and ambush me with rolling pins and wet dishcloths, ready to inflict damage. Like now.

I was startled out of my reverie by a burst of noise several notches above the ordinary market hubbub. Squawks, shrieks, screams and a torrent of French which I could not understand but which was unmistakably furious.

I took in the scene in a flash. A dwarfish man in overalls was holding upside down a huge red chicken. It was cackling in outrage, its wings flaying the air madly. Naomi was standing to one side with her hand over her mouth. Clara and the man were yelling at each other in their respective languages. A crowd was gathering. Clearly the stallholder had been about to send the chicken to the great henhouse in the skies and Clara, good English girl that she was, had raised objections.

'You disgusting, odious, callous little murderer!' she screeched. It was interesting that 'little' was by far the least insulting word she had hurled at him, but also the only one he had understood. His eyes were popping from his head, he pounded his chest with his fist, looked round at the bystanders for their support. Him? Little?

Wearily I began to elbow through the crowd to try and intervene. But someone tall, smiling, and with excellent French, beat me to it. Kostaki.

I stopped in my tracks. He produced a sheaf of notes. He took the chicken. He handed over the money with a cavalier gesture indicating that no change was required.

Was it my imagination, or did the affronted chicken quieten at his touch? Who could blame it? It was in the hands of an expert. Now Kostaki righted the ruffled bird, holding it in such a way that it looked nice and snug and motherly again, like one of those china hens made to hold eggs. He held it out to Clara. The onlookers smiled indulgently. Naomi blushed and giggled. Clara, to her credit, took the chicken with great aplomb and thanked its rescuer.

He lifted his panama. *'De rien.'*

Nothing? I stood there with my mouth opening and shutting. The rest of the bystanders relaxed, lost interest, became ordinary shoppers once more. The stallholder, handsomely paid, fumed but held his peace.

Kostaki melted away . . . blue shirt, white jeans . . . Say, who was that man? They call him the . . .

'Mum! Look what we've got!'

'I am not taking that thing home!'

'But it's really, really sweet. And that hunky man – by the way, I'm sure I know him – he rescued it for us. Did you see that bunce? I mean, this is a really wicked hen.'

Yes, I thought, my heart thundering somewhere just behind my wisdom teeth. Wicked.

CHAPTER NINE

'Look, I'm sorry, but I am not keeping that thing at the villa.'

'You said you wouldn't have her in the car. And here she is.'

'That's only because we needed to get away.'

'No, it's because you didn't want some vile French person to wring her innocent little neck.'

'I really don't feel strongly about that, Clara. Don't tell me you honestly believe those chickens you eat roasted on a Sunday at home died of natural causes?'

'No, but at least they weren't prodded and poked and scared witless before—'

'Clara, they have appalling lives! I bet that hen's had a marvellous time scratching around some nice sunny farmyard.'

'All the more reason not to subject her to the humiliation of a public execution.'

'Now you *are* being ridiculous.'

'She's so beautiful. I mean, look at her feathers.'

'We'll see if M'sieur Rindin will take her.'

'Of course he will! And she'll be in the oven before you can say *bon appetit!*'

'Perhaps, but you won't have to witness it. Look, I am not going to discuss this any further. We are not having a hen in that beautiful garden which doesn't belong to us. Anyway, what about Teazel? And Obelix? And I expect the place is alive with foxes. She wouldn't last five minutes.'

'I bet Royston would help us build a run.'

'Your father will go spare.'

'When you say that, you're weakening.'

'No I am NOT weakening!' I had to shout because the hen suddenly emitted a volley of piercing clucks and shrieks and batted its huge wings, sending a cloud of red feathers floating between me and the windscreen. Naomi screamed, Clara yelled at Naomi, and I swerved and only just avoided a Peugeot towing a camping trailer.

'The hen goes,' I said.

Had this incident, or anything like it, occurred in one of my novels, the next scene would have depicted the girls happily building a run for the hen while their mother looked on with a rueful smile and the father, also rueful but fond, told her what an old softy she was.

But this was the real world, and I was adamant. Apart from the obvious impracticality of introducing a lone chicken into a rented environment bristling with predators, I was anxious to test my independence of Kostaki. Admittedly he hadn't known I was there and had not (I sincerely hoped) recognised Clara who had been a child of eleven at the time of our association. Even so I felt he had been toying with my sensibilities, dabbing his hand in the heated waters of my innermost emotions and stirring them up with his customary casual ease. How dare he turn up when I was on an outing expressly designed to push all thoughts of him aside? And how dare he go buying my daughter a chicken, in one of those charming, useless gestures which have undone women since time immemorial?

I stopped at a roadside café where I could see other hens scratching about in a pen at the side of the house, and swept in. I demanded to speak to the *patron*, and offered him the hen. He was delighted, and tried to pay me, which I refused. He took the hen and placed it with the others. They were smaller, but the cock, strutting and peering, looked well up to the job. In recompense I accepted a free drink for the three of us. The girls took bottles of Coke and sat on the verandah wall with brows like thunder.

'I hope you're satisfied,' said Clara as we drove off. 'It'll be *poulet maison* at that place tomorrow.'

'Guilty?' said George. 'Why on earth should you feel guilty?'

It would have taken too long to tell him. 'I don't know really.'

'Exactly. No one, not even us, takes a hen on holiday.'

'Of course. But you know how it is. Those two could make St Francis of Assisi feel like a heel.'

We were sitting on the verandah, sipping iced coffee which George had made in my absence. The girls were in the pool, not swimming, but clinging to the side and talking in an undertone. Teazel lay flat and limp as a pair of discarded socks on the tiled floor. In the empty melon field the cannons popped intermittently. I was a bundle of nerves, but George had either ascribed my condition to the hen or simply did not notice. He was being unusually solicitous, which didn't help. His iced coffee and soothing words brought Kostaki rearing up before me to mock my duplicity.

'I don't suppose you did any shopping for the party?'

'What?'

George leaned back and crossed his legs, a

149

classic defensive pose. 'The supper party. I wondered if you'd thought about it while you were over there.'

'No. You said you were going to do that.'

'Yes, yes, you're right, that's absolutely right, I did. Only I'm glad you didn't, because it seems as if we may have to call it off.'

'Oh?' This was good news.

'Yes. I've got to pop back to the UK.'

'What?'

'I had a word with Eloise this afternoon and I'll have to pop back for a few days.'

I wished he'd stop using the word 'pop'.

'Why?'

'Too tedious to tell. But if I don't there's a possibility of a major cobblers.'

The message was now coming into focus. I put down my glass of iced coffee: it had become a poisoned chalice.

'Look,' I said, 'if you hadn't handed out your number they'd have had to uncobble the cobblers on their own, wouldn't they? I mean that's what people do when other people are on holiday.'

'In theory, yes. But in point of fact the mess would just have been left to fester till I got back.'

I stared at him. I was conscious, yet again, that it was not George's absence I resented, but the fact that he was clearly doing exactly as he pleased. Taking a comfort break from his holiday, and from the rest of us. Getting back into harness. Feeling indispensable and important. And I would be left here with no company but the rumbling rebellion of the girls, the insinuating presence of Royston, and my torturing reflections on Kostaki.

I must have looked pretty hostile, for George's manner became more conciliatory.

'I'll be as quick as I can.'

'What about the car? There's no way I can be stuck here without the car.'

'If you could bear to run me to Bordeaux, I'll fly.' I saw him make a swift mental leap, before adding: 'Don't worry, I'll din them for exes.'

I shrugged. They say daughters get more like their mothers with age, but I could feel myself inverting the process and getting more like Clara by the second.

George decided to become bracing. 'Anyway, it's an ill wind. You'll be able to cry off the party.'

'I'll do no such thing,' said a voice which I took to be mine.

'But I foisted it on you in the first place. Now you have a cast-iron excuse to cancel it.'

'I have, yes. When do you need to go?'

'There is a flight tomorrow afternoon, if that's not—'

'That's fine.'

*

151

It's funny how quickly paradise can turn into a bus queue. The Villa Almont, which only a week or so ago had been very heaven, was now a wasteland of boredom and irritation. The heat, the silence (which I now saw as a row of dots broken by occasional exclamation marks as the cannons fired), and even the flat, blue waters of the pool mocked my restless impatience. Deprived of the domestic displacement activities afforded by Basset Magna I was driven back to *Down Our Street* as the only way of maintaining my tenuous hold on sanity.

The novel was changing under the influence of my altered state. A new sensuality quivered through the text like a tropical breeze. I had decided that in view of the fact I was working with a biro and not on the typewriter (I was a Luddite concerning word processors), I would concentrate on key scenes and link them together when I got back. With half the book already typed, I reckoned by this method to be finished at the end of September.

There was only one scene I could write this afternoon and I started a fresh page and launched into it.

'I'm not staying!' shouted Mattie, and without listening to what her uncle was saying she stormed out of the corner house, slamming the door behind her. For a

moment she stood there, catching her breath, her cheeks on fire with anger and embarrassment. From the corner of her eye she caught sight of Mrs Bickerthwaite at Number 22 ducking back inside, her head doubtless full of the gossip that was her stock in trade.

'Yes, you get back in, you nosey old witch!' yelled Mattie, heedless of the shame to her uncle and aunt. 'At least I've given you something to talk about!'

Did she imagine it or did several net curtains twitch as she marched up the street?

She had no idea where she was heading. And in her haste to be gone she had come out with no coat, nor even a wrap against the wind that swept off the moors this late October afternoon. Even so she had reached the end of the town before she began to feel the cold, so incensed was she by her uncle's suggestion.

Stay? Stay here? Here, in Marsdyke, where the men worked in the mill, or down the mine, and the women whited their front steps and black-leaded their grates, and did their washing on a Monday? Stay and live like that after what she had become used to? Even though she was alone she tossed her head and gave a gasp of impatience. Why, she had had men waiting for her at the stage door, she'd been fêted and flattered, and she'd sipped champagne into the small hours. How could Uncle Gransden ask her to stay to mind Aunt Clarice?

Mattie had been walking swiftly. Now the moors spread before her in their stern glory, rippling green, grey and purple like a wild sea beneath a stormy sky.

Even in her rage they caught at Mattie's heart. Tears sprang to her eyes. It was not the moors she feared and despised, but the small, confined life of the streets of Marsdyke. The thought of months — years, perhaps — spent tending an ailing, aged woman in that cramped little corner house . . . she shuddered. She could not, would not, do it.

Like all spirited romantic heroines Mattie was in danger of becoming insufferable. Admirable ambition could so easily turn into egomania, and fieriness into good old-fashioned rudeness. And as for misplaced passion, well! Before I was through my readers would want to take Matilda Piper by her pretty shoulders and shake her till her fine white teeth rattled in her generous mouth.

Scarlett O'Hara had started it. She had been the prototype minx, beautiful and bloody-minded enough to inspire devotion, and sufficiently wrong-headed to make the reader feel superior. An inspired creation. I often wondered whether Margaret Mitchell realised, when she set pen to paper after the long years of exhaustive research, that her epic novel would chiefly be remembered for the transcendental corniness of Rhett and Scarlett's final exchange, captured on celluloid by an Englishwoman and an actor with taxicab ears . . .

At any rate, since I was no Margaret Mitchell,

and *Down Our Street* was assuredly no *Gone With The Wind*, I was going to have to do something to restore Mattie to her senses and make her once more the wholesome, home-loving, tender-hearted girl she had once been, albeit with an added dash of assertiveness courtesy of her time in the big city.

Her arms wrapped tightly round her against the cold, Mattie walked on until she had reached the cluster of great tumbled stones which as children they had called the Witches. From a distance they looked like a group of hunched, black-robed old women sitting in a circle on the wind-combed hillside. Two hyphenated adjectival phrases here. I debated which one to excise, decided I liked both of them and would leave them in for the moment. I knew very well that in all likelihood a respectful copy editor (it was a sign of my advancing years and reputation that the copy editors seemed younger) would let them slip by and they would annoy me for ever after, but there was no point in wasting time on them now, with the story waiting to be told.

Mattie sat down on the hard, moss-covered lap of the largest of the Witches. It was more sheltered here, but the wind still whipped her hair across her face. Tears of cold and self-pity welled up in her eyes. She was on her own in the world, and no one understood her.

Because of the wind, which had snatched away the sound of his approach, Oliver Challoner was upon her before she saw him. The great black horse fretted and stamped among the rocks as she dashed the tears from her eyes with her wrist.

'There was a time, Matilda,' said Oliver in that mocking way of his, 'when you were not so vain as to walk out on the moors with nothing but a flimsy frock to protect you.'

Not trusting her voice, she didn't answer him. To her consternation he dismounted and stood surveying her, the reins looped casually over his arm. I tried to picture this. I was by no means sure how feasible this casual looping would be in a stiff moorland nor'easter, and jotted a question mark by it.

'What is more,' continued Oliver, 'the dresses you had then suited you better.'

Now Mattie was stung. She got to her feet, her eyes flashing green fire.

'I won't ask you what you mean by that,' she said with all the cold contempt she could muster, 'but I'd thank you to keep your unwanted opinions to yourself.'

'The dresses you wore then,' went on Oliver as though she hadn't spoken, 'may have been hard and homespun, but you looked fine in them, Matilda.'

'Because I am a hard and homespun woman, I suppose!' snapped Mattie, (in case my readers should have failed to draw the inference).

Oliver let go of the reins of the grazing Lucifer and

walked slowly towards her. She could not step back for the rock behind her, and he came so close that the scented ruffles on his shirt front almost brushed her face. (I made a note: Ruffles okay?) *When he spoke his voice was no longer mocking but silky and insinuating.*

'*So you are a woman, are you, Matilda?*' *he asked, and she could feel his hands resting lightly on her waist.* '*Let us see . . .*'

Before she could move or struggle his arms slid round her and his mouth came down on hers.

After a long moment he released her. She swayed back against the rock, her legs weak. She expected him to speak: to say that she was indeed a woman. But he remained silent, and only his eyes sparkled with malicious amusement as he picked up Lucifer's reins and swung into the saddle.

Then and only then did he speak. Holding out one black-gloved hand, he said:

'*Well, Matilda, may I offer you a ride back to Marsdyke before you catch your death of cold?*'

She was so incensed that she could not at first find words to answer him. But he must have read her feelings in her eyes, for he wheeled the horse and cantered away. And his laughter was carried to her on the wind.

She shook her fist. '*I would not take a ride with you, Oliver Challoner, if you were the last man on earth!*'

*

In my mind's eye I could already see the cover which the Erans would produce to accompany *Down Our Street*: the Lysette Anthony lookalike with her hair streaming in the wind . . . the rolling moors, the scudding clouds . . . Oliver Challoner as played by Daniel Day-Lewis, all cheekbones and eyebrows . . . in the middle background Seth Barlow, arms folded, cap on the back of his head . . . in the distance the huddled rooftops of Marsdyke, the black skeleton of the mine, and the smoking towers of the mill . . .

The trouble with being a published writer, I reflected as I went downstairs, was that you learned about publishing. And about publishers, their whims and predilections, the way their minds worked. And it corrupted you. Unless you were an Iris Murdoch on the one hand, or an automaton-like producer of pulp romance on the other, you began to think like Them. For novelists, there was no 'Us'. When two or three of the scribbling persuasion were gathered together in the name of hype, hustle, workshop or seminar, they sniffed round each other with the stiff-legged walk and rolling eyes of mongrels in a park, unable (or unwilling) to establish any real intimacy. The dark secrets of their respective contracts ensured that they remained for ever isolated.

I poured myself a glass of wine and stood staring out of the kitchen window. The white gravel of the driveway glittered and glared in the sun. Dennis Potter was on record as saying that the best writing came out of repression. If this were so, *Down Our Street* was destined to be a real bobby-dazzler.

'He's doing what?' said Clara, with all the scathing incredulity at her command.

'Going back to England. Just for a few days.'

'What for?'

'Problems at work.'

'I see.'

'Gosh, that's really tough on your dad,' said Naomi. They were both standing, dripping, on the verandah. I couldn't tell whether Naomi's intervention was ironic, or offered in a spirit of arbitration. I gave her a hard look which she returned stonily. She had made a turban of her towel, and was an imposing sight.

'Yes, poor George,' I agreed shamelessly.

Clara looked daggers at both of us. 'Poor nothing. Can *we* go?'

'Certainly not. We're on holiday.'

'Yes, but we're nearly halfway through. You know perfectly well Dad won't come back once he's over there.'

I wasn't going to argue hypotheses and principles. Practicality was the only way to stymie this move.

'He's flying home,' I said, 'on expenses. There's no way we can afford for you two to fly.'

'Come on, Nev,' said Clara. The slap of their feet went away in the direction of their room.

That night in bed, George said: 'Don't be angry about this.'

'I'm not.'

'Yes, you are, you're bristling.'

'Then it's a little late to advise against it.'

'You know what I mean.'

'I think a holiday's a holiday, that's all.'

'No, you don't, you think a holiday's a necessary evil.'

This 'I know you better than you know yourself' line was one of George's most infuriating attributes. I turned my back on him with a flounce, and listened to the small, self-satisfied rustle as he sought the companionship of the Queen of Crime.

By the time I dropped him at Bordeaux airport at three the next afternoon, I just wanted him gone. I had already begun to make those mental preparations and adjustments which were necessary to contemplate ten days (for I believed Clara) without George's improving influence. It would not, for instance, be necessary to spend every waking hour in breathless admiration of things

Gallic. Neither would there be any need to be civil to Royston, since I had not the least interest in his tabletop facilities. I could be sloppy and celibate and eat bread in bed. I could row with the girls and buy tinned food.

What I couldn't do was stop thinking of Kostaki. That was another thing that annoyed me, as I stood outside the departures terminal at Bordeaux and watched George get his case from the boot. Did he have some kind of death wish? Why was he never there when temptation stalked our relationship? Why, in God's name, did he trust me?

We bumped cheeks and he said he'd be in touch. Realising this would mean a visit to Royston's office, I told him not to bother, but he insisted that it was the least he could do. Driving back I realised I never wanted to arrive. I felt safe in the car. Safe from Royston, safe from the girls, safe from Kostaki. Safe from myself. I took a loop off the main road and drove along a lane flanked by plum and apple trees already groaning with fruit. There was no traffic to speak of. A couple of farm trucks, a tractor, a woman on a bike. So there was no chance of missing the white MG parked at a roadside *vente de fruits*. Nor of missing the legs, once more in shorts and even more tanned than before. I slowed down, not because my foot was on the brake, but because I was suddenly incapable of exerting pressure on the accelerator. But when he turned, a brown paper bag of plums in his arms, my foot shot down reflexively and I almost dislocated my neck. A panic-stricken glance in the rearview mirror revealed Kostaki and the walnut-faced fruit seller sharing a joke at my expense, with much shoulder slapping.

As soon as I was out of sight I pulled over and switched off the engine. A casual observer would have seen a fair-haired Englishwoman in a pink T-shirt sitting at the wheel of a Ford Sierra, but this would have been a chimera. The reality was a creature from the imagination of a Hieronymus Bosch, all fangs, claws, wild hair and mad eyes. And far from sitting in silence, I was screaming like a banshee.

CHAPTER TEN

Out popped Royston like a weatherman as I emerged from the garage.

'Get him off all right?' he asked, with a curious inflection which made me suspect double entendre.

'I dropped him there, yes,' I replied crisply.

'He can always let you know if there's a problem,' agreed Royston.

I ignored his implication that I would return to Bordeaux at a moment's notice to bail George out of trouble, and headed grimly towards the house.

'I suppose,' Royston called after me, 'that you won't be wanting to entertain with the lord and master away.'

'What on earth,' I threw back, 'makes you think that?'

We were getting further and further apart, and each trying to have the last word. Infuriatingly, it was Royston who had it.

'Only slipped out to say you had a call.'

I stopped, and waited for him to elaborate.

'The girls have got the details . . .' He gave an insouciant wave and sloped off.

I followed the sound of MC Hammer and discovered the girls in the shade behind the barbecue. They were lolling in the hammocks. Teazel lay on Clara's stomach. Everybody's eyes were closed.

'What's this about a phone call?' I asked.

'Oh, your agent called,' mumbled Clara.

'My *agent*?'

The cat shifted slightly, otherwise there was no response.

'You mean Lew?'

'If she's your agent—'

'He.'

'—then it must have been.'

'Actually,' put in Naomi, who contrary to early indications was assuming the role of mediator and advocate in the Blair ménage, 'Royston did say it was Lew somebody.'

'But how on earth did he get in touch? I never gave him the number. The only person I gave the number to was Gareth. Somebody's playing silly—'

'Well, it wasn't us,' said Clara. 'And he wants you to call back.'

'He can whistle for it,' I said.

'Urgently.'

It was not even a matter of conscious decision. I simply went back to the garage, climbed in the car and reversed out at speed, the wheels churning on the gravel. I was rewarded by the sight of the cat streaking away from the hammock area in alarm, fur on end, like a jet-propelled sea urchin. On the way down the drive I noted, with grim satisfaction, Royston's baffled glance as I roared past.

'Yes, sure, help yourself,' said Priscilla. 'D'you have a card?'

'Yes, but I'm not going to use it,' I said. 'I shall reverse the charges.'

'Might as well live dangerously,' she said.

Common sense dictated that the cool thing to do was simply wait for Lew to ring again. If it was that urgent, he would. But I was so furious – with him, with Royston, with George (the rat) – that I wanted to take the initiative. It was early evening, the publishing world's happy hour, and Lew would doubtless be retrieving a couple of bottles of white from the fridge for a session of mutual ego-grooming with one of his clients, or an antic hay of gossip and negotiation with an editor. I badly wanted to disturb him.

Also, I had to admit I was curious. This was

Reality knocking at my door. This was proof that people thought about me in my absence in the way that Eloise et al thought about George. It was only a shame that George was not here to witness both my righteous (and rightful) indignation, and my importance in the world of letters.

After a brief interlude during which it sounded as though the operator were swimming the channel with the receiver between her teeth, I got through. Lew was talking to someone else as he lifted the receiver.

'. . . don't know a first-rate commercial property when they see one. Hallo, Lew Mervin – oh, yes, sure . . . Harriet?'

'Well?'

'Is that – uh – Harriet, is that you?'

'Yes.'

'Harriet!' He sounded, as always, genuinely delighted and quite impervious to what I had fondly imagined to be my iciest tone. 'This is so serendipitous, you have no idea—'

'Lew, you called. Someone gave you a number and you phoned. I am on holiday. Or was.'

'That was your husband, Harriet. He's such a great guy. He really understands you, and how many women can honestly say that about their husbands?'

'He does not understand me!' I barked.

'Okay, but he knows you love your work. A

writer never stops working. Life is work, for the writer, right?'

'Up to a point.'

'But you don't know how great it is that you called. I wonder if you can guess who's sitting on my sofa with a glass of wine in his hand and your name on his lips?' enthused Lew. I tried to picture whoever it was sitting on the plump, chintzy cushions beside the piecrust occasional table covered with photos of his ex-wife and nubile daughters.

'I have no idea.'

Lew chuckled. A deep voice said something in the background.

'Only Sonny Beidermeyer,' said Lew.

I was momentarily stumped. 'Who?'

Lew lowered his voice and I detected a hint of anxiety as he repeated: 'Sonny Beidermeyer, from Aurora.'

Now I remembered. Aurora Publications of New York. The biggest, swankiest, and certainly the most bumptious of all the big, swanky, bumptious American publishers. The company who were always two moves ahead of the game, and who had invented the game in the first place; whose deals were the most audacious, whose hype the most breathtaking, whose commercial success awesome. And yet who always managed to have at least one svelte, brilliant book adorning the review pages to ensure their continuing literary integrity. Sonny Beidermeyer. Well, well, well.

'Harriet? Are you there?'

'Yes.'

'Sonny is here, and we were just speaking of you.'

'Nicely, I hope.'

Lew chuckled. 'Of course! She says she hopes we're saying nice things about her.'

There was another distant rumble and Lew's laugh went up a couple of semitones. 'Sonny says he wouldn't speak ill of someone he hadn't met.'

'Right.' My mental silhouette of Sonny, which had been that of a large walnut whirl, broadened slightly at the top. Beidermeyer was obviously no pushover.

'So,' I said, rather more briskly, 'what can I do for you?'

Lew lowered his voice again for the non-public part of the conversation. I could picture him wrapped round the receiver, his glasses halfway down his nose, his narrow shoulders hunched in an attitude of Woody Allenish intensity.

'Harriet, how is the novel?'

People often referred to the work in progress in this way, as though it were a dependent relative or delicate pet; or perhaps some awkward and unlovely medical condition.

'It's okay. Not finished, or anywhere near it, but I'm managing to do some most days.'

The voice went public again: 'She works even on holiday, this lady!', and then returned to me. 'That's great. Only Sonny is a great admirer of your work, he really loves your writing, and he is in town hunting for a traditional English saga. Something with heart and integrity. Real emotions, real feelings, real people – a sense of history, you know?'

I knew, but was by no means sure what it had to do with me.

'I think,' said Lew, 'that *Down Our Street* may be just what he's looking for.'

I digested this. 'You do?'

Another nervous laugh intended to display cavalier confidence to Lew's unseen audience. 'I know it!'

It was a while since I'd had an American success. *A Time to Reap* had not even found an American publisher, due (Lew said) to its degree of sophistication and brilliance. The word turncoat might have been invented for my agent, who was capable of hijacking the moral high ground no matter how shifting the sands, and who could snatch credit from the jaws of the most crushing condemnation.

'Harriet?'

'Yes?'

'I keep losing you.' There was a tapping sound. 'Must be the line. I take it we are interested?'

'All things being equal.' I was playing it cool, but actually I could feel a distinct prickle of excitement at the thought of Sonny Beidermeyer and his customised cheque book.

'She says all things being equal!' laughed Lew. This time there was no answering rumble, and he went on. 'Now the point at issue here, Harriet, is that I've been able to give Sonny a fair idea of the novel from your excellent synopsis, and incidentally I've let him have a copy, but he is dying to see a few chapters . . .'

Lew left this hanging in the air for me to grab I didn't somehow think that Beidermeyer was the sort of chap who 'died' to do anything. That was pure Lew Mervin. On the other hand, I must be as shadowy a presence to him as he was to me. I would play hard to get. It was tough on Lew, but I was sure his small store of business acumen would come to his assistance.

'I'm sorry,' I said, 'there isn't a lot I can do about that. We're here for another ten days, and I've got the whole thing with me. I'm writing in longhand at the moment. It's really not a good time.'

'I understand that perfectly, Harriet,' said Lew solemnly. He loved his clients to behave like serious writers. 'The book must come first, and I know Sonny would be the first to appreciate that

. . .' His voice faded again as he glanced round for endorsement of this view. 'I'm wondering how we can get round this.'

'I'm pleased with the way it's developing,' I added.

'She's pleased with the way it's developing,' relayed Lew.

There was an answering rumble, which drew closer and suddenly and alarmingly became a voice in my ear.

'. . . exactly how we can get round it. Mrs Blair, this is Sonny Beidermeyer of Aurora, New York.' He introduced himself as though nothing Lew had said till now had done the job adequately.

'How do you do?' I gave cool detachment my best shot.

'Mrs Blair, are you interested in being published by Aurora?'

He was alarmingly direct. His use of my married handle recalled the Great Man of Era Books, whose best girl I had been for so many years until the unfortunate Fartenwald incident. His voice was deep, thick and gravelly, the sort of voice used to promote American beers and Kentucky Fried Chicken.

'Yes,' I said tamely.

'Good. In that case I want to see this manuscript your agent has been telling me so much about.'

'The trouble is I'm on holiday in France.'

'And I'm in London on business,' countered Beidermeyer abrasively. 'But I see no reason why young Lew here shouldn't fly down and pick up the book.'

I could hear Lew no-no-noing and sure-sure-sureing in the background.

'At my expense,' added Beidermeyer.

'Isn't that a bit drastic?' I asked. 'I could post it.'

'You could post it, Mrs Blair, but I have only a few days in your lovely capital, and very little faith in the postal system. If your novel is as commercial as it is said to be then I want to read it while I'm still in the UK.'

'Right,' I said.

I'd had to make some pretty swift decisions. This would undoubtedly have been my opportunity to make use of Royston's much-proffered fax machine, but I could not bring myself to give him the satisfaction. Besides which I rather liked the idea of Sonny Beidermeyer, the big man, sending an envoy scurrying to France to collect the precious manuscript.

By the time I put the phone down three minutes later I'd arranged to pick up Lew in Bordeaux the following afternoon. We had been out-hustled by an expert. Beidermeyer had seized control and exercised it with the assurance of a master. I was torn between wondering how I had allowed this to happen, and excitement over the possibility of a fat American sale.

'Everything okay?' asked Priscilla, floating by with a tray of beers.

'Yes, fine.'

'Only it can be the very devil getting a decent line from here.'

'No problem.'

I sat down outside and ordered myself a *demi-pichet*. No problem? I could see little else.

'Where exactly are you staying?' asked Priscilla when she brought my drink.

'The Villa Almont. Do you know it?'

'God, yes, how funny, it's one of Annie and Chris's places.'

'Annie and Chris?'

'My sister and brother-in-law, the Rutherford-Pounces. I dare say you'll have corresponded with them before coming.'

'What a coincidence.'

'It's a new acquisition, that house. They wanted something in this area to keep an eye on me, really,' explained Priscilla. She seemed to accept her role as prodigal with equanimity. 'Have you met them?'

'Yes.'

'What did you make of them?'

'They were very nice.'

Priscilla guffawed. 'They're perfectly okay,

actually. Underneath all that.'

I remembered very clearly our visit *chez* the RPs. Annabel wore an upstanding collar, a Guernsey, pearl earrings and the sort of jeans that only well-bred women wear. Crispin had sleek hair with a high parting, and chukka boots. Their house was freezing cold.

'So you're Annabel's sister?'

'That's right.' Priscilla sat down at the table and lit herself a Marlboro with quivering, orange-stained fingers. 'Hard to credit, isn't it? She did all the right things and I did all the wrong ones, but we are absolutely devoted.' She recovered from a coughing fit and added: 'As a matter of fact one of Chris's envoys is over at the moment so you'll probably get a visit. But you mustn't worry. He's an absolute honey.'

Royston was swimming with the girls. Or at least he was bobbing about on our giant inflatable turtle, sitting astride and urging it forward with his heels as though in some aquatic Rotten Row.

'We invited him in!' called Clara gaily. 'It must be so awful to be next door and not be able to use the pool!'

Royston dismounted and pulled himself up on to the edge. He was very thin and white with immensely pointed shoulders and knobbly knees like the ten-stone weakling in the Charles Atlas ads.

'I'll be off now your mother's back,' he said, as though I were a termagant in crimplene and he some kindly guardian standing in loco parentis.

'There's no need to rush,' I muttered.

'Where did you go, anyway?' asked Clara. 'You never said.'

'I went to town to make a telephone call.'

'Whatever did you do that for?' asked Royston. 'You should have come round to me.'

'I had one or two other things to do,' I said. 'And I had my card with me.'

They were not sufficiently interested to ask what my agent had wanted to speak to me so urgently about, and I was too pigheaded to tell them.

'Hey,' said Naomi from the lilo, 'Royston, show Harriet your eye.'

'She doesn't want to see it,' said Royston, in the tone of a man who takes his harp to parties and is invariably asked to play.

'Oh yes, go on,' added Clara. I sat stolidly on the grass. Royston turned round, made an 'O' with his finger and thumb round his right eye, somehow popped the eye through it, caught it in his other hand, treated me to a quick flash of the empty socket and replaced it. The whole grisly trick was over in a few seconds. The girls shrieked and clapped.

'Amazing, isn't it?' they chorused.

'Amazing,' I agreed.

Royston spread his arms as though acknow-ledging the applause of a vast audience. 'It was nothing. I got it when I was but a lad. I came off my bicycle on to a neighbour's chickenwire fence. Stood me in good stead with the girls ever since.'

I tried hard to see Royston as some kind of spoiled romantic hero, fatally attractive to women. But it was no good.

'He's got a spare one,' said Naomi from the lilo.

'And there's not many guys can say that!' shrieked Clara.

'Does it ever just – drop out?' I asked.

'Never fear. Once it's in, it's kind of sucked in place like a sea anemone.'

'What's the spare for then?'

'Security,' replied Royston. He got to his feet. He was wearing those strange long bathing shorts, printed with orange, black and purple psychedelia. In my view they were only just acceptable on youths of Gareth's age, and on someone of Royston's feather not at all.

He misread my expression. 'I see you like my shorts.'

'I wouldn't say that.'

'I thought I'd branch out.'

'Good for you,' put in Clara. 'They're really up to date.'

There was clearly no point in being rude,

especially as he was going.

'We'll see you the day after tomorrow then,' I said pointedly.

'Yes, indeed. I'm looking forward to it.'

I wished I could say the same.

Later that evening I saw Rindin paddling about in the dewpond and sure enough, at about eleven, the drainage pump started up. I decided not to go to bed until I was ready to fall asleep.

It was a sultry night. At half past twelve I was still out on the terrace when Obelix came down for a swim. She swayed heavily down the steps till her front feet were in the water and drank noisily. Thirst slaked she looked about her for a moment with water dripping from her muzzle before taking a great leap, ears flying, and belly-flopping on to the surface of the pool. She then did several stately lengths in a determined manner, like an old lady in a leisure centre.

This time I didn't resent the intrusion. But it brought home to me the fact that my struggle to regain the status quo, which only a week ago had seemed moderately successful, was beginning to lose ground.

George, whose exhaustively presented views on the virtue of family holidays had led to this trip, had buggered off to the office at the first opportunity. Agents and publishers were determined to winkle me out and involve me in deals. Lew was coming. Royston was lurking, one-eyed and insinuating, on the sidelines. Rindin and the Count were conducting their war of attrition across the no-man's land of the Villa Almont. Priscilla Shaw was RP's sister-in-law. The roving scout was about to descend.

And somewhere out there in the hot, scented, buzzing night was Kostaki.

I rose from my seat, charged the pool and did a racing dive into the water in my shorts and T-shirt, narrowly missing Obelix, and sending her floundering and yelping for the steps.

CHAPTER ELEVEN

I went to Lalutte early next day to shop for the dinner party. My plan was to acquire the ingredients, do whatever cooking I could in advance and stow it in the fridge, and give over the afternoon to the collection and settling-in of Lew.

The town had a brittle, biscuity quality as if, were one to rap the yellow walls with one's fist, it would disintegrate into a pile of crumbs. Pru's Bar was empty, and the dogs not in sight. I did my shopping without a pause for refreshment, and set off for home. On the way back I glanced through the gateway of the Château Forêt Noir and saw Isabelle and Véronique working on the front border with long-handled hoes. They looked like a couple of gawky wading birds as they dibbled about among the weeds. Of the Count and his house guest there was no sign.

Indoors, perhaps, putting a final polish on their Valse Valeta. Back at the Villa Almont the girls were still in bed asleep and Royston was not at his work centre. Through the window I could see the fax machine sporadically dribbling documents into an empty room.

As I put my purchases away and got on with the fairly simple cooking to which I was committed, I tried to look on the dinner party as an opportunity to claw back some self-esteem.

At the airport, Lew was last through, in spite of having travelled first class courtesy of Aurora, NY. He was an experienced traveller – every year saw him breaking new ground in places like Nepal and Alaska – but he appeared flustered.

'You're never going to believe this, Harriet,' he said, sublimely unaware that as far as he was concerned I was ready to believe anything. 'But I picked up the wrong bag.'

'It's easily done,' I conceded, remembering the Scotsman in Perth.

'Happily the other guy found out right away. He went to get a present he'd bought for his mother.'

I pictured the poor man opening the case to be confronted with piles of Lew's designer mistakes. Mind you, Lew was wearing a few of them. Enormous white-rimmed sunglasses bestrode his nose, and a lemon seersucker jacket topped a white T-shirt and white peg-top trousers which made Lew, a small man, look as if he were entering for a sack race. His feet were shod in painfully new white HiTecs picked out in silver like the hooves of a circus pony.

'I guess I may have brought too much,' he observed as we toiled across the concourse with his trolley, 'but I've learned that to travel light can be a false economy.'

We emerged into the afternoon sun.

'Wow,' remarked Lew, 'this is serious heat.'

'Yes, it's topped the hundred mark for the past few days.'

We climbed into the car and I rolled back the sunroof. Lew sighed and stretched his arms. His state-of-the-art plastic watch looked like a toy on his bony wrist.

'You're *en famille*, Harriet?'

'Yes. Well, in theory. Though actually George had to go back to the UK yesterday.'

'Surely not, when you're on vacation! Why was that?'

I accelerated sharply out of the slip road. 'Some business hitch or other.'

'Gee, poor George,' said Lew. 'And I'm here.'

I glanced at Lew. Was he suggesting that he might in some way be able to fulfil George's role in my life? It was unthinkable. In all the years I'd known him, and despite his devotion to me and unalloyed admiration for my work, there had never been in our relationship a hint of what my headmistress would have called 'silliness'. At this moment Lew was polishing his outsize sunspecs on his handkerchief, leaving his exposed face looking even more thin and worried, and his large nose even more bulbous. No, it was guilt that had been the impulse for Lew's remark. Guilt, at being here in sunny southern France with a bestselling author while poor old George grafted in the smoke. There wasn't a trace of arrogance in Lew's make-up. I was sure this was what had led to the breakdown of his marriage to the breathtaking Marisa, scion of a noble house and from a long line of mad, bad people. You only had to see Marisa's photograph – flaring nostrils, curling lip and hooded eyes – to know that she needed three blazing rows a day and a beating before breakfast to keep her amused. The initial attraction was even harder to fathom. Perhaps in those far-off days Lew had come into Marisa's life trailing clouds of glory, the rough diamond from Hoboken, New Jersey, the Sinatra of publishing . . . Lew finished polishing his specs, replaced them on his conk and blew his nose on the handkerchief. No again. Marisa had wanted something to wipe her feet on.

'How long can you stay?' I asked gently.

'A couple of nights. Will that be quite all right?'

'Fine. I've got one or two people coming to dinner tomorrow night, so you'll be able to play host.'

'Sounds wonderful. I tell you what, though, Harriet. What I'm looking forward to most of all is reading *Down Our Street*.'

How little it takes, I thought, as we turned on to the autoroute and hurtled south, to make some people happy.

Lew was predictably bowled over. 'Too much . . . it's exquisite . . .' he breathed, drinking in the house, the pool, the garden, the hammocks, the view over the parched sunflowers to the heat-smudged horizon. 'How did you find this place?'

I decided against describing the Rutherford-Pounces. 'Oh, friends of friends, you know the kind of thing.'

'I should have such friends,' said Lew wistfully.

He went for a swim. His trunks weren't quite as funny as Royston's, but only because they were more expensive. They were Black Watch boxer shorts, from which his thin legs protruded like a couple of lolly sticks. The girls lay motionless on their loungers by the *sous-sol*, faces greasy with sun oil, eyes shielded by Ray Bans, but I knew they were watching. Suddenly I felt rather protective of Lew. I should not be on my own tomorrow night.

*

He pleaded tiredness and went to bed early. But the knowledge that someone would soon be reading the work in progress for the first time had filled me with a fresh enthusiasm for it. The girls were sitting on the side of the pool enjoying a quiet fag in the moonlight, and Royston was safely behind his shutters, so I went up to the *atelier* to add a few telling paragraphs to *Down Our Street*.

I had left Mattie Piper alone on the moors, tear-stained and windswept and quivering in the wake of Oliver Challoner's importunate embrace. So far, so star-crossed. But in the nature of the beast, things were going to have to get a lot worse before they got better. Mattie's behaviour, for a start, had to bottom out, and this was next on the agenda.

Perhaps, I wrote, *it was that rough, demanding, unasked-for kiss that fanned Mattie's resentment to a fury. Left to herself with only the whispering moors for company she might very well have come to terms with her uncle's request, and seen that since her aunt had not long to live it was her place to be at her side, supporting the frail old woman at the end of her life as she had been supported by her as a child.*

I paused. This last sentence had so many pronouns that I was by no means confident my reader would be able to navigate through them to the meaning: that Mattie owed her aunt one. I put a wiggly line under it, and continued:

Mattie's heart was in the right place, but that kiss had given it an unpleasant jolt. Furious now with herself as well as with Grandsen she set off for Marsdyke, running as fast as she could, her head bowed beneath the pouring rain.

She slammed the door of the corner house behind her and leaned back on it, panting and bedraggled. Gransden was sitting at the table, peeling an orange. Mattie guessed it was for Clarice. He was making a mess of it, his large, gnarled fingers were clumsy and kept tearing away the fruit with the pith. The sight of him doing this small task infuriated Mattie.

'Oh for goodness sake!' she snapped, snatching the orange from him and beginning to peel it herself with fierce, quick movements. 'I'll do this for you because I can't stand to see you make such a mess of it. But I'll not stay, Uncle! I will not!'

'Very well, lass,' he said quietly. She glanced at him from beneath her lashes as she peeled the orange and saw that there was no fight left in him. He was an old, tired, unhappy man. And why should she, young, beautiful and ambitious, spend her time with him? It was out of the question.

'There you are,' she said, returning the neatly peeled orange on its plate. 'And now I must go and get ready.'

The next day the heat changed. It took on a

sullen, threatening quality. The girls complained bitterly about the few clouds which gathered on the horizon like a group of louts in a bus shelter. Teazel retired to the woodshed. Rindin reset his cannon and withdrew. Lew roosted in the *atelier* reading *Down Our Street* with admirable concentration considering half of it was in longhand.

As I was sweeping the verandah in the morning Royston came out to do some illegal watering.

'Storm's a-brewing,' he called cheerily. 'Hot enough for you?'

'Do you think it'll hold off till after tonight?' I asked.

He stood arms akimbo and gazed about him like an old salt on the sea wall. 'Very like. This kind of thing can go on for days.'

I wasn't sure whether to be comforted or not. It was only ten thirty and I was already running with sweat.

'You have a visitor, I see,' observed Royston.

'That's right.'

'Family friend?'

I should have told him to mind his own business but I wanted to clarify matters. 'My agent, actually. We have a business transaction to discuss.'

Royston shook his head indulgently. 'Honestly, what a pair you are. No sooner has George gone rushing back to the UK to see to some problem or other than you've brought in your agent. If this is the Blairs *en vacances* I'd hate to see them under pressure!'

'It was an unavoidable coincidence,' I said. 'And none of it would have arisen,' I added frostily, 'had you not been so keen to share your desktop facilities with George. One can only avoid work if one is incommunicado.'

I didn't wait for him to top this one, but went in and put the kettle on.

'Coffee, you two?' I bawled through the girls' door. They were playing a rap tape, three minutes of funky hectoring against which the normal, unamplified female voice was powerless to compete. It was Lew who came to the *atelier* balustrade, and called down:

'What was that, Harriet?'

'Oh, Lew. Coffee?'

'Sounds great. Black no sugar, but I'll come and get it.'

He came trotting down the stairs. Today he wore a pink golf shirt with the same baggy white trousers and a red sweatshirt knotted carelessly about his shoulders. The sweatshirt had risen up round his ears so he looked like a sheep in a muffler.

'I can't tell you how I'm enjoying your book,' he said. 'It has such narrative drive, such feeling. You do have a knack, Harriet, of taking a popular genre and making it your own. Giving it the Blair touch.'

'Well, thanks,' I said. Dear Lew, peeping out of his red sweatshirt. 'Do you think it's what Aurora want?'

'I think Sonny is going to be bowled over. It has such authenticity.' It was as well it was dark in the house, or Lew would have seen me blushing. 'We may get ourselves a really good deal here.'

He went back happily with his coffee. The girls' door slammed open and Clara emerged in her George Michael outsize T-shirt. 'Is that coffee?'

'I did try to offer you some but I couldn't make myself heard.'

'That's okay.' Clara assembled mugs and yelled: 'Nev! Coffee!'

'Why don't you turn the music down?' I suggested. 'Lew is trying to read upstairs.'

'Tough titty,' responded Clara. 'We're on holiday. He could go to the hammocks.'

'It's too hot out there. He's not acclimatised.'

As it turned out Nev switched the machine off before emerging. True to type she wore a blue baby-doll nightie which hung from her chest like a bell tent.

'It's your dinner party tonight,' she said sunnily. 'Is that going to be a problem with us going out?'

'Going out?'

'Yes, you know,' said Clara, 'it's that dance in the town. Dad said he'd take us.'

I remembered now. George had said just that,

and it would be pretty mean of me to back out of it, especially when feasting and fun were planned on the home front.

'No, that's all right, I'll get you there.'

'Great!'

'Where is it?'

'At the town hall.'

'It will be jolly good for your French, that's for sure. And you can ring Royston's number if you have any problems.'

As they carried the coffee back into their lair I heard them choking with laughter and repeating: 'Jolly good for our French!'

Dinner parties no longer filled me with alarm, because I'd long since stopped giving them. I went out of my way to tell invitees that the meal would be supper. This meant that they could only be pleasantly surprised by whatever amusing little dish I threw together. The men didn't have to wear suits, the women could look as beautiful as they liked while still being comfortable, and it didn't matter that none of the crockery matched, nor that we did not own a complete set of dining chairs. George was mortified by our deficiencies in the chair and crockery departments, but I kept telling him that it showed we were free spirits, happy with nothing more than a crusty loaf, a rough red wine and some spirited conversation among good and trusted friends.

Mind you, things weren't quite the same at the Villa Almont. It was an odd feeling entertaining in someone else's house, with guests who had very probably been here before under the regular management.

I tried not to let it put me off my stroke. But I kept coming across Jules and Antoinette's notes urging me to use the antique glasses, the Limoges china, the silver candlesticks, the lace tablecloth and napkins . . . Would it look like downright rudeness to use the kitchen stuff when such an *embarras de richesses* was on offer?

In the end I decided it wouldn't matter so long as we ate out of doors on the verandah. The atmosphere out there was as humid as a weightlifter's armpit, and the sky was boiling with uncertainty, but I put my faith in Royston's prognosis. I covered the table with a check tablecloth, found some plain green linen napkins, fetched out the kitchen cutlery and a couple of brass candlesticks, and offered up a prayer of appeasement to Thor.

I had dispensed with a first course and constructed a feast of delicious, low-labour options as the centrepiece for the meal. *Charcuterie*, marinaded cold fish, pasta in homemade tomato sauce, and assorted salads of my own devising, to be accompanied by a choice of breads. For afterwards I had made a stupendous fresh fruit salad, and there was cheese, celery and (I had tracked them down in the Lalutte supermarket) Bath Olivers to please the English contingent. I picked some trailing nasturtiums and a few coral and white roses from the garden and put them in a pottery vase. It was going to look very pretty and inviting, and unmistakably informal. Teazel sat beneath the bellpull and watched me with languorous expectancy. In this mode he reminded me strongly of our own cat, Fluffy. A feeding trance was a feeding trance no matter where one found it.

The guests had been invited for seven thirty, so I told the girls they must be dropped at the town hall in Lalutte not a second later than seven p.m., whether they liked it or not.

'That's miles too early,' Clara complained. 'It's so naff to be hanging about waiting for things to start. Can't you take us after you've eaten?'

'No, I can't!' I replied, scandalised. 'I'm not going to jump up and abandon my guests for half an hour at that stage in the proceedings. Besides, I shall have had a glass of wine or two by then.'

'That's an idea,' put in Naomi. 'We can go to that café and have a couple of drinks while we're waiting.'

I began beating on their door at a quarter to seven, and at five to they emerged in full battle colours. Clara wore the same ensemble she had worn to the château, but this time her hair, usually a farouche cloud of tangled ringlets, was up in a Bardot-esque style, backcombed on top, stray tendrils hanging round her face and on her neck. She looked quite indecently seductive. Naomi had swapped the black miniskirt for calf-length flares. I had to admit that if I had been a casual observer asked to say which one was the nice girl, I'd have gone for Naomi.

'Won't you be cold?' I asked Clara.

She not only interpreted this correctly, but treated it with the contempt it deserved. 'I am not dressing like a nun to go to a disco.'

'Don't worry,' said Naomi, 'we'll be good.'

I left Lew opening red wine and putting clean teatowels over the dishes, and took them to the town. The château, as we went by, was studded with lights.

'They're getting ready for your party,' said Clara.

For some reason this remark, intended to encourage me, made my heart sink, but once I'd deposited the girls in the town square and reminded them of their rights and responsibilities it bobbed up again. Everything was ready. It might even be possible to enjoy the evening.

As I walked back into the house Lew handed me a glass of champagne.

'Here's to my favourite author!'

'Lew! How lovely – when did you get this?'

'In the duty-free. Here's to *Down Our Street*. I know it's going to be your breakthrough book in the States.'

'I'll drink to that.'

We clinked glasses. Lew was looking quite fetching tonight, in oatmeal slacks and an oatmeal and white striped matelot jersey. He spent such a lot of time and money on his clothes it was a shame he so seldom looked right. You either got or you hadn't got style, as the song said, and Lew hadn't.

Just before seven thirty, as he and I stood on the verandah with our drinks, speculating on the imminence of the *orage* to end all *orages*, Royston appeared and told me I was wanted on the phone.

'You go and take the call,' he said bossily. 'I'll introduce myself.'

Breathing a prayer for poor Lew I picked up the phone. 'Hallo?'

'It's me.'

'Oh, hallo.'

'I just thought I'd wish you *bonne chance* with your dinner party.'

'Supper.'

'Sorry, supper, quite right. Are you quorate?'

'Not yet, only Lew and Royston.'

'Who and Royston?'

'Lew Mervin.' Of course George didn't yet

193

know the results of his officiousness. 'In consequence of your dishing out this number to all and sundry I've got Lew here for a couple of nights.'

'Stap me – you mean the blighter invited himself? I am sorry.'

'No, as it happens he's been sent to pick up my manuscript. There is what is known as transatlantic interest.'

'Oh, so that's good!' George was not going to lie down and accept guilt. 'But – um – couldn't you have put it in the post?'

'No time. The bloke from Aurora isn't in town long.'

'And you need to strike while the chequebook's hot,' agreed George. 'Well, well, well. I am missing a lot.'

I sensed he would ask why I hadn't used the fax, but now there was a flurry of activity in the drive as a white Citroën and a motorscooter jockeyed for position.

'They're arriving. I must go.'

'Okay. Have one for me. See you soon.'

I rang off hurriedly, realising as I did so that George had mentioned nothing of his own doings, or the likely date of his return. Before closing the office door I saw the battered 2CV from the courtyard of the château rattle through the still-settling dust outside the window.

I arrived at one end of the verandah as the Count

arrived at the other. Royston, still bearing the mantle of host, threw his arms in the air.

'Guy! *Bienvenue*! And who is this?'

I looked at the young woman accompanying de Pellegale. I held out my glass, nervelessly, to be replenished by Lew. I knew exactly who it was. I'd have known that bright, freckled, challenging face anywhere. It was Monica Ball.

'Hallo, Monica,' I said. 'What on earth are you doing here?'

Monica shrieked and fell upon me, slapping my arms, massaging my shoulders and tousling my hair as if I were some faithful mongrel dog while the others looked on in amazement.

'I don't believe it!' she squealed. 'Way to go, Mrs Blair, I never thought it would be you!'

I introduced her to Royston and Lew, and cautiously permitted the Count to kiss my hand. It turned out Monica was on a footslog of Europe, as she put it, had spotted the Count's flag and availed herself of the hospitality. It was not the moment to ask what else had been on offer, because the remaining guests were arriving thick and fast. First came the British couple invited by Royston.

'Keith and Denise hail from outside Basingstoke,' said Royston, a remark to which there was no possible response. The Platfords were trim and tanned, the sort of couple who

195

have got everything so well organised that nothing can dent their self-satisfaction.

'This is an exquisite place,' said Keith, 'but an energy conservationist's nightmare.'

'We decided right away,' added Denise, 'that whatever we bought we'd made sure it was just as lovely in the winter.'

'And it is,' confirmed Keith. 'You must come over and see for yourself.'

During this exchange Monica's attention had turned to Lew, and Véronique and Isabelle had arrived – theirs had been the bone-shaking 2CV.

We were, as George would have said, quorate. Royston was passing among the company with a bottle, so I slipped away to the kitchen.

I'd only been there thirty seconds when Monica came bounding in. 'Is there anything I can do?'

'No, it's all organised. Just a case of putting it on the table. It's only supper.'

'Mmm!' Monica bent over my cold collations, peering and sniffing and making foodie noises.

'Only simple stuff,' I said. 'I am on holiday.'

'That's right!' agreed Monica. 'So where's George?'

From the way she said this it was clear that my husband's name had been on her lips – and very probably those of others – quite frequently since I'd last met her. His rarity value in having remained twenty years married to the same woman had elevated him to the status of conversation-fodder.

'He had to go back to the UK.'

'Oh no, whatever for? And I really wanted to meet him.'

'A business problem,' I said curtly, sprinkling chopped chives on the fish.

'M-hm. Too bad,' said Monica. I could almost hear the cogwheels whirring.

'How long are you in Europe?' I enquired, shaking the jar containing the salad dressing and not bothering to disguise the slightly threatening note in my voice.

'Another month,' replied Monica. 'I'm not even sure I'll go back to Oz then. I might pack in the job and look for something in London.'

'Goodness, what a big decision.' My heart sank at the prospect of lunches at the Gadfly during which fresh revelations about Monica's social life would make heads snap round all over the dining room like a pinball machine.

We carried the various dishes and plates through to the verandah and laid them out on the table. It was prematurely dusk and so hot that on exposure to the air the food broke into an instant sweat. Beyond the trees the horizon was lit by the occasional sickly electrical flicker. Even the arrival of supper couldn't bring the palpitating Teazel to his feet. The candle flames were stunted and motionless.

'A veritable feast!' exclaimed the Count, which compared to the catering at Forêt Noir it undoubtedly was.

'Sit anywhere,' I said. 'There's no plan.'

There may have been no plan, but Keith and Denise soon devised one. It involved putting me in the middle of the long side of the table with my back to the double doors 'for easy access', with the Count on my left and Keith on my right. At the end of the table next to the Count was Monica, with Royston opposite her. Facing us were Véronique, Lew, Denise and Isabelle.

'Best we can do with nine, I'm afraid,' said Keith, a man used to trouble-shooting.

'Shall I dish up?' asked Lew, always eager to please. As plates were passed and filled to order, the Count leaned towards me and breathed in my ear: 'You know our little traveller?'

It was the kind of euphemism that in the purlieus of Basset Magna would have referred to some embarrassing bodily pest – a headlouse, thread worm or pubic crab – but it seemed unlikely to have such a connotation here.

'I'm sorry?'

'Monique. Our little waif from the other side of the world.'

I had never thought of Monica as a waif. I wondered if the Count made her wear her thongs and haversack when they conjoined.

'Yes, I met her when I was in Australia. She worked for their branch of my publishers.'

'I think she is wasted in publishing,' observed the Count, glancing libidinously at Monica who was telling Denise that vaginismus afflicted four out of ten Australian women on their wedding night.

'Perhaps,' I said. 'She was very good at her job. She was on the publicity side of things.'

'But of course,' said the Count. 'What else?'

I heard the first faint rattle of thunder, and resumed my relationship with the Almighty long enough to assure Him of my good offices at future times if He would only pull rank on Thor forthwith.

On my other side, Keith was saying to Royston: 'You need one of these laptop efforts. I reckon mine saves me twenty-odd hours a week and a millimetre or two on the arteries . . .'

I looked across the table at Lew. Isabelle and Véronique were silent and smiling as usual, presumably planning fresh refinements to the 'Teddy Bears' Picnic' for later. Lew was safe with Denise, though.

'. . . be on the books of an agent such as yourself when one has not yet had work published?' she was asking, fork poised, teensy furrow in place between the brows.

Lew demurred, but honourably, in case it was my closest friend he was addressing. I longed to tell him that this was a woman who would be first off the Russia sledge in my book, and that anything he could do to crack her smug, gloss top-coat would really make my evening.

'It's difficult,' he said earnestly. 'These are tough times for publishing, and no matter how much faith an agent has in a writer it's not an advantageous climate to take on someone with no track record.'

Unfortunately, he had not slammed the door firmly enough and there was an aperture wide enough for Denise to get her foot in. 'I have lots of ideas,' she said. 'And English was my best subject at school . . .'

Next to Denise, Véronique sat smiling. She had cleared her plate – well, she'd had nothing else to do – and quite suddenly she leaned across and spoke in English. 'Madame – there is music?'

'Please, call me Harriet. Um, yes, the owners said we could use what was here. It's mostly modern jazz and classical, I think.'

'No!' Véronique shook her head. 'To play on? Player?'

'Yes, there's a sound centre. But—'

Véronique patted the capacious hessian shoulder bag that hung on the back of her chair. 'Records here.'

She leaned back, switching once more into spectator mode, and I concluded that our exchange was at an end, and that Véronique was only here for the dancing. I felt panic rise in my throat like milk about to boil over. This was when I needed George, to tell me not everything that happened was my responsibility, and no one was going to blame me if my supper party was subverted by lunatics and sabotaged by the weather. I recalled a similar occasion some years ago when an innocent after-dinner party game had nearly wrecked my reputation, and almost ruined my chances with Kostaki before they'd begun. The auguries were not good.

'Hey, do you put mustard in this sauce?'

Monica's voice cut across my inner panic.

'No.'

'It's so good. But you ought to try a smidgin of Dijon, it makes it really memorable.'

'I'll remember that.' I saw that she was mopping her plate with a piece of bread. 'Do have some more. Everybody, help yourselves.'

'Where are your two delicious daughters?' asked the Count. He was one of these people who always had to get too close to you when he talked, revealing the piece of watercress on his front teeth and the gold virgin nestling between his gleaming paps.

'They're not both mine,' I said. 'Just one. The

other's a friend. They've gone to a dance at the town hall.'

'And you let them go unchaperoned?' put in Royston with a ho-ho intonation. 'You're trusting!'

'Girls these days are incredibly mature,' said Lew. 'They can handle most things.'

'It's the handling I worry about!' said Royston.

Keith patted the back of my hand. 'Take no notice, Harriet, they'll be fine.'

Denise dabbed her mouth with her napkin. 'You'll never stop a good, responsible parent from worrying. It's like telling the stars not to shine, isn't it, Harriet?'

I weakly agreed, simultaneously realising that I had not given Gareth a thought since I'd arrived.

After supper, the inevitable happened. Véronique put on her Dance Hits compilation, and the storm broke. Had the rest of us been able to remain on the verandah, the ghostly bossanovas and rumbas being executed inside might scarcely have impinged. In fact the distant Latin rhythms, and the removal from the table of the conversational dead wood might have been positively beneficial. As it was, the Almighty turned on the celestial tap with such force that two of the hanging baskets plummeted to the ground, and the verandah floor was awash inside a minute. We scuttled for cover, taking the plates, cheese and Bath Olivers with us.

We re-established ourselves indoors with our plates on our knees, trying to pretend that there was nothing noteworthy in two elderly women doing the *pasa doble* as we ate.

'This is fun!' said Lew. 'It's really quite cosy.'

Then there was a power cut.

'Don't worry!' shouted Royston. 'I know where the candles are!'

I sat in the dark, hoping my fates would do something right for once and get me out of this one. The rain hammered down outside in a solid sheet and the thunderclaps overhead made the ping-pong balls rattle in the atelier. The occasional flash of sheet lightning revealed Véronique and Isabelle, music gone but still gamely strutting and weaving, Royston rummaging in the drawers of the sideboard, and Lew, Keith and Denise on the sofa like the three wise monkeys. Of the Count and Monica there was no sign.

'Oh dear,' I said, 'I'm really sorry about this.'

'It's not your fault, Harriet,' said Denise. 'It happens all the time around here. And this house has no independent generator.'

It was clear from her tone that theirs did. I sat miserably, trying to scoop up overripe brie with a broken biscuit.

'Blast,' exclaimed Royston, 'and double blast. I'll have to go round to the annexe.'

We sat there quiescent in the tumultuous

darkness as he stumbled to the door, tripped on the Chinese rug and fell into my lap. I suppose the berserking of natural forces must have prevented us from hearing the arrival of the car. The first we knew of the approach of anyone else was the double door slamming open, a roar of wind and water as the storm gatecrashed the gathering, and an intrusive glare of torchlight.

I couldn't see who was holding the torch, but I could, unhappily, see the rest of us. Royston struggling to get off my knees like an upturned dung beetle. Véronique and Isabelle in an attitude of quasi-hauteur like some second-rate civic statue. The Platfords and Lew sitting in a row with their plates on their knees. And, oh yes, there were the Count and Monica – engaged in deep petting on the *atelier* floor cushions.

'Who is that?' I asked, pushing Royston unceremoniously on to the floor. 'Can you tell me who that is?'

'The name's Ghikas,' said Kostaki, closing the doors behind him. 'I've brought your girls back.'

CHAPTER TWELVE

'*Pas de* sweat,' said Royston, 'Constantine can sleep in the annexe.'

'I feel bad about this,' I quavered. It was the truth, but not for any reason Royston would suspect. 'Do you have room?'

'Plenty of room. For a chap,' said Royston.

'This place was next on my list,' said Kostaki, who had emerged from the bathroom with his hair in fetching disarray and a towel round his neck, like an ad for men's toiletries. 'So this is quite providential.'

He flashed me the smile which spelled instant lubrication and receptivity. I mumbled something I couldn't quite catch.

'What list is that?' asked Royston.

'Properties to be looked at. For the villa company, France Vacances. For the past week I've been based at a little auberge on the Cahors road. I have what you might call a roving brief.'

Roving briefs? I'll say. I made a bolt for the kitchen. Outside the thunder and lightning had abated, but not the rain, which was descending with the force of a massed army of Black and Deckers intent on screwing the Villa Almont into the ground. The electricity had returned, but was still queasy, dimming and flickering from time to time to keep us on our toes. The Platfords and the de Pellegales had left, and Lew had discreetly retired.

'Would anyone like a cup of tea?' I asked. I didn't know which I wanted more: Kostaki to stay, or to go. I was shell-shocked.

'That would be nice,' he said.

I felt as though I had been boiling kettles for him at midnight all my life. At least this time I wasn't wearing my towelling dressing gown with the spots of hair dye. Even while he and Royston were talking. I could feel the old, familiar dishonourable intentions wafting my way.

I opened the door of the girls' room. The light was out and they were sitting on the floor, their tear-stained faces and bedraggled locks lit only by the small glow of their cigarettes. Their present appearance contrasted starkly with the cruciality of their earlier toilette. It was going to be difficult to be as censorious as the situation demanded.

'Are you going to tell me what happened now, or later?' I asked in as firm a voice as I could manage.

'Didn't Dr Ghikas tell you?' asked Clara.

'He sketched in the outline,' I replied. 'I suspect he's too polite or too kind to go into details. I'm expecting those from you.'

'There's nothing to tell. We got stranded, that's all.'

'I told you to ring if you needed a lift.'

'Well, we weren't near a phone, were we?'

'You're telling me there was no telephone in the town hall, or anywhere near it? What about Priscilla's place? Or the public one in the square?'

'I told you we weren't near those!'

'Well, why not?'

I heard Clara give the grunt that generally accompanied a shrug. Naomi said:

'We went for a walk.'

'What, on your own?'

'With some boys we met at the dance.'

'I see.' It was axiomatic that the more I itched for Kostaki, the more reproving I became about the carnal whims of others. 'And then what happened?'

'The storm started, and they wanted to go back to the house where one of them lived and we didn't fancy it, so we went off on our own but the weather was so awful we couldn't find our way . . .' Naomi tailed off, having shot her bolt on the excuses front.

'Clara?'

'What?'

207

'Do you have anything to add?' Talk about the Grand Inquisitor.

'No. Naomi's told you.'

'We'll talk about this again later,' I said threateningly. 'I hope you've thanked Dr Ghikas profusely. In the meantime put out those disgusting things, clean your teeth and get to bed.'

The cigarette sparks glowed as they took a last, long, rebellious drag.

Kostaki was pouring water into the pot. In the steam that wreathed about his head I could see my Fates clutching their misshapen sides with mirth.

'You haven't said what you were doing in Lalutte,' I said.

'Oh, visiting a friend . . . just as well I was, don't you think?' He held up the pot. 'Shall I be mother?'

A little later, when Royston had borne him away to the snug, all-male preserve of the annexe, I tried rationally to assess my situation.

I was in France, on a family holiday, without my husband. My daughter and her friend had narrowly escaped rape in the middle of a thunderstorm on the streets of Lalutte. My nearest neighbours were a crazed porno king and a bloodthirsty peasant. And I was sharing the villa with three men – a neurotic American divorcee, a one-eyed lecher and the object of my wildest and guiltiest sexual fantasies. Good heavens, it was nothing!

It was evidence of my disturbed state of mind that I began to think quite fondly of the Platfords. I could have done with some of their inspired banality to balance things. As I tiptoed across the living area towards my bedroom door, Lew emerged from his room. He was swathed in a richly piled and satin monogrammed cream towelling robe, but still looked like a hamster peeping from its bedding.

'Sorry, Harriet,' he said, as though it were I, not he, who had been caught *en déshabillé*. 'I'm going to the john.'

'I don't suppose you feel like a nightcap?' I asked. I don't know what made me say it. I was not in the habit of taking nightcaps – in fact, to the best of my knowledge I'd never even used the word before – but after the baleful girls, and the uncomfortable company of my own thoughts, Lew offered the prospect of some comfort and reassurance.

'Hey! Well – sure! Why not?' was Lew's reply, a response which contrived to be both timorous and over-emphatic. 'I must just—'

'Cognac?'

'You have some?'

'No, but I can nip into Lalutte – of course I've got some!' I didn't bother to conceal my exasperation.

'Great.'

While Lew was in the bathroom I poured the drinks, and by the time he emerged I had done mine some damage.

'Shame about the storm,' he said, sitting down and crossing his legs, making sure the flap of his robe was tucked between his thighs. 'And after all your hard work.'

'Act of God,' I said. It was that time of night which encouraged indiscretion and unconsidered confidences, and we both knew it.

'Never mind,' he said heartily, as if I had indicated that I did. 'Tomorrow I'll be getting on that plane with *Down Our Street*.'

'Yes, indeed,' I said dully.

'I'll get Camilla to type up the handwritten chapters for Sonny. We may as well present him with a perfectly enamelled document. It all helps.'

'Why not?' I agreed. 'Lew, there are one or two things I'd like to explain.'

'There's no need, really.'

'No, I'd like to. It's about Constantine.'

'That guy who brought your daughter back?'

'Yes.'

'A charming fellow. About the closest thing I've encountered to a proper old-fashioned English gentleman, and he has to have a name like that!'

I would not be deflected. It was offloading time. 'He's what you might call an old flame.'

'Really? You knew him way back when?'

I could see Lew was entertaining a picture of high school proms, complete with corsage, sweetheart neckline and brylcreem.

'No, more recently than that. And in the biblical sense.'

'An affair?' Lew looked genuinely aghast. 'Harriet, you astonish me!'

'You disapprove?'

'Hell, no – I mean – I don't know what to say –' Lew retreated behind a flurry of Jewish gestures. 'I just never thought you were the type.'

'Married twenty years, Lew. *Twenty years* . . .'

'Is it that long?'

'It can happen to anyone. The *coup de foudre*.'

'I guess so. And this Constantine . . .'

'Your quasi-English gentleman, yes. He was insatiable and inexhaustible, if you want to know. And indiscreet! It was like those burglars who carry freezers and videos out of a house in broad daylight and no one thinks to query it.'

Lew's eyes widened. 'He stole your freezer?'

'No. He loosened my fridge on its moorings, though.'

'You're kidding,' said Lew. Our wires were now so hopelessly entangled that it didn't much matter what I said.

'Yes,' I murmured. 'Reputations, electrical equipment . . . it was all the same to him.'

'At the risk of sounding obvious,' said Lew, a proviso that came rather late in the day in his case, 'you can't tell a book from its cover.'

'He's good-looking, isn't he?'

'A heart-throb, I should say,' conceded Lew generously.

The mere word 'throb' made me move restlessly in my seat.

'Harriet,' asked Lew, 'why are you telling me this?'

'I thought you ought to know. You might wonder why I was behaving strangely.'

'I swear to God I hadn't noticed a thing,' he said. Though I knew he meant nothing by it this didn't say a lot for my moral behaviour. 'You know,' he went on, 'this makes me realise I've never met your husband.'

It was no good. He simply couldn't see me in this new and unwelcome light. I decided on the direct approach.

'Lew – could you stay here?'

'I beg your pardon?'

'Could you stay here for a bit? While George is away? I'd feel so much more – secure.'

Lew's face was a study. 'But Harriet, what about Sonny Beidermeyer?'

'I don't know him well enough.'

My very tiny joke was lost on Lew. 'I have to get the typescript back to him.'

'Can't we use an international messenger service or something? Aurora can afford it.'

Lew's face folded in on itself in a frown of anxiety. 'That's not exactly the point, Harriet.'

'You said yourself we were talking big bucks here.'

'I did, but naturally that presupposes a certain awareness of the situation on our part.'

'Come again?'

'We are the people trying to sell something.'

'Yes but – forgive me – I was under the impression Beidermeyer was trying to buy.'

'He is.' Poor Lew, the fence was such an uncomfortable place to sit. On the other hand he was there so often he must have got corns on his bottom. 'He is, but he is a powerful guy – it wouldn't look good if I didn't go back.'

'I suppose not . . .' I sighed heavily. There it was. I had tried to prevent the occasion of sin, but without success. It was hard to tell whether my sigh was one of despair or relief. Maybe it was neither, but simply an exhalation of lustful anticipation. 'What time's your flight?' I asked.

Lew's face unclenched. He beamed. 'I knew you could be relied on to do the sensible thing, Harriet,' he said.

I wondered what on earth had given him that idea.

*

The flight left Bordeaux in the early afternoon. Working backwards, I reckoned we could justifiably leave at about eleven thirty, and that if I lay in bed late, and then went into a huddle with Lew over *Down Our Street*, I could probably avoid seeing Kostaki that morning. Do not imagine, gentle reader, that I was loth to see him: I was simply loth to precipitate those events I knew would follow. Looked at in its most regrettable light, this prevarication could be seen as a kind of foreplay. It was only a matter of time.

By nature an early riser I remained determinedly in bed, sweating it out literally as the sun rose, and even the girls stumbled from their room and fell into the pool. At about ten I heard Lew moving about on the stairs and in the kitchen, and decided I'd better get up. I still didn't venture out, but scuttled to the bathroom and spent a further twenty minutes in intensive washing, shampooing, depilation and creaming. It was the adulteress's equivalent of putting on clean underpants, and the bus I hoped to get knocked down by was Kostaki.

When I was dressed I went to the kitchen to make myself coffee. The heat was already creeping up towards the pre-storm status quo. Clara and Naomi were outside working on their backs. When Lew leaned over the *atelier* balustrade and called me I nearly jumped out of my skin.

'Harriet! Okay if I get the book together? Hey, I'm sorry, did I startle you?'

'Yes – yes, you carry on. I'll join you in a moment.'

I turned back to stir my coffee, and was met by the sight of Kostaki's legs in all their lean, tanned splendour, at eye-level beyond the window. I hadn't even had time to compose my features into an expression of leaden indifference when the legs bent, and the rest of him whooshed into view.

'Morning!'

'Morning.' It was tricky sounding politely indifferent.

'Weather back to normal.'

'Yes, indeed.'

He was crouching, and must have been well aware that smile, crotch and legs were now nicely aligned and presented a prospect which few heterosexual females would have wished to resist.

'This is a fantastic place,' he remarked. 'The best I've been to so far.'

'Yes, we're very pleased with it.'

He glanced this way and that in a leisurely manner and then trained the smile back on me. 'I'm going to try and dry out the car. I'm afraid the soft top wasn't designed to withstand the kind of downpour we had last night.'

'No!'

He stood up, stretching. His face disappeared

for a moment and then came back into view as he leaned down and said: 'Royston's very kindly said I can stay in the annexe while I cover this area, so perhaps we'll be able to see something of each other.'

I had no doubt Royston would have filled him in on the details. 'Yes.'

'You look your old self this morning, by the way.' My God, had it been that bad last night?

'Thank you.'

'Don't think I've forgotten those little yellow jogging shorts of yours. Cheerio for now.'

He went. I stood my full cup of hot coffee in the sink and ran cold water into it. Little yellow jogging shorts? I myself had certainly forgotten about them till that moment. But by such simple means are old passions enflamed. Fancy him remembering ... He who must have been through many such shorts since then ... I joined Lew at the desk in the *atelier*. Actually, he was not at the desk when I got up there, but kneeling on the floor by the Building of Stonehenge.

'Oh ... Harriet. Sorry, I was waiting for you. They are shocking time-wasters these things, huh?'

He went to the desk and picked up *Down Our Street*, both the typed and handwritten sheets, and blocked them into shape with his hands.

'I think I've got it all here. Are there any corrections or modifications you want to make before I take it away?'

There was no answer to this question. Or the answer was 'yes', but it would have taken too long to put everything right so it had to be: 'No.'

'Fine. Sonny will understand that it's only a first draft. He's nothing if not a pro . . .'

Lew's voice tailed away as he followed my gaze to where Kostaki, just visible from this vantage point through the kitchen window, was wiping the inside of the MG with a towel. Small cars were no problem to Kostaki. I recalled all too vividly the bright green Fiat, and the contortions necessary to mutual pleasure in such a confined space. The MG would present a thrilling challenge . . .

'Harriet?'

I realised I was in a trance. Lew was looking at me with an expression of anxious concern.

'I was wondering when we should go.'

'Quite right.' I glanced at my watch. 'Whenever you're ready.'

I hung about at Bordeaux long after I'd said *au revoir* to Lew. I actually watched his plane take off. I felt a sort of superstitious dread about waving off the only copy extant of *Down Our Street*, and being sundered from these factors – Lew and the book – which might have offered some protection, or at least distraction, from what now awaited me at the Villa Almont. On the way back my driving was erratic. I had Jennifer Rush on the tape deck, and when she soared into 'I am your lady' and I allowed myself to think of Kostaki, I would hit a hundred. When the song finished and there was nothing but the hiss of the tape rewinding my spirits plummeted and I fell back to a matronly fifty m.p.h.

I had got so accustomed to the mental picture of Kostaki waiting for me on my return, with a smile on his face and a bulge in his shorts, that it was disconcerting to find no sign of him. But there was plenty of other activity at the villa. In fact there was quite a crowd in the drive, what with Royston and the girls, and the Count and Monica, both astride his motorbike and with Asti in the saddle bag.

'Aha, there she is,' cried Royston as I climbed out.

'Can they stay for a bit?' asked Clara, positively animated. It was the sort of request she hadn't made since I'd met her at the school gate about a hundred years ago. But de Pellegale and Monica were not the tousle-haired moppets of Basset Magna C of E primary.

'Harriet's had a long drive,' said Royston unctuously. 'Why don't you all go and make yourselves comfortable and I'll do refreshments.'

It struck me that he wouldn't have been out of place on the Magna Church Tower Fundraising Committee. He had the vocabulary.

The Count, unzipping his puce leathers with one hand, released Asti from the saddlebag with the other. The creature was on one of those extending leads which operate on a ratchet. As soon as it was placed on the ground it shot to the end of the lead, a distance of some six metres, and stood on its tiny hind legs, yapping frenziedly at Teazel who was taking his ease in the woodshed.

The Count reeled him in and tucked him under his arm. The leathers were obviously aids to dog-handling.

'*Tiens-toi tranquille*,' he admonished the foaming Asti, then said to me: 'We wished to say how much we enjoyed your dinner.'

'I'm glad you did,' I said. 'It was a pity about the storm.'

'An adventure, I think,' he replied. I remembered the heavy petting, and agreed that it had been.

We sat down on the verandah. The girls had gone to help Royston get the drinks. The Count stroked Asti, who now nestled like some luxuriant chest wig in the open zip of his leathers.

'I don't suppose,' said Monica, 'you fancy a swim? Because I'm dying for one.'

'Please,' I said, 'feel free.'

By the time I emerged from my room in my bikini, Monica was already in the pool, starkers. She had an athletic figure and frighteningly little pubic hair. The minute I hit the water she did a motorised freestyle to my side and let me have it.

'That man,' she said, 'is an animal.'

'Who?'

'That cunt de Pellegale.' She obviously intended no pun. 'I reckoned it was quite fun to begin with. He's a game old guy, I'll give him that, but when he offered me work at his poxy club in Paris—!' She rolled her eyes and smoothed back her wet hair. 'Elbow time.'

'What work was that?'

'Oh, messing around for the punters. You know, sapphic delights, schoolgirl romps, that kind of thing.'

It wasn't something of which I had much first-hand knowledge and I would have pressed her on the subject, only she continued at once: 'I'm moving on tomorrow. But be warned. The old sod has developed a yen for your Greek boyfriend.'

At least here was someone who had no illusions about the nature of my relations with Kostaki. My pleasure in knowing that I was no longer a mere housewife of twenty years' standing delayed my reaction to the rest of her remark.

'You don't seem too put out, I must say,' she remarked. 'And to think I had you down for a—'

I got there. 'He has a what?'

'A yen. And I'm not talking Nip currency here. He fancies the Greek.'

'Kostaki?'

'Is that what he's called? Far out. I don't mind saying if he was a touch younger I could go for him myself.'

This stung me. Younger? 'Monica, for heaven's sake, you were sleeping with the Count!'

'But that wasn't fancying. It was shared interests. Or so I thought. Anyway, watch out for your boyfriend.'

As the MG snarled up the drive, Monica threw her head back and did a reverse flip into the water, waggling her feet in the air and disappearing to surface after only seconds at the far end of the pool. I was left gasping.

I swam a couple of lengths and pulled myself up on to the edge. Royston had brought a tall jug of something and glasses on to the terrace.

'Drinks, girls!' he called.

I clambered out as Kostaki appeared from the direction of the annexe.

'By the centre,' he exclaimed, 'gorgeous women and cool drinks. It beats working. What have you all been up to?'

221

CHAPTER THIRTEEN

'*Attends! Attends!*'

The Count, holding up one fleshy palm as if directing traffic, sprang from his seat. Asti dropped on to the floor and began to draw his lips back in a ferocious snarl. Monica, who had presumably achieved some kind of armed truce with the beast during her spell of shared interests with its master, scooped it up.

'I wasn't going anywhere,' said Kostaki, removing his shirt and flopping down on the verandah step.

The Count waddled off in the direction of his car, trailing yards of unravelling dog lead. I would have said something, but Monica simply gave it a sharp tug which almost had the tea table over, and the Count's pace quickened as though he'd been sprung from an elastic catapult.

'So tell me about yourself,' demanded Monica,

sitting down by Kostaki. She held Asti's vibrating muzzle clasped in one hand.

'Was your friend's flight on time?' asked Royston.

'He's not a friend,' I snapped. 'At least, he's only secondarily a friend. He's my agent.'

'Oops, sorry,' said Royston. The girls giggled. It was curious and disobliging the way they seemed to like him. 'I hadn't realised the two were mutually exclusive.'

Fortunately I didn't have to argue this one, because the Count came back round the corner carrying a posy of flowers, the blooms framed by a doily, their stalks stiffened with wire. I prepared myself to be suitably touched and delighted, but the Count strode past me, leapt down the steps like the Cookeen Fairy and spun through 180 degrees to face Kostaki.

'For you, M'sieur,' he said, executing a portly bow.

'For me?' Kostaki could be such a ham, but it stood him in good stead with eccentrics. I was stricken with dread. 'But how delightful – what did I do to deserve these?'

'You assisted the young ladies in their hour of need,' declared the Count. He was utterly shameless. Monica gave me a speaking look as Kostaki buried his nose in the flowers and inhaled deeply.

'I'm sure I did nothing,' he said, 'that wasn't in the normal line of duty or common courtesy.'

Royston sucked his teeth and the girls smirked. I seemed to be the only one who wasn't enjoying this charade.

'You rescued them!' trumpeted the Count. 'You returned them, in the teeth of the storm!'

'It was no more than anyone would have done,' Kostaki assured him. Damn right it wasn't. 'But thank you anyway. It's a charming thought.'

I was gripping my glass of lemonade so tightly I was in danger of crushing it. I had competition. How easy it would have been, I reflected, to offer some little *cadeau* of my own in recognition of Kostaki's chivalry. But no – I had been too obsessed with my own reactions and now de Pellegale had outflanked me.

The Count relieved Monica of the dog, and returned to us, his face glowing with feeling.

'Guy, you old rogue, what are you playing at?' asked Royston, refreshing glasses. The girls made 'ooh!' faces at one another.

'*Comme il est charmant!*' rhapsodised the Count. He was a disgrace. I could even sympathise with Monica, who was now admiring Kostaki's flowers. She didn't seem to be issuing her dire warning. Perhaps she considered her duty done in that department, and that I would leap to protect my interests. I pressed my hand to my brow.

'Poor Harriet,' said Royston, 'we're giving her *mal à la tête*.'

'It's not you,' I said.

'Chucking-out time!' he cried. 'Glasses, everyone!'

Monica and Kostaki got up and came over. The Count beamed. From the safety of his master's leathers, Asti gave a series of spluttering yaps.

'You don't have to go,' I said. 'I simply have a headache. You can stay here for as long as you like. I'm going for a lie-down.'

For once I didn't dither. I went. As I walked to the bedroom I heard their voices start up again in a more muted vein as they discussed my plight.

I closed the door and cast myself down on the bed. The glint of the pool beyond the muslin curtain was like a mirage. There were a lot of mirages . . . the picture of Kostaki and me locked in each other's arms, for one . . .

I heard the scrape of chairs, and the voices of my guests returning to normal as they prepared to leave: the Count's oily chuckle, Monica's abrasive whine, Royston's unctuous patter . . . Someone knocked on the door.

'Come.'

Clara put her head round. 'Can we get you anything?'

'No thanks, love.' My weak voice sounded like Toad of Toad Hall in his malingering vein.

'Are you okay?'

'I've just got a head, that's all.'

She peered at me for a moment as if trying to work out whether I was telling the truth. I smiled faintly.

'Right then,' she said.

Next to appear was Monica. 'Sorry you're crook, Harriet. Don't mean to disturb you only I'll be gone tomorrow.'

I leaned up on one elbow. 'Well, good luck. Where are you heading?'

She shrugged, a true daughter of the jolly swagman. 'See where I end up.'

'Take care.'

'And you. Look out for the Greek. See you, Harriet.'

Shortly after that I heard the motorscooter start up, and the long, stuttering diminuendo as it climbed the hill to the château. Glasses chinked together on a tray, the annexe door opened and closed. The glint of the pool fragmented as the girls went in for a swim.

He may have knocked, but I didn't hear him. He was suddenly there, closing the door softly behind him with one hand, holding the Count's posy in the other.

'How are you feeling?'

'Fine.' It was suddenly true.

'This was a good wheeze. I told them I'd come

and give you the once-over – in my medical capacity.'

'Of course.'

He moved to the side of the bed. 'I think you ought to have this.' He laid the posy on the bedside table where it looked rather like one of those lizards which display an enormous ruff when on the attack. Or when courting.

He'd put his shirt back on, but it was undone, and now he shrugged out of it and slipped out of his shoes. As he unbuttoned his trousers he said conversationally: 'I have to make an inspection of this property, you know.'

This was at least as plausible as most of Kostaki's chat-up lines, and a good deal more romantic than some. And what did it matter? It was as though he'd never been away. I was swept up and churned vigorously in the familiar tumble-drier of his embrace. The earth didn't merely move – it boogied furiously for a full fifteen minutes. Clara and Naomi could have been going down for the third time and I should not have noticed. In fact it was curious, as we surfaced, sweating and gasping, to hear them splashing in the pool as though nothing had happened.

'We really shouldn't be doing this,' I murmured. Kostaki and I were still joined at the hip, and he responded to this observation by giving one of his famous corkscrew thrusts, a movement with a hint of whiplash like the jump of a bucking bronco, designed to restart a flagging motor.

'Don't do that,' I begged.

He did it again. 'I said don't . . .'

'I know . . .'

'Then why . . .?'

'That means you like it.'

He was right. As we started all over again I heard the girls' music by the *sous-sol* and knew we were safe for the moment.

The Villa Almont had once been paradise; then purgatory; and now it was very heaven.

'So,' said Kostaki, 'I shall be here for a few days yet.'

We'd been for a swim and were sitting in the evening sunshine by the pool. The girls were indoors making pancakes: an autumnal smell of burning floated from the house.

'That's wonderful,' I said.

We sat in silence for a minute or two in contemplation of our good fortune. Then Kostaki said:

'That Count is a bit of a card.'

'Yes.' I attempted to marshal my thoughts and concentrate. 'I ought to tell you about him.'

Kostaki picked a sprig of lavender and twirled

the stem between his finger and thumb. 'No need. So the old boy cheats at leapfrog.'

'It's not just that.' I elaborated on the need for extreme caution. Kostaki seemed to find it hugely funny.

'You don't say!'

'I do. He's in it commercially. Monica's leaving tomorrow because he wanted her to join his line-up in Paris.'

'Really? He might offer me a job.'

'You're not taking this seriously.'

'Not very, I must admit. He seems a harmless old pussy cat to me.'

I felt too indolent to take the matter any further. Kostaki was a big boy. He could look after himself.

'What happened to medicine?' I asked.

'You mean general practice. I'm a radio doc these days. I make soothing, non-controversial noises over the airways. I put some money into the RPs' business, and this job' – he waved a hand – 'is a free holiday. I check up on existing properties and scout around for new ones. At the beginning of September I'll be back in the studio three times a week.'

It figured. He'd be on TV before you could say scalpel. I just hoped his producer was prepared for the postbag from female viewers craving a private consultation. I suppose it was jealousy of those future fans that made me say what I had never intended to mention.

'How long were you with Vanessa?'

'Vanessa?'

'My editor, remember? The party?'

'I scarcely remember. It was nothing.'

Of course he would say that, wouldn't he? But for now I was prepared to accept it. Unexpectedly I had been handed this second bite at the cherry. I'd have been mad to dash it from my lips.

'Are you staying here for supper?' I asked, mindful of the numerous delicious leftovers in the fridge.

The bell tinkled. '*A table le docteur!*' called Royston.

'Prior engagement,' said Kostaki. '*Dommage.*'

We got up. I was so replete with sex that I felt I might be getting a tan on the inside.

'Come along, now,' said Royston. 'The lady's had a long day.'

That evening the drainage pump started up once more. Its faint, insistent drone was like the sound of sap rising. The girls and I pigged out on the leftovers and got mildly drunk.

'You're in a good mood,' said Clara. 'What brought this on?'

I'd half expected – and certainly hoped for – a

nocturnal visit from Kostaki, but Royston must have decreed a cup of cocoa and an early night. I sank at once into a deep and dreamless sleep, and only awoke at nine a.m. with the noise of the MG farting and snarling in the drive. I went through to the kitchen in time to see it flash past the window, off on another day's inspection of the Rutherford-Pounce empire.

When I emerged for my swim the surrounding fields were a positive hive of activity. In the melon field Rindin, along with a huge henchman in a vest and black trousers suspended from braces, was attending to his cannons. On the grassy lower slopes of Château Hill beside the villa's drive, three local women appeared to be cutting turfs. They straightened up and stared at me as I prepared to dive in.

'*Bonjour!*' I called, waving. This did the trick and they returned silently to their labours.

The weather had gone from brilliant to perfect. The sky was high and infinitely blue, with tiny wisps and feathers of cloud borne on the thermals. The countryside buzzed and twittered with contented wildlife. Butterflies bobbed over the geraniums and Teazel reclined like a pasha on the verandah steps. The girls had been feeding him on the most expensive cat food the Lalutte supermarket could offer, and his figure reflected this opulence. I hoped Jules and Antoinette didn't hold strong views about overweight animals.

I was suddenly drawn to *Down Our Street*. With the chapters to date removed to London, the table in the *atelier* was invitingly empty. I could have some fun. In order to reach the amusing part I would have to skip a couple of chapters, but I knew what they contained. Shortly after the incident with the orange, Mattie had learned of her Aunt Clarice's death. This had finally activated her conscience and she agreed to remain with her Uncle Gransden for a while. There would be strong hints that conscience was not the only factor at work here – memories of Oliver Challoner's kiss on the windswept moors were also fresh in Mattie's mind, and though she reminded herself continually of how much she disliked him, the reader would be left in no doubt that passions had been aroused.

However, unable to leave well alone (otherwise there'd have been no story, for heaven's sake), Mattie's desire to revenge herself on Oliver had prompted her to accept the hand in marriage of Seth Barlow. This development would end Part Two of the book. The third and final part would find Mattie and Seth some two years into their union, with Mattie still childless (it was so much easier) and Seth a champion of the local miners' rights. But Mattie is bored with Seth, and feeling once again the restrictions of life in Marsdyke.

She takes to disappearing from time to time for a quick burst on the boards in Haddeshall. And it is on one such occasion that Oliver Challoner (but recently returned from abroad) discovers her . . .

Mattie made sure she was looking her best before leaving the Palace. There were always one or two eager stage-door johnnies waiting outside, and she wanted the real Mattie Piper to be even more alluring than the Northern Nightingale who sparkled in the spotlight. She came out into the winter's night glowing, fragrant and smiling, aware of her charm and ready to use it. She was in her element. This, this was life! Not the humdrum servitude to which she had committed herself as Seth Barlow's wife.

She stood for an instant, framed in the stage door, enjoying her small moment of glory. Then, suddenly, a firm hand grasped her wrist and a voice said: 'Come with me, Mrs Barlow.'

'What – who are you?' she cried as she was dragged away from the warmth and light of the door.

A young man remonstrated with her captor. 'This is no way to treat a lady, sir!'

'And this is no lady!' came the reply. Mattie's heart pounded. The voice was unmistakably Oliver Challoner's, and the commanding tone and tall stature frightened away her potential saviour.

'Leave me alone! Let me be!' she hissed, but the grip on her wrist only tightened. A carriage stood waiting on

the corner, the horses' breath steaming in the cold. Oliver bundled her unceremoniously into the cab, and said a single word to the driver: 'Marsdyke.'

'What is this?' she gasped. 'How dare you, Oliver Challoner! By what right—'

'By the right of common decency.'

'What do you know of decency?'

'A little more than you, I believe.'

Mattie glared at Oliver, her eyes flashing. He had released her, and was now lounging back in his seat, the ankle of one long, booted leg resting on the knee of the other. (These anatomical details could be so confusing.) He regarded her with that lazy authority which so enraged and disturbed her.

'I demand to be allowed to get out!'

He shook his head. 'I am taking you home, Mattie Barlow. Home to your husband.'

'I do not need to be taken! I shall return home when I will, and when I am ready!'

'Does Seth Barlow know that you are here?'

'He knows I am in Haddeshall, of course.'

'And what you are doing?'

She averted her eyes. 'That is no business of yours.'

Now he leaned forward, his face hardening. 'But it is business of your husband's.'

'Oh!' *She covered her face with her hands to conceal her fury.*

'My husband, my husband! What do you care about my husband? Or about me? He is a dull, virtuous man *and I am nothing but his dull, provincial wife! Am I not entitled to a little fun, a little life of my own? Or must I moulder in Marsdyke with nothing to do but be Mrs Seth Barlow and die of boredom?'*

She scarcely knew what happened next, it was so quick. Two strong hands grabbed her waist, and she was pulled forward and laid across Oliver's thighs, her nose merely inches from his mud-spattered boots. The first blow made her shriek, and she heard him laugh.

'Sing out all you like, Northern Nightingale. No one's going to hear you. You've been owed this a long time.'

She struggled, and even bit his leg, but he held her fast until the sixth and heaviest slap had been delivered. Then he simply let her roll on to the floor of the carriage.

'I hate you, Oliver Challoner!' she shouted, through her tears of humiliation. 'You'll never know how much I hate you!'

'No,' he said softly. He had leaned back and his face was unreadable in the shadows. 'And neither do I wish to know. You owe me no kind feelings. It is your husband you must love.'

No more words passed between them on that long and bitter journey. Oliver sat grim and silent. And Mattie thought of Seth, and the lie that was her life.

I put down the biro with a sigh of satisfaction. There was nothing like a good spanking.

CHAPTER FOURTEEN

When I came downstairs the villa and its surroundings glittered, spellbound, in the midday heat. Rindin and his colleague were gone, and so were the mysterious digging women. The girls were washing their hair. Royston had gone to lunch with Keith and Denise (an invitation extended to myself as well, but which I had declined). Even the insects were silent.

I went for a swim, and then stretched out on a sunbed. I removed my bikini top and luxuriated as the sun reached those parts it didn't normally reach. My Fates must have had a good snigger over this little aberration. Not only was the Count on his way down the hill, but he had chosen today of all days to abandon the scooter in favour of a leisurely stroll through the woods with Asti and Obi. In his kaftan and espadrilles he was silent as a wraith, and the first I knew of his approach was the twin crashes of the dogs hitting the surface of the pool. I was spattered by a shower of drops which felt icy on my sunbaked skin. I yelled, which brought Clara to the door of their room, hot tongs in one hand, *baguette* sandwich in the other. 'Only those mutts,' I heard her say as she withdrew.

I glanced wildly around for the dogs' owner as I struggled into my bikini top. The garment's scantiness did not, unfortunately, make it easy to put on in a hurry. It was like trying to cram an oven-ready turkey into a couple of finger stalls.

When I'd finally got it in place the Count had not materialised, but his dogs were still paddling around in our nice clean pool. Obi's midnight dips were one thing, but this flagrant trespassing in broad daylight was too bad.

'Get out! Come on, out! Asti, Obi, out!' I yelled, but they continued to paddle around aimlessly, their faces wearing black-eyed grins of satisfaction. I picked up the inflatable turtle, hurled it into the water and jumped in after it. Seeing this pop-eyed silver monster bearing down on her at a rate of knots, Obi headed at once for the steps and safety but Asti, true to form, went on the attack, sank her teeth into the turtle's front flipper and began to savage it in earnest. Instead of simply releasing the turtle and opting for a dignified retreat. I entered into the spirit of the engagement and tried to rescue the mass of tattered, bubbling, and rapidly sinking plastic from the jaws of its assailant. The result was that I floundered, capsized and sank. Asti swam round triumphantly, a large piece of green and silver plastic protruding from her jaws.

'*Asti? Qu'est-ce que tu fais là? Viens ici! Vite! Imm-éd-iate-ment!*' It was the Count.

I righted myself, gathered the ragged turtle and waded for the side. Asti, well ahead of me, splashed up the steps to join the baying Obelix and shook himself vigorously, like a scaled-down version of one of those cylindrical brushes in the car wash.

I stood there, chest heaving. I tried to hurl the remains of the turtle to the ground but it's actually quite hard to hurl several square yards of waterlogged PVC. It simply slumped and lay there at my feet, its silly face leering up at me from the tiles.

The Count wagged his finger at the dogs – not, I suspected, for invading my pool and my privacy, but for failing to come when called. 'Bad dogs! *Cochons!* But Harriet – you look magnificent!'

I glanced down at myself. My tussle with the turtle had caused the three strips of bunting to come adrift and I stood before de Pellegale in the buff.

'Excuse me,' I said. 'I'll be with you in a moment.'

I walked with all dignity to the sunbed, wrapped myself in my towel and retreated to the bedroom. What with swearing and tearing my hair I took a great deal longer than necessary, and rather hoped the Count and his wretched dogs would leave. When I emerged in shorts and T-shirt it looked for a moment as though my prayers had been answered. But then I saw the familiar bulbous figure amongst the scrub by the compost heap, and spotted Rindin's battered pick-up truck parked at the top of the melon field. The two dogs were charging about amongst the plants, putting up the numerous birds which had learned to ignore Rindin's cannon. Rindin himself was standing a few metres from the truck with a large gun held at hip-height and pointing down the hill. The Count burst through the bushes, arms waving. Rindin was motionless as a scarecrow, but there was a fixed, vengeful menace about him that made me think I had better act no matter how much I would secretly like him to pepper the Count and his curs with grapeshot from point-blank range. I raced over the lawn as fast as my sandals would allow, shouting *'Non! Non!'* As I drew closer I could make out the Count's voice over the barking of the dogs, a stream of highly coloured French the gist of which was that Rindin was a shit-headed antichrist born out of wedlock.

I passed through the gamey atmosphere of the compost heap and then through the barrier of prickly scrub. Once in the melon field – the first time I'd actually stood on this contentious piece of ground – Rindin looked even more menacing, gazing down from the upper reaches of the slope, the black eye of the gun trained motionlessly upon us.

'*Arrêtez! Arrêtez!* Please,' I added, feeling better able to express my feelings in English. 'Please, Guy – do stop all this.'

The Count turned on me a face practically bursting its skin with fury. 'He is once more firing the cannons! I will not have it!'

'But please,' I said, 'leave it for now. We're the ones who have to put up with it. We're much closer than you, and we've become quite used to the noise. In fact I really don't notice it any more. This shouting and bad feeling is much worse, I assure you. We're on holiday – we don't want to be caught in the middle of a war!'

The Count looked from me to Rindin, and back. Pulses were palpitating on his face, neck and chest. He was like a duvet full of bullfrogs. For a long moment I could see him struggling with himself as the dogs returned to his side and flopped down, exhausted by their depredations.

At last he brandished a fist at Rindin, and unburdened himself of a few choice observations to the effect that the farmer copulated with his mother, soiled his own bed and was a cheap criminal for whom disembowelling would he laughably inadequate.

Apparently content that he had covered everything, the Count stormed back through the hedge, dogs in tow, and left me to make placating gestures in Rindin's direction. As I bowed and smiled he very gradually lowered the gun. But he was still staring at me as I stumbled across the lawn after de Pellegale.

The Count cast himself down on the sunbed, bosom heaving, hand over his eyes, emitting a long hissing mutter of invective. I was half afraid he would toss a wobbler and die on me, right there and then. The dogs were in the shade on the verandah, their combined panting like the brisk sawing of plywood.

'Everything okay?' called Clara, in a tone which suggested she had been watching the whole thing.

'Sure, never better,' I replied with ponderous irony. I went into the house and poured a glass of chilled Perrier from the bottle in the fridge. When I brought it back to the Count he was looking more composed.

'Thank you,' he said. 'My apologies.'

'That's all right. And do feel free to re-open hostilities after we've gone. But just for the moment. . . .'

'Of course, of course.' He waved a hand. I let him sip his water in peace for a few seconds, and then asked:

'What brings you down here this afternoon?'

'Oh – psschfft!' He made one of those quintessentially Gallic sounds to which it is possible to ascribe almost any one of a whole arsenal of emotions. 'A letter!'

'You were delivering one?'

'Yes, but the box is broken, and Royston has no mouth.'

'No mouth?'

'No mouth for letters.' The Count made a shark-like grimace to show what he meant.

'I see. Why not give it to me? I'll pass it on.'

'How kind. It is for the doctor.' The Count gave me a richly collusive look and produced an envelope from the pocket of his kaftan. 'I find him utterly delightful.'

'He is, isn't he?' I agreed. 'I'll make sure he gets this.'

There was a short silence, broken only by the dogs' panting, and the sound of Rindin driving his truck out of the field. The Count's eyes glittered dangerously. I needed to steer his attention in some other direction.

'I wonder if you could tell me something.'

'Madame.'

'Early this morning there were lots of people in the meadow over there.' I pointed to the slope beside the drive. 'It looked as though they were cutting turfs. Is that what it would have been?'

'Uuuuhh . . .' The Count nodded and smiled mysteriously as though I were an exceptionally observant child. 'Yes.'

'What do they use them for, fuel?'

'Uuuuhh . . . It is our secret.'

I assumed he meant he wasn't going to tell me, but he went on: 'The hill is full of Germans.'

I misunderstood him again. 'They were German? I thought they were local women.'

He shook his head, obviously delighted with my mistake. 'The Germans are in the ground.' He ran a plump index finger across the second of his chins. 'Dead.'

It took a moment for this to sink in. 'Dead Germans?'

The Count nodded again. 'During the war. The Resistance.'

I digested this. 'You mean the local resistance picked off German soldiers and actually buried them up there?'

'Uuuuhh . . . *oui*!' said the Count.

'Good heavens.' The story had a Clochemerle-ish *grand-guignol* charm about it, but just the same

. . . I wondered about the villa's water supply.

'So what were the women doing?'

'*Il y a un passage souterrain,*' explained the Count, making a snaking gesture with one hand. 'Underground corridor. From time to time it sink . . . collapse . . .' He lowered his hand palm downward as if depressing a plunger. 'The women must fill in the holes.'

I realised that for the past two weeks I had been completely unaware of the real nature of my surroundings. The information the Count had given me made me feel that all local eyes had been, and were still, upon me. Like one of those sets of Russian dolls, the answer to one question simply disclosed another question waiting to be asked.

'Where does the tunnel lead to?'

Guy de Pellegale closed his eyes and steepled his pudgy fingers before his face.

'*Au Château Forêt Noir!*'

As soon as he'd gone I steamed open the envelope. I felt elated, and slightly crazed. The world had gone mad (or had evidently been so for some time in this neck of the woods) so I might as well join it. The stench of murder and exotic vices wafted on the air with the scent of lavender and ripening melons.

'My dear Constantine,' said the note, in an

extraordinary hand that left no line, dash or dot unembellished. 'I should be enchanted to know you better. Can you come for dinner at the château on Wednesday? Just an informal gathering of family and friends' – I'd heard that somewhere before – 'but your presence would be such a delight. Yours in anticipation, Guy de P.'

Carefully I replaced the note in its envelope, sealed it and put it in my bag. Then I knocked on the girls' door and called: 'Who fancies a drink up in the square?'

I intended to go to Pru's Bar, but as we approached Clara remarked: 'Oh look, isn't that Dr Ghikas?'

'Yes,' I said, 'so it is. Tell you what, why don't we try this one for a change?'

I turned briskly into the other café. We placed our order with the sad-faced proprietor, and the girls swigged Kir Royale as I squinted into the late evening sun at Kostaki. He was, as they say, well in, sitting at a table with Priscilla, talking, laughing and availing himself of one of Mad Max's stupendous platefuls.

I felt oddly detached. At that moment I decided I would do nothing to prevent Kostaki from going to the Château Forêt Noir for an informal evening of spaghetti hoops, choc ices and Sir Roger de Coverley.

*

On the other hand, when he popped round after supper to check out my power points and electrical equipment, I allowed him to perform thorough and exhaustive testing.

Afterwards I gave him his letter. He didn't read it at once but put it in the back pocket of his white jeans which were lying beside the bed. We knew we had an hour because the girls had gone round to the annexe to watch the French equivalent of *Top of the Pops* on Royston's TV. Even so, I was annoyed that he hadn't read the note. I got up and began to get dressed.

'What's the matter with you?' he said, lying back with his hands behind his head as I fished a dress out of the wardrobe. 'Why so jumpy? You don't honestly suppose that Royston thinks we're just good friends?'

I tried to look haughty. 'I had hoped as much, yes.'

Kostaki shook his head indulgently. 'Harriet, Harriet . . . For one who bangs like a shithouse door you are an innocent, you know that?'

'Look,' I said, looming over him with the hairbrush. 'Don't patronise me.'

He rolled over. 'Give me six of the best, teacher, do! Okay, okay.' He slipped out of bed and stepped into his clothes. 'I meant no harm.'

He came up behind me as I brushed my hair and ran his hands over me, turning me this way and that as though admiring himself in a new suit. I could feel my knees turning to butter.

I said sternly: 'Have you been discussing us with Royston?'

'Of course not.'

It was an effort, but I turned to face him and pushed him to arm's length. 'Then how would you know what his view of us is?'

'Knowledge of human nature picked up over years in provincial consulting rooms,' said Kostaki.

I supposed that would have to do. I made coffee and we went and sat on the verandah. The first stars were coming out in the dove-coloured sky. Moths tapped against the shutters. The faint chitter of Europop drifted from the annexe windows. I mentioned what the Count had told me that afternoon concerning the underground passage.

'It runs between the château and this villa,' I said.

'That's right,' said Kostaki. 'Royston told me. So that the old milords from the original château could exercise their *droits de seigneur* several times a night with comely peasant girls without getting their feet wet. This place was just a farmhouse – animals on the ground floor, people upstairs, plenty of nice soft hay. Lovely.'

It was jolly annoying that he knew about this

too. 'Ah,' I said, 'but did you know what's in the tunnels now?'

'If you're referring to what's been in there since the mid-forties, yes. One of the reasons the soil's so good, I imagine.'

I sulked. 'I wonder why Royston didn't tell me about this.'

'Well, for heaven's sake, you are the holiday tenant. It's not the kind of local colour you necessarily want to bruit about when people are paying several hundred smackers a week for the privilege.'

'I suppose not.'

'That's where the name came from.'

'What name?'

'Villa Almont. It's actually Villa Allemand.'

'Damn Royston,' I said. 'I do think he might have mentioned it.'

'Why?'

'I feel like a laughing stock.'

'You're certainly the laughing stock I like to feel,' said Kostaki in a smoky voice, laying his hand on my thigh.

'Stop it,' I said, and meant it.

'Okay.' He withdrew the hand at once and I did not wish for it back. 'Besides,' he added, 'you mustn't be so hard on Royston. If it wasn't for him I wouldn't be here. And he does have a glass eye, you know.'

*

About half an hour later the girls came sloping back round the corner.

'Programme's finished,' said Clara. 'And there's a call for you.'

'Oh, no,' I said, getting up. 'Who?'

'Lew Mervin,' said Naomi crisply. 'Calling from London.'

Kostaki and I entered the annexe and found Royston sitting cross-legged on his divan eating peanuts out of a packet and watching a game show.

'Hallo all,' he said. 'Help yourself, Harriet.' He nodded in the direction of the office.

Kostaki joined him on the divan and I went through to the office.

'Hallo, Lew.'

'Harriet! I'm truly sorry to call you at this hour, and drag you away from the moonlight on that glorious *piscine*, but I've just got back from such an exciting dinner.'

'Oh.'

'With Sonny Beidermeyer.'

'Oh, yes?' It was actually quite hard to keep the note of anticipation out of my voice.

'Yes! And he is so taken with *Down Our Street*. It was he who invited me to dinner – Gay Hussar, no less – expressly to say that he loves every word and is looking to buy it.'

'Looking?'

'Wants! Wants to buy it. No, really. No ifs or buts, he is totally sold on your book.'

'That's great,' I said. 'How much?'

'We didn't get into the detail, but from the general tenor of our conversation over dinner you can rest assured we are speaking of a six-figure sum.'

I plucked a six-figure sum out of the air and divided it by two to account for it being US dollars. 'How much do you think?'

'Now, Harriet!' Lew gave a teasing, squeaky laugh that hurt my ears. 'Patience! He has to consult one or two other suits back in New York.'

'I thought he was The Man at Aurora,' I said pettishly.

'He is The Man, he definitely is, and none other. But they're obviously planning a complete re-launch of the Blair *oeuvre* in the States, and that's not something to be undertaken lightly.'

'No,' I said, trying to keep the impatience out of my voice. 'I suppose not.'

'You get back to that mellow wine and those twinkling stars, Harriet,' advised Lew. 'And leave everything to me.'

CHAPTER FIFTEEN

Only George would have sent a postcard of an English provincial town to a luxury villa in the heart of rural France. The card was one of those multi-shot efforts, with four rectangular pictures of Basset Regis (Corn Exchange, Town Hall, Market Street and Parish Church) and a circular one in the middle (Municipal Park). Nothing about it would have made me want to visit Regis had I not known it already, and as a local it inspired no pang of nostalgia for the place.

'Having a tedious time, wish I was there,' George had written. 'Based in town for convenience, but went to check on the homestead. No signs of wild debauch, though a small party is mooted. Eloise sends her regards and says you are a heroine. Was hoping to get back to you for at least a few lengths and a good dinner before next weekend, but it's looking unlikely. All love, George.'

I wasn't too happy about the 'small party' but I imagined if there was one then George as the parent on the ground, so to speak, would keep an eye on things. I must say I thought it was a bit much him staying in London and not in Magna where he might have supervised the domestic scene at close quarters. Then I remembered that he was supposed to be on holiday, and was actually at work: with the adoring Eloise. Heroine, forsooth! I had not exactly been sitting in the shade with my needlepoint during his absence.

I showed the postcard to Clara. 'God, a party!' she wailed. 'And we're missing it!'

'Only a small one,' I said soothingly. 'And with a bit of luck it won't happen at all.'

'You must be joking. Why else does a bloke stay at home when everyone else goes away?'

'I'm sure your father will have advised him against it in the strongest possible terms.'

I could tell they weren't convinced. They retreated groaning and grimacing to their sunbeds, convinced they were set to miss a bash on the scale of the Chelsea Arts Ball.

I met Kostaki in the drive as I returned from hanging up some washing. He was climbing into the MG.

'You'll never guess what that letter was,' he said. 'Only an invitation to dinner at the château.'

The simple soul was reacting as we had done to our own invitation. I wondered if Royston had filled him in on what to expect. I might as well test the water.

'Gosh,' I said, 'you jammy thing.'

'Bit of a social coup, eh?'

No, he knew nothing. For once, I was grateful to Royston.

'Absolutely,' I agreed. 'You'll have to tell us all about it. When are you going?'

'Well, he left it fairly open, but I thought I'd drop in on my way back today and suggest tomorrow night. It's quite informal, apparently.'

'Super.' Not for the first time I noticed a fleeting resemblance between Kostaki and George. Or maybe it was just the Y chromosome at play.

I decided we needed shaking up a bit. I riffled through the numerous leaflets and brochures left by our landlords and decided on a day out.

'But we're perfectly happy dossing around here,' said Clara.

'I dare say, but we could do with a change of scene.'

'I don't get the reasoning.'

'You'll enjoy the dossing more if you have a day away from it.'

'It's our holiday too, so why can't we do what we like?'

'You do do what you like, all the time. Look at it

253

this way: I'd like a day out and I'd appreciate your company as your father's not here.'

'Come on Clara,' said Naomi. 'It might be all right.'

It was more than all right, it was absolutely brilliant. With QVQ blaring we drove to a small market town set high above the Tarn. The mediaeval grain market had been lovingly restored, the church was a gem, the views lyrical. The greasy spoon where we ate four courses for the equivalent of £4.50 a head served up roast poussin swimming in a winey gravy with caramelised shallots and the biggest pile of featherlight golden *frites* we had ever seen. When we finished one bottle of the house red, another was immediately plonked down, cold from the safe-like 1950s fridge in the corner. Madame, all BO, gold teeth and oily black curls, served at table and a fair proportion of her extended family were involved in the cooking. The *chef d'équipe* was M'sieur, who followed his corporation into the room while we were demolishing the chicken, and stood over us, sweat trickling through the stubble of his lower face to join the mat of black hair on his well-upholstered chest, and encouraged us to eat up. He tweaked the girls' cheeks and admired their hair, their legs, their eyes and everything about them, adding that it was hardly surprising such exquisite blossoms had grown from such a beautiful tree. By which, I realised, he meant me.

By the time they were halfway through their *glaces variées* with hot chocolate sauce and chopped pistachios, and I was well on the way to finishing the second bottle, the girls were positively mellow.

'This is an ace place,' said Naomi. 'Thanks for lunch.'

'My pleasure,' I said.

'Can we look round the shops afterwards?' asked Clara, striking while the iron was positively molten.

'Sure,' I said, 'why not?'

There was a very good reason why not: the shops were shut. I was not broken-hearted, since the heat outside was enough to make me reel, especially with half a litre of house red swilling inside me. But I was sorry for the girls' sakes that the unexpected success of the day couldn't have been rounded off by the purchase of a couple of wicked little tops.

'Can you believe this country?' Clara said as we idled to the car between higgledy-piggledy white and apricot houses with blazing flowers and peeling shutters. 'Not a thing open at three thirty in the afternoon.'

'But when they do open they'll be open till dark,' I pointed out. 'They take their eating seriously in France, as you may have noticed.'

Clara slid me a sly glance. 'You're doing a Dad again.'

On the way back we saw the white MG parked outside the Château.

'What's he doing at the funny farm?' asked Clara.

'He's dropped in to accept a dinner invitation,' I said. I couldn't help it. I smiled.

'You're joking!'

'Honour bright.'

'Good luck to him,' said Nev. 'Does the Count fancy him, then?'

What the hell. 'As a matter of fact, yes.'

They shrieked, and clutched each other and fell about in the back seat. I accelerated merrily down the hill, borne on a warm tide of *vin de table* and sisterly fellow feeling.

I was on the sixtieth of the projected hundred lengths needed to shift my headache when Kostaki came bounding on to the verandah. 'Mind if we join you?' Royston was with him.

'Sure.'

They leapt in making the surface bob and heave so that I did the nose trick. I escaped to the house to stem the flow of snot, and then made some tea. When I returned with the tray they were sitting by the *sous-sol*, with the radio playing.

'Tea!' I called, feeling like old mother slipper-slopper.

'Our friend here is going to dinner at the château,' said Royston as they joined me.

'I know.' While the girls collected their tea and retired I tried to work out who knew what about whom.

'I was just saying, he'll have a beezer time,' added Royston.

'Yes, I didn't realise you people had been up there,' said Kostaki amiably. 'You never said.'

I shrugged. Royston said: 'The Count's hospitality is legendary.'

'I can't wait.'

There was a short pause. My eyes flicked frantically from one to the other like a rattlesnake on speed. Both men looked blandly affable, but it was unmistakably Kostaki who was being duped, and he who changed the subject.

'Tell you what I've been meaning to say. Did you see there's a play on in the town square on Wednesday? Why don't we go?'

'Yes, why not?' agreed Royston. 'I saw the poster.'

'I have it here,' said Kostaki. He felt in his back pocket and pulled out a folded sheet of paper. ' "*Le Chien du Jardinier*" *de Lopez de Vega, mise en scène Archimède Pollu, place des Cornières, Lalutte* . . . "The Gardener's Dog"?'

' "Dog in the Manger" would be the idiomatic translation,' said Royston. 'Actually Pollu's band

257

of strolling theatricals come every summer They're not bad; it's usually quite a jolly evening.'

'How good does one's French have to be?' I asked. 'I mean, would the girls enjoy it?'

'Oh Lord, yes, it'll be stuffed with talent,' Royston assured me, with a keen grasp of the essentials.

Kostaki was continuing to read. 'Here we are. *"Le chien du jardinier ne mange pas les choux, mais il ne permet pas non plus que quelqu'un d'autre les mange."* I get the drift.' He folded the paper up again. 'So it's settled, then. Wednesday night we'll have a few jars at Pru's and then take in the show.'

Pru's? I was only sorry I wasn't going to be there to watch him free fall into panic at the Château Forêt Noir.

That night he went out. I poured myself a cognac and went up to the *atelier*. I didn't work. I just turned on one light and sat on a cushion next to The Building of Stonehenge. Various people had been adding to it in an offhand way and it was more than two-thirds completed. What remained were the difficult bits: sky, hills, unbroken areas of grey rock and so forth. I sifted idly through the pieces. And as I did so I realised, quietly but blindingly, that I no longer cared for Kostaki.

It was a revelation. I sat back on the cushion, gobsmacked. It took me a full minute or two to adjust to the idea, and the next stage was a tremendous sense of relief. I was no longer addicted!

Even the past had lost its rosy glow. The kaleido-scope of selective memory shifted so I recalled not the wild passion and forbidden ecstasy of that earlier summer but its terrors and embarrass-ments, and the mortification I'd endured as it drew to a close. Nothing is so shaming as a backward glance at infatuation.

Like a damp and shrivelled butterfly emerging from its chrysalis, I stretched my wings and gave them a tentative flutter. I could feel myself becoming once more my own woman.

The next day I determined to do nothing but suit myself. Not the girls, not Royston, not Kostaki – especially not Kostaki – were going to influence my behaviour. There was enough food in the villa, so I didn't need to shop, and neither did I intend to cook. I arose early and pinned a note by the verandah bell announcing that I was incommu-nicado for the day. I applied myself to *Down Our Street*, chronicling Mattie's return to Seth, and her somewhat late resolution to be a loyal and suppor-tive wife to this excellent man. This did not, I told myself, parallel any particular patterns in my own life, it simply showed Mattie growing up and beginning to think for herself. No matter what loin-stirrings and heart-trippings were occasioned by the masterful Oliver Challoner, she had seen at last where her duty lay, not to mention the error of her ways. I even introduced a touching scene in which she returned to the corner house and expressed her remorse to Gransden over past folly.

I wrote all morning. At twelve thirty the girls said Royston had offered to take them out for lunch and I said that was fine. Kostaki had set off on his rounds (old expressions die hard) long ago, and I waited till I heard the motor going up the drive before taking a swim.

There were only four full days of the holiday left. It was plain that George would not be returning. I was going to have to clear up, pack, load and drive through France without the aid of another adult. A matter of hours ago this prospect would have put me in a sweat of anxiety. Now I felt positively invigorated by the thought. In fact, I decided, we might drive overnight and arrive home a day early.

That evening I asked the girls if either of them fancied a walk through the woods. Naomi pleaded urgent nail-care but rather to my surprise Clara heaved herself off her bed and said: 'I don't mind' – an expression which in her book conveyed something close to enthusiasm.

As we walked up the hill between the rustling oaks, she said: 'I tell you one thing, I won't be sorry to be on my own again.'

'Naomi?'

'She's really beginning to get on my nerves. She

keeps going on about the GCSE results. I don't even want to think about them.'

Neither did I. I felt a surge of affection for my daughter.

'Holidays are difficult,' I agreed. 'One's rather stuck. I thought we might head for home on Friday night.'

'Good idea,' said Clara, and then added more cheerfully, 'We saw Dr Ghikas at Pru's again at lunchtime. I think they're an item.'

'It figures,' I said.

We finished our walk to the top of the hill in a friendly silence which contrasted pleasantly with the grim armed truce that so often characterised my dealings with Clara. By some unspoken agreement we went as far as the château gates. The windows this side were dark, but there was a faint glow at the back of the house. And as we stood there we heard, faint but unmistakable, the sound of the 'Birdy Song', and smiled at one another.

It was Wednesday, the night of the play, before I spoke to Kostaki again. We had been joined by the Platfords, and were having drinks outside the annexe – served by Royston through his living room window – before going to Lalutte. The de Pellegales were due to meet us in the town, and Kostaki had indicated that Priscilla would be taking time off from her bar duties to join us. This information caused me not the slightest flicker of jealousy. I was cured.

'How did you get on at the château?' I enquired when the two of us drifted together.

He smiled ruefully. 'I can see why you didn't warn me.'

'Did the Count behave himself?'

'Depends on one's criterion.'

'You know what I mean.'

It was one of the extremely rare occasions when I'd seen Kostaki look uncomfortable. 'He was a genial host. But, Harriet, he's after me!'

Poor Kostaki. The biter bit.

'I take it you're not keen?'

'Please.'

'And you've told him you're not?'

'I – er – I tried, but I have a suspicion he thought I was being coy.' Kostaki swished his drink around in his glass. 'He was pouring great vats of some vicious plonk or other. I'm afraid I was ratted. He said he was going to pay me a visit . . .!'

'You'll just have to be firm.'

'That's exactly what he's hoping.'

'What sort of visit does he have in mind?'

'A clandestine one. He intends using the secret passage,' said Kostaki glumly. 'No, don't laugh, it isn't funny.'

*

Pollu's strolling players were a professional company, but they were reaching the end of a trying spate of one-night stands conducted in extremely taxing conditions and in the sort of heat which would have left a Kalahari bushman begging for mercy. When we arrived in the Place des Cornières at eight twenty for an eight thirty start, the hundred or so metal chairs set out before the stage were largely empty. This was for the excellent reason that the set was still under construction. Not only that, but most of the lighting was lying in a tangle of wires on the cobbles while a couple of youths in slashed jeans wobbled about on an insecure gantry fighting off the pigeons from the church tower. Background music filtered from some invisible (and unreliable) source, now submerged beneath a crackle of interference, now deafeningly loud. The Count waved his arms at us from Pru's Bar and, when we joined him, muttered disparagingly about the shambles. He needn't have bothered. I felt entirely at home. I only wished George could have been here to see for himself the proof that no matter what the qualifications in the Art of Living a village cock-up was a village cock-up on both sides of the English Channel.

'Besides,' said Keith, 'it's always like this. Why we continue to turn up early year after year I'll never know.'

'Perhaps,' suggested Royston, 'they want our critical faculties to be thoroughly dulled by drink before they start.'

'Pru!' called Kostaki. 'Come and join us!'

There was a definite sea-change in Priscilla's appearance this evening. She wore a blue printed dress with a cross-over bodice and cap sleeves which could have been a Paris original or a jumble-sale find: impossible to tell. I got the impression that the frock's long skirt was meant to be worn with staggeringly high, peeptoe shoes, but Priscilla had on a pair of flat basketwork sandals with a T-strap like Mary Jane's. Her fine, stringy hair was done up in a knot on her head and there was a suggestion of mascara about her eyes. The home counties collecting rings and tea tents seemed suddenly closer, and I reminded myself that Kostaki was working for this woman's brother-in-law. It was indeed a small world, and getting smaller.

The café belonging to the sad-faced man was closed, since the cloisters on that side were being used as a backstage area by Pollu's players. In consequence, by the time we were on the third round, Pru's Bar was packed, not only with the habitués of both establishments, but with quantities of disaffected theatre-goers killing time and not a few actors in full seventeenth-century rig awaiting the call for beginners. Mr Sprigg, the

estate agent, was putting himself about, lit up like
a neo-Georgian coach lamp.

'Joint's jumping,' said Royston. 'Perhaps we
should put the show on right here.'

The girls went to play the fruit machine. Priscilla, when not attending to her patrons, sat down
by Kostaki, and the Count changed places with
Keith in order to sit on his other side. I watched
this with a quiet satisfaction that would have been
unthinkable a short while ago. It was suddenly as
clear as crystal that Kostaki had designs on Priscilla and her private income, that she was not
unreceptive to his manifest charms, and that the
Count's elephantine attentions were not just a
grave embarrassment to Kostaki, but placed the
whole enterprise in jeopardy. For the first time I
felt I had something in common with Royston: I
understood the pleasures of detachment and
manipulation. It didn't occur to me to blame
Kostaki for having so flagrantly toyed with my
affections while pursuing self-interest elsewhere.
Ours had never been a relationship conspicuous
for its emotional sensitivity. I had been a bored
housewife, rusty with disuse, and he had been a
ladykiller not in the least interested in the thrill of
the chase. Things had turned out exactly as one
might have predicted.

'*Prenez vos places!*'

The order came from Archimède Pollu, the

harassed producer of *The Gardener's Dog*, who over an hour ago had been pacing the assembled flats, rostra, drops and benches of the production grey-faced with stress. Now the stress appeared to have given way to rage with the world in general and his unfortunate audience in particular.

Dutifully we filed out and took our seats in the darkening square. The lights illuminated (finally) a spare and minimalist set enlivened by a couple of trees in tubs and a trellised arch of roses. But it was scarcely needed. The whole scene was so beautiful and timeless it snatched my breath away. The Disney-picturesque rooftops of Lalutte were silhouetted against the early night, squadrons of brilliant stars hovered overhead, and the pigeons from the church tower flew home to roost, their wings flashing a petrolly silver in the shafts of white light from the gantry.

The actors, released like greyhounds from the slips and fortified by several *boissons*, were in form and on song. The smooth, cultured French flowed over us and the action – knockabout stuff as easy to follow as any provincial panto – unfolded sweetly and merrily before us. We were halfway through the first act before I even noticed the girls were not with us. When I did notice it was inevitable that several other things should impinge on my consciousness at the same time.

With my concentration broken, I was suddenly

aware of male voices raised in hot dispute coming from the direction of Pru's Bar which was doing business for those of a philistine cast. A dim murmur of conviviality had underpinned the play from the beginning without in the least disturbing it. This, however, sounded like a bloodbath in the making.

Straining as one does to hear what one is not supposed to hear I caught the odd phrase, none of them edifying. I glanced along the row but the Count and Priscilla were still flanking Kostaki like warders, the attention of all three rigidly on the stage. In the other direction Denise and Keith appeared to have noticed nothing, but Royston caught my eye and grinned.

The dispute grew in volume and ferocity. On the stage a romantic episode was in progress, the lovesick Countess being solaced by a young musician on the mandolin. The unfortunate troubadour had without doubt drawn the short straw tonight as he warbled and strummed against an ever-more intrusive background of obscenity and abuse.

The interval followed, and not a moment too soon. I struggled to the side of the square in an attempt to reach the front of the surge towards liquid refreshment. Outside Pru's Bar a few enterprising local braves were attempting to separate and hold fast the two combatants whose confrontation had so disturbed the closing scenes of Act

One. Beneath the dirt, grazes and contusions I identified Mad Max and the sad café proprietor, his melancholy transmuted to violent rage by the manifest unfairness of this evening's arrangements. I had to sympathise with him. With the square containing a record number of thirsty people he had been forced to sit in his darkened, shuttered premises and watch as Pru's Bar burst its seams with free-spending revellers. However, my concern was the girls, and I was very relieved to find them sitting unharmed at a table near the café door, drinking Coke.

'It's perfectly all right,' Clara said accusingly. 'We can see and hear from here, and Max said we could keep an eye on Priscilla's dogs.'

The animals were lolling in a malodorous heap at the end of the bar.

'But Clara,' I said, 'Max is drunk out of his mind and engaged in a fight.'

'Only for a little while,' said Naomi soothingly. 'It's over now.'

The bar was filling up, but over the tops of heads I could see the sad-faced man being led rebelliously away, and Max raising a meaty fist at his retreating back view.

'Please can we stay here?' asked Clara. 'It's nice.'

To be sure they looked safe enough, and the Count was standing near the bar waving a couple of bottles of red in the air, so I left them to it, with stern warnings as to their behaviour.

Priscilla, like the good sport she was, had gone back behind the bar for the duration of the interval, and was not able to rejoin us at once. As we returned to our seats Denise said to me:

'Do I detect romance in the air?'

'Very possibly,' I said.

'I do hope so. Keith and I have been saying for ages that Priscilla needs a man in her life. It's such a strange existence for a young woman stuck here serving drinks to foreigners all day.'

I reflected on this as we took our seats. Royston tapped me on the knee.

'Potential scene-stealers on every hand. Look up there.'

An extremely old man in the characteristic overalls and flat cap of the older *citoyens* of Lalutte, a bag of tools hanging from his belt, was climbing a ladder to the crazily slanting roof of the building adjoining Pru's Bar. On reaching the top he settled himself – it was apparent he was taking advantage of the lighting to mend some guttering in the cool of the evening – took a bottle and a piece of thin rope from the bag, and lowered the bottle over the edge of the roof.

'Jolly smart idea,' I whispered as the mandolin began to play. 'He can haul it up when he wants a drink.'

'That's what we're afraid of,' put in Keith. 'He's over ninety.'

The first twenty minues of the second act passed without interruption and I was beginning once more to lose myself in the spectacle, atmosphere and performances. Only the occasional rattle and scrape of the gutter-mender's bottle punctuated the action. But sadly Max, his duties in the bar over for the night, had sought out his opponent with the intention of picking up where they'd left off. A roar of pain and fury split the night, and caused even the ineffably camp Fool to forget his lines for a second.

From then on the fight raged through the cloisters behind the stage, occasionally disappearing behind flats or into premises unwise enough to have left their doors unlocked, but always re-emerging, like some many-limbed monster, to continue on its inexorable way from backstage right to backstage left. The local youths who raced round the perimeter of the square to interpose their bodies did not have the air of people approaching their task – that of protecting the sacred rites of Thespis – in the proper spirit. The effect of their arrival was to turn the fight into a full-scale brawl. The actors soldiered on like good 'uns as their scenery quaked and rocked and obscenities rent the air, while the wretched Archimède Pollu could be seen approaching apoplexy in the wings, alternately remonstrating with the combatants and exhorting his players to greater efforts. The audience frowned and leaned forward in their seats, putting their collective will behind performance art.

And in fact the crisis was well on the way to passing, as the brawl was ushered out at the far corner of the square and moved spluttering and roaring down the steep hill past the *mairie*. But as it did so and an audible sigh of relief ran round the assembled company, two things happened in quick succession. The first was that the nonagenarian on the roof reached for his bottle, missed both the string and his footing and slithered down, landing – luckily, but with a fearful crash – on one of Priscilla's tables. Several customers rallied round to succour the old fellow but the dogs, ever alert to the possibility of mass mayhem, escaped from the girls' unrigorous supervision and bounded, barking joyfully, to the spot they had been coveting all evening: centre stage.

It was mere unhappy coincidence that the Countess's lap dog, Fleurette, was participating in the action at that moment. The poor creature could not have been on heat, but Heinz the Alsatian (as we could attest) was not above seeking relief with dogs of the same sex and a different breed. A little thing like lack of female receptivity was not likely to deter him. As Zac and Pedro began to rend crinolines and knickerbockers, and to leave their calling card on the tubbed trees and rose trellis, he began energetically to press his suit with Fleurette. Archimède Pollu rushed on from the wings with a pike and tried to separate the two, while the strolling troubadour attacked the others with his mandolin. The Countess and her attendants, lifting their shoulders and their eyes to heaven, left the stage.

'*Exeunt omnes*,' said Keith happily.

'*Les chiens de la patronne* . . .' extemporised Royston. I glanced along the row. The Count, obviously stimulated by the activities of Heinz and Fleurette, was gripping Kostaki's thigh and staring at him with glowing eyes. Kostaki looked ashen.

Priscilla had not yet returned to her seat, but now I heard her call:

'Harriet! Harriet! I think you'd better come. I'm afraid your girls are absolutely plastered!'

CHAPTER SIXTEEN

I could feel myself beginning to emerge from the holiday. We were thirty-six hours from our return and I was thinking in terms of eating things up, checking the tyre pressures, and buying presents to take home. I debated whether George should be included in the latter department, and concluded that he would be catered for by our duty-free wine allowance. I dragged the girls, morose and suffering from their self-inflicted alcohol poisoning, into Torcheron and instructed them to use what remained of the holiday wad for PR back home. I was fairly certain they would collapse in a convenient watering hole, revive themselves with cappuccino and then move on to the nearest inexpensive fashion outlet, but it didn't matter. What I wanted was the pleasure of shopping alone. To a dispassionate observer my life may have appeared somewhat ragged at the edges, or even a downright shambles, but as far as I was concerned it was beginning to come right, and such minor problems as existed were nothing some judicious shopping wouldn't put right.

I got a T-shirt for Gareth and some of the ubiquitous local honey for Declan and Mrs O'Connell – this last was only a fairing, since I knew Declan would be extending his corny palm to be crossed with folding money on my return. I then went in search of a stall I'd noticed the last time we were here. It was a permanent site in the covered market, presided over by a villainous-looking youth who made jewellery. His manner was calculated to keep custom at bay, but I braved it and bought a necklace and earrings of such bizarre and beautiful originality that I knew I'd love them for ever. The young man really should have been more amiable, for his prices were as breathtaking as his wares, but I was in no mood to penny pinch. I felt lucky.

On the drive back we compared our purchases. The girls were much recovered and, now that the holiday was on the home straight, no longer getting on one another's nerves. The imminent prospect of showing off their tans and embroidering the facts to their associates back home had raised their spirits considerably. They even touched on the sensitive subject of the exam results without falling out. And I myself was not averse to the idea of what George generally referred to as 'getting back in harness'. Every now and then I recalled my last conversation with Lew, and my heart, avaricious organ that it was, gave a little leap.

Maybe, just maybe, this was going to be It.

As we drove past the rear windows of the annexe Royston stuck his head and shoulders out, waving the telephone receiver in one hand.

'It's Lew Mervin from London!'

'Hang on, I'll come round.'

Talk about winged feet. I zoomed round the corner of the annexe and in at the open door, noticing in passing that Kostaki was sitting on the divan with his head in his hands.

In the office Royston thrust the telephone into my hand like a relay runner doing a baton change, and slid out of the room.

'Lew?'

'Harriet! Are you sitting down?'

'Why?'

'You ought to be sitting down when you hear the news I've got for you.'

I subsided on to Royston's swivel chair. 'Go on.'

'I just heard from Sonny Beidermeyer in New York.'

Lew was enjoying this entrepreneurial fore-play.

'And?'

'You've done it, Harriet. You've cracked the States. You've hit the big one.'

'Yes?'

'Aurora Books want to buy up your previous stuff from that other chickenshit place you were with.' He referred to the New York publishing house who had up to this moment launched a small selection of my books on to a largely indifferent American public. 'Aurora want to re-launch you over there. They want to colla-borate with Era on a three-book contract, the first of which will be *Down Our Street*.'

'Gosh! So?'

'The offer they are making is conditional upon your being able to give them a completed typescript for *Down Our Street* by the end of September. I told them I was pretty sure that would be no problem.'

'No problem at all.'

'And Harriet – they want the two of us, you and me, to go over to New York as soon as possible to talk ideas, and so you can meet the folk on the farm and so forth. Harriet,' he breathed rever-ently in case I might have missed the point, 'this is such a compliment!'

The tension finally got to me. 'Lew.'

'Yes, Harriet?'

'I hate having to ask this but – how much?'

He told me. It wasn't a six-figure sum. It was a seven-figure sum. Even divided by two it was a stupendous, gobsmacking, drop-dead lump of money.

'Congratulations, Harriet,' said Lew, like a midwife presenting a new mother with twins. 'You did it.'

This was not the moment for modesty, false or otherwise. 'I did, didn't I?' My head swam. 'So – what happens next?'

'When do you get back?'

I made a lightning survey of my revised plans. 'Saturday morning.'

'Could I book tickets on Concorde for the Sunday? I know it's a rush, but then we have Monday and Tuesday clear in New York. And they're paying – Harriet?'

'Concorde . . .'

'There's a ten thirty flight. Can you manage that? Only I have to ring Sonny back tonight.'

It was going to be a scramble, but I was playing with the big boys now. 'Tell him no problem!'

'Terrific. By the by, I told the folks at Era and they are over the moon! I better go – uh-oh, before I do I've got someone here who wants a quick word with you. We were about to crack open a bottle in your honour.'

There were some mutterings and shriekings from beyond Lew's cupped hand, and then:

'Harriet, you beaut!'

'Monica . . .?'

'Get you! I'll know who to come to when I need a few bucks, won't I?'

'I suppose you will.' I was a huge silly grin on legs, but even so there was something I wanted to know. 'What are you doing there?'

'Neat, huh? Lew was the first person I bumped into when I hit town, so he's putting me up till I find myself a job.' There were some more muffled sounds, and then: 'He says to tell you we're an item.'

Not many days before I would have been downright incredulous at this. Now it seemed perfectly in keeping with current trends. 'Well I never,' I said. 'That's great.'

'You can buy us dinner at Le Gavroche as soon as you get back from the States,' Monica promised me. 'Now go to it, girl. I'll hand you back to the boss.'

'I'm so pleased for you, Lew,' I said.

'We're very happy. I thought another serious relationship was never going to come my way, but Monica's changed all that.'

I pictured little Lew tucked up in bed with Monica taking him forcibly in hand.

'I wish you both all the luck in the world,' I

said, meaning it more than they would ever know. Lew thanked me, and went on to explain how and where we would liaise at Heathrow, and to indicate that if I were able to bring any more of *Down Our Street* with me that would be even more wonderful.

'Remember, Harriet,' he concluded, 'it's not just one book that Aurora are buying into here but the whole Harriet Blair package – the popular reads, the literary novels, everything. It's *you* they want. They've finally cottoned on to what we've always known, that you're an author for all seasons.'

After I'd replaced the receiver I sat for a moment, dazed. An author for all seasons . . . this was a new title, but one I could very readily learn to live with. I liked the sound of it.

Royston put his head round the door. 'Cup of tea, Harriet? Or something stronger?'

'Something stronger, please . . .' I got unsteadily to my feet.

'Oh, dear. Bad news?'

I was sure he must have heard, whether by design or accident, a fair amount of my conversation with Lew, and was simply being nosey. He needn't have worried. I was stinking rich and I didn't care who knew.

'Exactly the opposite. I've sold American rights for a huge sum of money.' I put my hands to my head. 'A *huge* sum.'

'Hey!' Royston rushed into the living room. 'Doctor! Crank your face up and look cheerful. Harriet's hit the big time!'

Kostaki got up like a man with lead in his socks, came over and gave me a kiss. 'Well done. You deserve it.'

Royston scampered out and called the girls, and then returned to fetch glasses and a bottle from the kitchen. Kostaki just stood there looking miserable.

'Sorry,' I said, 'I realise there's nothing like someone else's good news to make a bloke depressed.'

'It's not that. I'm pleased for you. I really am.'

'And I'm pleased for you,' I said daringly. 'And Priscilla.'

'Oh—' He gave a rueful jerk of the head. 'That.'

I wasn't going to let him off so easily. 'So there is something?'

'Yes. I'm sorry.'

'Don't be sorry! What's the matter with you?' I put my arm about his shoulders and beamed bossily at his ear, as the girls arrived in the doorway and Royston returned with drinks.

At intervals during that evening when I could summon sufficient coherence I reminded myself to take note, because this was what happiness felt like. Not contentment with its deep, deep peace, nor the white-knuckle ride of ecstasy, but the bright, untarnished sunshine of happiness. It wasn't only the money. I had escaped the demeaning shackles of lust, and there was considerable evil pleasure to be had from watching the Count clank his chains at poor Kostaki.

I was fit, filthy rich – and free.

Long after the girls had gone to bed I floated out into the night. It was warm and still. Kostaki joined me. Not realising how benign I felt, he appeared sheepish.

'About Pru,' he said. 'Actually, we're thinking of getting hitched.'

'Marvellous!' I cried. 'A wedding – you will invite me?'

'No hard feelings?' he asked wistfully.

'Of course not.' Now there was a definite shadow of disappointment. 'So what's up?'

He heaved a tragic sigh. 'It's that old fart at the château. Honestly, Harriet, I wish I'd never been halfway civil to him. He's completely obsessed. He says he's going to give me a surprise.'

'The secret passage . . .'

Kostaki nodded grimly.

'You'd have thought a tunnel stuffed with cadavers would have been enough to dampen anyone's ardour.'

'Come on, Harriet. You've met him. It would take half a dozen panzer divisions in full battle order to make him think twice.'

'Why don't you simply move out?'

'I plan to. But I gave this number to the RPs, and Crispin's calling first thing tomorrow morning. I simply must be here to prepare the ground about Pru. You've seen for yourself what a stuffed shirt he is. If I just bugger off it won't look good. And where his wife's sister's concerned he'll expect to see evidence of honourable intent, solvency, reliability. Blood on the sheets, I shouldn't wonder. Christ, they're coming over in a few days' time! They're not going to be too impressed if that fat old goat's still prancing about the place treating me like some kind of superannuated rent boy! What's the matter?'

I was paralytic with laughter. I was enjoying this every bit as much as Kostaki had enjoyed my discomfiture at the hands of Era's Great Man, all those years ago at the Fartenwald Buchfest. Revenge was sweet. But Kostaki was rather sweet, too. And in spite of the alcohol I was razor-sharp.

'What he needs,' I said, 'is a fright.'

'What would you suggest?' said Kostaki. 'That hairless skin of his is like vinyl flooring.'

'If he turns up, I think you should prepare to accommodate him.'

'*What?*'

'I only said prepare. Don't worry,' I soothed. 'I have a cunning plan. Come round to the verandah. I'll make us some coffee and have a quick word with the girls.'

The little bats were darting and swooping like airborne minnows when I rejoined Kostaki and explained what I had in mind. His jaw dropped.

'You're joking, I hope.'

'Do you see me laughing?'

'To be frank, yes.'

'That's a smile of quiet confidence.'

'I can't do it. It's undignified.'

'And fighting off the château-bottled shirt-lifter isn't?'

'Point taken,' said Kostaki. 'If he shows tonight, I'll do it.'

After he'd gone, with only the most chaste of valedictions passing between us, I went for a swim. Intermittently the cannons popped. The girls had switched their music off. The only other sound now, apart from the silken ripple of my breast-stroke, was the distant barking of a dog in the woods. A tiny speck of light moved here and there in the melon field – Rindin perfecting his scourge of those feathered banditti bold enough to conduct raids in the small hours.

When I'd showered and dried I got into bed, but left the door and curtains wide open. I knew what I was waiting for. On cue at about one thirty there was a heavy splash as Obelix took the waters. I watched her quite tenderly as she sculled back and forth with that matronly motion, her large jowly head lifted high above the surface. Not wanting to disturb her I tiptoed out on to the verandah and pulled up a chair at the far end, facing the annexe. There was nothing to do now but wait for the fun to begin.

Only five minutes or so later I heard a kind of muted commotion in the living room of the annexe where Kostaki slept on the divan. This was followed by an urgent whispered exchange between two voices, one low and tense, the other a swift, excitable patter, rising to an occasional shrill squeak. The Count was paying court. I absolutely hugged myself in pleasurable anticipation.

Like a watched pot, it took rather longer than I thought, and the silence during the intervening minutes was profound and impenetrable. What on earth were they doing? Had Kostaki changed his mind and bottled out? Were they talking things through? Drinking coffee? Or were they actually – doing it?

Unable to contain my curiosity I had risen from my chair and was about to creep closer when the shit hit the fan. A wail like an air-raid siren went up, followed by a babble of confused French in which it was possible to distinguish *le bon Dieu* being frequently and urgently invoked.

The shutters went back with a sound like a football rattle. Another wail went up from the far side of the annexe, heading west. I flew along the verandah and up the path past the bedroom doors. I just heard the girls' sleepy voices complaining bitterly about the din. Obelix hurtled from the pool and rushed past me, cannonading off my legs like a wet sheepskin rug.

There he went, Count Guy de Pellegale, scampering up the hill like an inflated Wee Willie Winkie, with his robe gathered about his knees and Obelix galumphing in his wake. As I watched him go, one of the cannons went off with a louder than usual report, and the Count squealed and leapt in the air before disappearing amongst the trees. A faint smell of cordite tickled my nostrils.

I told the girls it was nothing, only the Count and his dog having an altercation. They were sleepy enough to accept it. With the utmost self-satisfaction I went back to the verandah and sat down.

Lights had gone on in the annexe, and I heard Royston and Kostaki talking. Then all but one of the lights were switched off again, and Kostaki emerged in his short, black kimono. Seeing him thus attired my vital organs gave a very slight nostalgic lurch.

'Well?' I asked.

He stood looking down at me. The kimono was not that firmly tied.

'Harriet,' he said, 'you're a wonder.'

'I know.'

'It was so marvellously apt. It caught him off balance, literally. I can't thank you enough.'

'Please . . .' I made a feathery gesture of dismissal. 'Glad to be of service.'

'And me. Can I be – of service?'

He put his hands on the arms of my chair and leaned forward. The kimono fell open. His breath smelled of wine. His voice took on that unique timbre, an erotic frequency which seemed to thrust deep into the eardrum.

'Harriet . . . how about it? For old times' sake.'

I put my face very close to his. 'Old times . . .?' I breathed. I rose so we were standing chest to chest and I could feel all too clearly his sentimental attachment.

'Old times?' I repeated. 'I'm afraid not, doctor. Time for you to settle down with a good woman.' I pushed the chair back with my foot and sidestepped him. 'And as you know,' I added, going to the French window, 'I was never that.'

I slipped inside, closed the window, turned the key and blew him a kiss. My last impression of him standing there on the verandah was of a man left holding an unwanted present.

CHAPTER SEVENTEEN

The following day, Friday, I woke at six with a buzz of excitement. I knew that this shiny, perfect happiness would in the nature of things become tarnished, and that today – the last of the holiday – was the one to savour.

I let Teazel in and left the verandah door standing open. Duvets of mist lay over the fields and dew-covered spiders' webs festooned the verandah pillars like glass rosaries. The cat's fur as he pressed against my legs was cool and slightly damp. I pulled on a track suit, made tea, and went up to the atelier to write the final episode of *Down Our Street*.

Mattie Piper, thankfully, had turned the corner and become a halfway decent human being. Looking back I slightly regretted having made her such a madam to begin with, but that could be altered in the second draft. The important thing

now was to end triumphantly. A certain nobility
was to emerge in all three of my protagonists.
Satisfaction had to be given, and seen to be given,
on every side.

The spanking episode had represented a nadir
of behaviour for those concerned. This final
chapter was to have a different feel altogether:
grey, gritty, elegiac – but with the faint traces of a
new dawn on the rain-smudged horizon. A pit
disaster had struck Marsdyke. Seth Barlow,
having refused an early chance of escape in order
to stay below ground with his men, was trapped
with over a hundred others. The wives and
families of the endangered miners were gathered
at the pithead, silent and watchful in the freezing
downpour. Mattie, as Seth's wife, was their
natural leader.

She felt the other women looking at her, I wrote, *asking
something of her which she felt unqualified to give. But
she knew she must try. She had to do something, say
something – not to allay their fears, but to give them
strength. Had she been religious she might have led
them in prayer. Had she been gifted in oratory she
might have found fine words to lift their hearts. Had she
been political she might have stirred them to action. As
it was, she recalled with sudden clarity the words of her
uncle, now grown so old and infirm that he could not
leave the house to be with her at this vigil.*

'Mattie,' he had said to her, 'don't change. Be true to yourself, lass, and use those qualities you have. It's pretending to be what they're not as makes fools and villains of folk.'

Remembering this, she knew what she could do. She drew a deep, ragged breath, and felt the grimy air of Marsdyke rush into her lungs. It was a while since she'd sung, and the first couple of notes came out rather thin and faint. But as she grew in confidence so her voice grew in resonance and volume, and by the time she reached the line 'And was the holy lamb of God/On England's pleasant pastures seen' other voices were joining hers. By the time they got to 'Bring me my bow of burning gold' the whole crowd was singing, their faces sombre, but their voices full-throated and thrilling. Mattie knew it wasn't much, but it was a way of binding them together, and so easing the terrible tension of this long and fearful wait.

It was as they finished 'Jerusalem', with the final 'green and pleasant land' hanging in the cold air, that she heard the clatter of hooves and looked over her shoulder to see Oliver Challoner dismounting from his horse on the fringes of the crowd.

He tied Lucifer to a railing and began to make his way through the throng towards the mineshaft. His face was grey and strained. He looked, Mattie thought, almost vulnerable. A hiss of resentment marked his path through the crowd of women. When he reached Mattie's side she did not realise he had seen her until he said, in a *voice devoid of all expression:* 'How long has it been?'

'Two hours now.'

'A rescue party has gone down?'

She nodded. 'But the air must be getting short.'

Oliver glanced at her face. 'Seth is there . . .?'

'Yes. He could have come out, but chose to stay.'

'Your husband is a brave man, Matilda.'

Mattie met his gaze, those blue eyes which had always had the power to unsettle her, and saw that for the first time he was using her full name not to tease or censure her, but as a mark of respect – and something else. But before she had time to respond he added almost brusquely: 'Here, wear this for me,' and removing his heavy topcoat he placed it over her shoulders.

She was about to say that she did not need or want his coat, but he was already striding away from her towards the pithead, his black hair plastered to his skull by the insistent rain.

A woman standing near Mattie gave her a sharp, vindictive look.

'I hope that Challoner's no friend of yours, Mrs Barlow,' she said, 'and you with your man stuck in t'pit like a rat in a hole.'

Mattie felt a clean, reviving flame of anger leap up in her. Fiercely, she rounded on the woman.

'My friends are no business of yours! And as to my husband, if more pairs of hands will help to save his life, and your son's too, then I'll not complain whose they are!'

It was as she turned away from the woman's gaping face, her own heart racing, that Mattie realised she had championed the man whom for her entire adult life she would have sworn was her enemy.

At this point I heard a small sound downstairs. One of the advantages of writing by hand was its quietness – one was alert to every sound. I let a few seconds elapse and then got up and went to look over the balustrade. An envelope lay inside the verandah door.

It was quite a dignified note under the circumstances.

'Dearest Harriet,' he had written.
'I have to move on this morning – a couple of properties near Torcheron need my attention. When I get back you will have left, and anyway I shall be staying in the town to be with Pru. I do hope you don't think badly of me. I was being such a good, about-to-be-married chap until I bumped into you. You always did bring out the beast in me. However, this little episode with de Pellegale has shown me the error of my ways. It's clean living for me from now on.'

I gave a snort, and as I did so the MG started up in the drive.

'I really can't thank you enough for your help in ridding me of the old boy. The creative imagination is indeed a wonderful thing. And you still have the best legs in the business. Read this In Loving Memory. K.'

I finished the note as the MG left, sending a spattering of gravel on to the kitchen window. Without hesitation I screwed up the piece of paper and dropped it in the pedal bin.

Back upstairs I crouched down next to The Building of Stonehenge. There were only about twenty pieces left to put in. The queue of ancient Brits scowling beneath the stormy skies of Salisbury Plain reminded me of the women gathered round the Marsdyke pithead. For a moment I saw myself as part of a great tradition of British popular culture, beginning with Druid monuments and reaching all the way to twentieth-century schlock fiction.

Infuriatingly, there was one piece missing. The head of the Arch Druid, bearded, open-mouthed and with eyes rolled heavenward (if the box lid was to be believed) was simply not there. I searched around for a few minutes, but in the end I had to admit defeat and went back to *Down Our Street*.

For another hour I wrote. I described both

Mattie's attempts to rally the forlorn womenfolk, and Oliver Challoner's heroic leading of the rescue effort below ground. I winched the tension up till I reached the really poignant part. Now only Seth Barlow remained imprisoned by the rock fall. Oliver had stretched his arm out to him to help pull him through the single narrow aperture. I was engrossed. This was real action: these two men locked together by need, circumstance, rivalry and mutual respect. For once the period didn't matter. Human drama was everything. Oliver did all he could, but a final flurry of stones broke his arm and separated him from the wretched Seth for ever.

When the first rescued man appeared at the pithead, I wrote, *it was gathering dusk, and only a few storm lanterns illuminated the cluster of dark figures. The women peered, then gasped and surged forward. Mattie remained very still as other women clasped their loved ones, or wept bitter tears as they realised their wait had been in vain. A sharp wind had arisen and the icy rain was thrown in handfuls against her face. She stood like a statue, with Oliver's coat pulled tight around her. On every side, families she had known for as long as she could remember were experiencing a grief or a joy they would never forget, and from which she was excluded. For the past hours they had looked to her for leadership, and had drunk deep of her spirit, pride and courage, but now she was forgotten in the tumult of their private emotions.*

As they had surged past her when the men had come

up, so they began to drift back through the dark and rain towards the small, mean houses of Marsdyke, to evenings of celebration or weeping according to their fortunes. Exhausted children were dragged by the hand or clasped in fathers' arms. The elated comforted the bereaved. Injured men leaned on their womenfolk. And still there was no one for Mattie.

At last she stood alone. A single storm lantern, bobbing in the wind, lit the pithead. The last few rescuers came up and moved away from the black mouth of the shaft with the heavy tread of defeat. As they passed her she felt their beaten glances slide across her face like the touch of so many cold hands.

He came last of all. He seemed to have aged twenty years in the two hours since she had last seen him. His face was scored by tiredness and despair, and his right arm was in a sling made from a bloodstained scarf.

'I'm sorry, Mattie,' he said. And his voice was so low she could only barely hear it for the noise of the wind and rain. 'I'm so very sorry. There was nothing we could do.'

He didn't touch her nor she him. For a moment she struggled to master her emotions. When she had done so, she said: 'You did all you could. Thank you.'

Then she removed his coat from her shoulders and placed it around his, whose trembling she could feel. His eyes were dark with pain.

When they reached the place where Lucifer stood, head drooping in the rain, Oliver looped the reins over his good arm and continued to walk with Mattie, back to the house where now she must learn to live alone. As she stood on the step her heart was full and she saw from his face that his was also.

'Farewell, Matilda Barlow,' he said. 'I should like to do what I can to help. Seth was a man I admired — more than any.'

'I shall manage,' she said, not meaning to be sharp, but fearful of her feelings.

'Perhaps I might call from time to time. To see how you are.'

'Please do. And now you must go. You should have your arm attended to. I would do it myself, but—' Tears threatened her, and he had the grace to turn from her and heave himself, with a ragged intake of breath, into the saddle.

They exchanged a last look, and then he rode away, slowly, down the street. Mattie opened the door and entered the house where she must mourn her husband, and bear his child, which only yesterday had stirred in her for the first time.

And where she must wait, perhaps years, for the man she truly loved.

I wrote the words 'The End', and went downstairs to wake the girls.

While they used the call box in the square to tell their fathers we'd be home next day, I went for a quick *citron pressé* at Priscilla's. A handful of regulars were obviously in the throes of some kind of celebration at the bar, and it was plain from her manner that Kostaki had not begun the great clean-up of his act by telling her about me. Thank God.

She was back in her Peace and Love get-up, and her appearance contrasted strangely with the manner in which she wagged a huge hand over the bar at me.

'Clock this,' she said. 'Constantine's making an honest woman of me at last!'

'This' was a very nice, very solid, diamond cluster.

'Congratulations.' I kissed her warmly, to moist chuckles of approval on all sides.

'Aren't you going to miss all this?' I asked, waving a hand at the faded posters, the oil-drum barbecue, the dogs heaped on their lopsided bench in the sun.

'Not a bit. As a matter of fact I'm really looking forward to getting a place down in Dorset with some land for a couple of decent horses.'

What a turn up for the books! Kostaki the media doc, the meanest, moodiest thing in jockey shorts, scourge of the surgery, Casanova of the couch – buried in Dorset with big Pru and her hunters.

'*Au revoir*, Priscilla,' I said. 'I hope you'll both be very happy.'

*

The afternoon was for packing, so on the way back from Lalutte we dropped in to say goodbye at the château. For the first time we rang the bell at the front door. Isabelle answered, and indicated with upraised finger that we should wait there while she consulted her husband.

We were in a long, dark hall stretching from the front of the house to the back. I dimly remembered having crossed it *en route* from the drawing room to the dining room. As we waited I wandered up and down. About halfway along there was a large framed jigsaw of a Brueghel painting – dozens of chunky figures in a snowbound landscape. I switched on the small strip light above it. The girls joined me and we peered at it together.

'What a basket case,' murmured Clara in awe.

Naomi said: 'There's a piece there that doesn't belong.'

'Surely not.' I looked more closely where she pointed. She was right. On the body of a stubby youth in well-filled yellow tights and a padded jacket was the head, unmistakably, of the Arch Druid. It had been cut about a bit to fit – the Stonehenge pieces were bigger – but there was no mistaking what it was.

Naomi got a nail beneath the piece and prised it out.

'Ooh look,' said Clara, 'a peephole.'

297

It was, too. The girls looked first, and their gloating expressions as they drew back gave me a pretty fair idea of what to expect.

'It's the Count's playroom,' said Naomi.

It wasn't large, but it was well appointed, and the Platfords were enjoying themselves in it. Against the red wall opposite, framed by black laquer dragons, stood Keith (naked but for his car keys on a thong) holding a video camera to his left eye. Among the scarlet satin cushions on a black futon Denise, also naked, was indulging in the sort of behaviour that made one glad their house was so well insulated.

I drew back, stunned.

'Not a word,' I said. 'Not one, single word. Ever.'

'Look out!' hissed Clara. 'She's coming back!'

We reassembled by the front door as Isabelle returned with a politely regretful expression. It was so sad, she said, but her husband was indisposed. He was *désolé* that he couldn't bid us farewell in person, but she was sure we understood . . . Oh dear, I said, and what could possibly be the matter?

He had a bad back, apparently. A bad lower back. In fact – Isabelle indicated the exact location of the indisposition by placing one hand on her generous buttock. But everyone was so kind – why even now M'sieur and Madame Platford were round with a quiche.

Trying with my stern tone to stifle the girls' snorts and squeaks I expressed our distress at the news, and begged Isabelle to give Guy our regards, and our thanks for his hospitality.

As we returned to the car we could hear Asti and Obi baying wildly in some distant chamber of the Château Forêt Noir.

On the way down the hill we had to pull on to the verge to make way for a dilapidated tractor coming in the opposite direction. When it was almost level with us, its ancient mechanism creaking and growling with the effort, I saw it was Farmer Rindin at the wheel. I jumped out and flagged him down.

I had only ever seen him as a vaguely sinister figure in the middle distance, or in the twilight of the château garden. Today, in full sunshine and at close quarters, he looked perfectly unexceptionable.

'*Bonjour Madame, ça va?*'

I told him we were going tomorrow morning and he extended a calloused blackened hand and wrung mine as if I were his dearest friend. I suppose in some odd, tangential way our presence in the Villa Almont had assisted his revenge on de Pellegale. He fished a couple of melons from a box at his feet and pressed them on me.

I explained that we had paid a farewell visit to the château. At once his face darkened. He informed me in a splenetic snarl that the so-called Count de Pellegale was a pervert of canine ancestry who should perform the physiologically impossible without delay. Shamelessly I nodded, and asked why he felt so strongly. He at once produced a dog-eared snapshot from the pocket of his overalls and held it before my face, tapping it energetically with his finger. '*Voici ma fille! Ma petite fille!*'

His daughter she may have been, but she was far from *petite*. If Guy de Pellegale had indeed corrupted this tasselled and feathered houri with her cantilevered chest and merc-radiator grin, then it had not been an arduous or unrewarding task. Still, poor Rindin wiped away the suggestion of a tear as he replaced the photograph and confided, lest I had missed the point earlier, that the Count was an evil pile of excrement which he spurned beneath his heel and spat on. Illustrating, he hawked with a sound like paper tearing and sent a large gob of viscous yellow matter zooming past me to land with a splat and a sizzle on the bonnet of the car.

Back at the villa I went up to the *atelier* and gave the Chief Druid his head. As I was standing back to admire the completed picture Royston appeared.

'Harriet? Hope you don't mind me coming on up. The girls said you were here. Just wanted to wish you *bon voyage*.'

'Thanks.'

'I say, you found it!'

'Yes. Guess where.'

'Guy's been using it to cover up his peephole. Before that he was using a bit of the Queen's Coronation regalia – the orb, I think. He likes to have something different to mark the spot. He pinches them when he comes down on visits.'

'He's laid up today,' I said. 'Rindin gave him a backside full of shot last night.'

Royston chuckled. 'Really? Good show. Speaking of spyholes, that was an inspired idea of yours.'

This knocked me back a bit. 'You knew about it?'

'Why not?' He winked. 'Liberty Hall, Harriet, you know that. Besides, it'll be great material.'

'Material?'

'For my novel. My *roman à clef*. About expatriate life in France. I'll be finished soon.'

The can of worms opened up by this revelation was almost too appalling to contemplate. 'You never said!' was all I could manage.

Royston patted my shoulder. 'Now come on, Harriet. We writers don't want to go giving away our trade secrets, do we? I shouldn't have to tell you that.'

*

Later on that evening, when we were packed and had drunk the last of the wine, I went upstairs to collect *Down Our Street*. I switched on the light over the table and re-read what I had written that day. Aurora notwithstanding, I was suddenly riddled with insecurity. Damn Royston. The signs had been there and I had not noticed.

I read, at first only scanning, but with increasing absorption. As I did so I was overcome with a sort of tenderness. My throat filled. I was choked. I saw that somewhere in *Down Our Street*, which had begun so inauspiciously as an exercise in genre-production, there was a decent story struggling to get out. At some point a conversion had taken place. I cared about Mattie and Oliver. And I was sad for poor Seth. I had always known that I was no more than a mediocre writer, but I was a story-teller. And soon I would have the capital to enable me to write what and how I wanted.

I scooped up the pages and ran down the stairs.

'Come on, girls!' I shouted. 'Let's head for home!'

CHAPTER EIGHTEEN

'Stay calm,' I said, patting George's knee. 'What's the worst that can have happened? A mess, that's all.'

'You think so?' said George.

'Of course. And if there's anything structural—'

'Jesus wept!'

'—if there *is* anything structural, so what? It's only bricks and mortar. And we're not short of a bob or two, remember?'

'That's not fair!' chimed in Clara. 'When I had my fifteenth you docked my allowance to pay for those curtains.'

'Oh, don't you worry,' I said. 'Gareth will have to cough. I'm just trying to persuade your father that damage to the house isn't the end of the world.'

We'd met up with George in London. Over brunch in a Pizza Express I'd informed him of my imminent departure for New York and the consequent desirability of his taking up residence at the homestead once more. I could see that this was going down like a lead balloon, and I couldn't really say I blamed him. I should have hated to be on the receiving end of it. But in my new persona as dollar millionairess and free spirit I was untroubled by guilt. And despite the all-night drive, a nap on the hovercraft and another on the way out of London had completely restored me.

'Um – you won't forget about me, will you?' asked Naomi.

'Damn,' said George, 'and double damn. Sorry.'

'Don't worry,' she said tolerantly. We were already on the road between Bassets Parva and Magna. The shortest route to the Nevilles' was along the A road we'd just left. George screeched to a halt and bounced irritably into reverse.

'Oh God,' said Clara, 'can't you take me back first?'

'Of course not,' I said, all queenly serenity. 'We'll take Naomi home.'

George executed a three-point turn as though auditioning for *Lethal Weapon 3*, and gunned back the way we'd come in the direction of the main road.

'Sorry about this,' said Naomi.

'That's quite all right,' I said, since George plainly wasn't going to. He was in the grip of the most diabolical home-coming blues. Served him right for ducking out of the holiday in favour of fawning over Eloise and her organisational lacunae. 'One good thing,' I said as we turned out and pulled straight into the outside lane, 'we can postpone looking at the mess at home for a few more minutes.' Even going at ninety I could hear George's teeth grinding.

At the Nevilles' house on the outskirts of Regis I stood in the drive and chatted amiably to Mrs Neville while George and Naomi's brother Luke, a goth, undid the rubber spider and hauled down her enormous case from the roofrack.

'Thanks for your postcard, sweetheart,' said Mrs Neville to her daughter. 'It's funny you mentioned that Lord de Pellegale – it's the name of the firm Marie-Laure's using to fit out her en suite.'

Naomi came over and kissed me. 'Thanks ever so much,' she said, 'it's been really great.'

I beamed indulgently. She advanced on George, but he stuck out a curmudgeonly pre-emptive hand. It was amazing how Naomi had improved. I could only think it was due to the polarising effect of so much thoroughly bad behaviour.

'She's looking so well,' said Mrs Neville. 'It was so kind of you to take her along. I do hope she's been no bother.'

'No bother whatsoever,' I reassured her truthfully, without adding that we had lately experienced so much bother on a Wagnerian scale as to render anything Naomi could have managed completely negligible.

The girls exchanged whispered promises to get back together as soon as possible, and we piled into the car. George negotiated the circular drive like Dick Dastardly on speed, and we headed for home.

'Wow,' said Clara, as we approached the house, 'there are plenty of people about.'

'So there are,' I said.

George moaned.

The place was a hive of activity. Most of the downstairs front windows stood open and the noise of a power drill was clearly audible even before George switched the engine off. A man in builder's overalls was doing something to one of the outside window ledges and Declan was applying a screwdriver to the latch on the gate. Through the landing window I could see Mrs O'Connell stopped over the Hoover.

We didn't bother to unload the car, but simply got out and advanced, intent on grasping the nettle. Declan, having caught our scent on the breeze, raised his head and glared at us like a bull surprised in a field.

'So you're back then!'

'Yes, indeed, Declan,' I replied sunnily. 'My goodness, what a lot seems to be going on.'

'They're animals, so th'are!'

George stalked past us to talk to the man working on the window frame, and Clara disappeared into the house.

'You really didn't need to come, you know, Declan,' I said soothingly, adding as a reminder: 'But then I suppose this counts as overtime, doesn't it?'

A glimmer, combining both avarice and resentment, lit Declan's beady eyes for a moment. 'He rang me, so he did! Said you were coming back a day early and he needed to get things straight. Jesus Christ almighty, I never thought I'd be rebuilding the place!'

I stepped back and ran an appraising glance over my property. Long experience had taught me that a bland affability was the best way to deal with Declan's ire. 'You've done very well, Declan.'

While he was still muttering and scowling I went into the house. It was very tidy: unnaturally so. This was due to last-minute ministrations before our arrival, and also because most of the surface items – vases, clocks, ornaments, plants and the like – had been removed. I applauded this precaution at the same time wondering where these items had been stowed. A glance through the half-open dining room door revealed a huge pile of mail lying on the table like an unexploded bomb. I closed the door.

Everything was slightly damp – walls, floor, carpets, surfaces – and there was a strong smell of disinfectant and cleaning fluid. I snuffed the air and wondered what other, less wholesome smells these had replaced. I opened the door of the downstairs cloakroom. Here it was the same story – scrubbed, clean, damp. There was no loo paper, and no hand towel: both must have fallen prey to some emergency that I did not care to picture. I looked into the sitting room, whence the sound of the power drill had emanated. The top bookshelf was now back in place, but the books were in piles on the carpet. The young man gave me a cheery jerk of the head.

'Soon have you straight, missis.'

'Good. You haven't seen my son anywhere?'

'In the garden clearing up a spot of litter.'

'Thanks.' Something he'd said prompted me to ask: 'And you haven't seen the dog?'

'Dog?' The man looked blank. 'Nope.'

A pity. Beyond the window I could see George testing the window ledge with an expression both grim and doubtful.

I went out into the garden. At once Fluffy the cat, who had sensibly been roosting in a tree until

the danger was passed, jumped down and came
to say hello in his perfunctory way. He seemed
small and streetwise after Teazel.

Gareth, dressed only in jungle-print cutoffs,
was at the far end, but moving in my direction.
He carried a black bin bag into which he was
dropping the empty cans, cigarette packets, fag
ends and worse which littered the grass. The bag
was already half full.

'Gareth!'

His face lit up. 'Oh, hi, you're back.'

'Yes.'

'Nearly there, shan't be a tick.'

He reached me, and put the bag down with a
clunk. 'I'll do the beds later.'

'I hope you mean the flower beds.'

'Good journey?' He scraped his bristly cheek
against mine. He had the warm, slightly rancid
smell that I was not too old and sere to associate
with a Great Thrash.

'Yes, thanks. Good party?'

'Brilliant. Everyone said it was magic. Best
party around here that anyone could remember.
And what do you think?' – he made a sweeping
gesture taking in house, garden and surroundings – 'not a bad job considering you came back
early.' My son's was a sanguine nature, capable of
snatching credit from the darkest shitstorm.

'I haven't looked everywhere, but it doesn't

seem too bad.'

'I had a bit of a ring round. Got the old bog-trotters over—'

'Gareth!'

'And Brett got hold of Si and Dave from Turner's, and two or three of us are getting together to pay them.'

'As long as your father doesn't have to.'

Gareth's face became wary. 'Where is he?'

'Making a tour of the affected areas. More in sorrow than in anger.' I heard a distant ping as Clara lifted the receiver on the upstairs telephone. 'By the way, I don't want to know whether anyone was in the bedrooms, but there had better not be the smallest trace of occupancy.'

Gareth slapped me on the shoulder. 'No worries.'

I didn't know whether this was a statement of fact or an exhortation, but from his complacent air I was obviously supposed to be reassured. I moved on to the last of the matters arising.

'And Gareth, where's the dog?'

'What – Spot?'

'Unless you've replaced him in our absence.'

'I'm not dead sure.'

'Hazard a guess.'

Gareth had the grace to look slightly uncomfortable. 'He got out – some time during the party. A woman did ring earlier and said he'd had a bit of a go at her rubbish, but when I went round there he must have moved on. He'll be back soon, you know what he is.'

I did know, that was the trouble.

'Oh,' called Gareth, as I went back to the house. 'A bunch of flowers arrived for you. I put them in the utility room.'

Goodness knows how he'd managed to stand the bouquet in the sink, because the utility room was where everything else had been shoved. He'd had the foresight to turn on the cold tap but not to turn it fully off, so a small trickle of water was running over the side of the sink. I turned it off, hoisted out the bouquet – a gigantic stook of glads, lilies, dahlias and chrysanths – and stood instep-deep in water as I read the card.

'To our very favourite and most successful author. Have a wonderful time in the Big Apple and come and celebrate when you get back. Lots of love, Tristan, Vanessa and all at Era Books.'

Well, that was nice of them. It was only a pity I shouldn't be able to enjoy the flowers. I wasn't staying.

Carrying the bouquet into the kitchen to put it in water I encountered Mrs O'Connell on the stairs.

'Mrs O'Connell, you're a hero,' I said. 'Let's have a nice cup of tea.'

*

Ten minutes later the kettle had boiled and a surprisingly large number of people had gathered in the kitchen for tea and biscuits. There was George, Gareth, the O'Connells, Si and Dave, Clara, and two strange, red-eyed youths who had wandered down from the garden, having presumably spent the night beneath the stars. Only George and Declan were surly. Everyone else was in rather high spirits. There was something akin to a party atmosphere.

'Right,' I said to George. 'I'll leave you to see this lot out. I've got things to do.'

He looked dismayed. 'Surely you can leave tomorrow morning? I thought the whole idea of coming back early was to have a day's grace.'

'Absolutely,' I agreed. 'But I'm not spending it here. It's an early flight, so I'm going to have a night at the club.'

'It seems a bit precipitate,' he said.

'Not at all. I'm only going to be away three nights. Better to go now, while I'm on the move. I'll buy you something expensive and preppy from Sak's.'

'There's really no need.'

I kissed him. Talk about the kiss of Judas. 'Oh, yes there is,' I said. 'You'd be surprised.'

I left the house at six. I may have been a rat leaving a sinking ship, but I was a jolly virtuous one. I had driven eight hundred miles, unpacked, turned round three complete washes and put them away, sorted frozen meals out of the freezer, done some domestic shopping, showered, changed, packed and put the post where it wouldn't be found till I'd gone.

As the taxi left the village, I saw Spot. He was trotting purposefully down the road in the direction of home. He looked self-satisfied and only slightly jaded. I knew that look. It did not surprise me that he was wringing wet: it had taken a hose to separate them. The enraged owner of the bitch in question was probably on the phone at this moment. But at least the call would interrupt George's lecture to Clara on the advisability of re-takes . . .

Lew seemed worn out. 'Bye, hon,' he said to Monica. 'Take care now.'

Monica made a face at me over his shoulder. 'He's such an old hen. For chrissakes, Lew, you're only away a few days. And in case it had escaped your attention I'm all growed up.'

'You don't have to tell me that,' said Lew soupily.

'Excuse me,' I said, 'there's a couple of things I have to get.'

I did the obligatory tour of the Sock Shop, Body Shop, Knicker Box, Boots and John Menzies. It was a funny feeling to know I could buy whatever I wanted – even one of those big, fancy baskets full of coconut milk foot salve and pine kernel skin freshener – and yet nothing took my fancy. It made me realise how potent a force was guilt in my shopping habit. With guilt removed, restraint returned.

I went back to Lew and Monica.

' . . . Marks and Spencer do great ready meals for one,' he was saying. 'And do be careful with my yucca. It can't stand over-watering.'

'I shan't go near it, honest Injun,' said Monica, and they kissed.

'I'll see you in the departure lounge,' I said, loudly and clearly in order to cut through the miasma of cheeping bluebirds and fluttering cherubs.

'Sure! Bye-bye!' they said without looking.

I went through to the Concorde passengers' lounge and availed myself of a courtesy buck's fizz and a dish of stuffed olives. This was the way to travel. I was fully refreshed after a night spent in one of the Gadfly Club's recently refurbished guest rooms. Lew was in charge of the arrangements. He had made the bookings and fixed the meetings with Sonny Beidermeyer and others in New York. As Monica had so rightly observed, he was an old hen. I had nothing to do but attend to my appearance, keep my smile in place and my brain functioning at a fairly undemanding level.

I had brought the last part of *Down Our Street* with me and intended to get it typed up by someone else after we arrived. Wasn't New York the city that never slept, and where anything could be bought if you had the money to pay for it?

I sipped my drink and let my mind cast about for whatever took its fancy.

It wandered, as it often had over the past couple of days, to the brilliant plan I had devised for Kostaki. So simple, so elegant, so fiendishly apposite.

My only regret was that I had not been there to see, as the Count had advanced on Kostaki's enchanting, invitingly upturned tush – only to see a bright, glassy green eye staring back at him.

'Now I know,' said Lew as he arrived, 'why the English call it gigglewater.'

☐ The Flowers of the Field	Sarah Harrison	£4.99
☐ A Flower That's Free	Sarah Harrison	£4.99
☐ Hot Breath	Sarah Harrison	£4.99
☐ An Imperfect Lady	Sarah Harrison	£3.99
☐ Cold Feet	Sarah Harrison	£4.99
☐ The Forests of the Night	Sarah Harrison	£4.99

Warner Books now offers an exciting range of quality titles by both established and new authors. All of the books in this series are available from:

Little, Brown and Company (UK) Limited,
P.O. Box 11,
Falmouth,
Cornwall TR10 9EN.

Alternatively you may fax your order to the above address. Fax No. 0326 376423.

Payments can be made as follows: cheque, postal order (payable to Little, Brown and Company) or by credit cards, Visa/Access. Do not send cash or currency. UK customers and B.F.P.O. please allow £1.00 for postage and packing for the first book, plus 50p for the second book, plus 30p for each additional book up to a maximum charge of £3.00 (7 books plus).

Overseas customers including Ireland, please allow £2.00 for the first book plus £1.00 for the second book, plus 50p for each additional book.

NAME (Block Letters) ....

....

ADDRESS ....

....

....

☐ I enclose my remittance for _____

☐ I wish to pay by Access/Visa Card

Number ☐☐☐☐☐☐☐☐☐☐☐☐☐☐☐☐☐☐

Card Expiry Date ☐☐☐☐